THE HUNT

ANDY HAYES MYSTERIES

by Andrew Welsh-Huggins

Fourth Down and Out

Slow Burn

Capitol Punishment

The Hunt

The Third Brother (forthcoming)

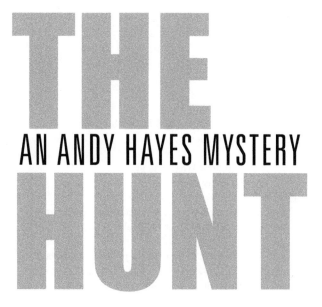

THE HUNT

AN ANDY HAYES MYSTERY

ANDREW WELSH-HUGGINS

SWALLOW PRESS
OHIO UNIVERSITY PRESS
ATHENS

Swallow Press
An imprint of Ohio University Press, Athens, Ohio 45701
ohioswallow.com

Printed in the United States of America
Swallow Press / Ohio University Press books are printed on acid-free paper ⊚ ™

27 26 25 24 23 22 21 20 19 18 17   5 4 3 2 1

First paperback printing in 2018
ISBN 978-0-8040-1209-6

Library of Congress Cataloging-in-Publication Data

Names: Welsh-Huggins, Andrew, author.
Title: The hunt : an Andy Hayes mystery / Andrew Welsh-Huggins.
Description: Athens, Ohio : Swallow Press, an imprint of Ohio University
  Press, [2017] | Series: Andy Hayes mysteries
Identifiers: LCCN 2017000575 | ISBN 9780804011884 (hardback) | ISBN
  9780804040815 (pdf)
Subjects: LCSH: Private investigators—Fiction. |
  Murder—Investigation—Fiction. | Columbus (Ohio)—Fiction. | BISAC:
  FICTION / Mystery & Detective / General. | GSAFD: Mystery fiction.
Classification: LCC PS3623.E4824 H86 2017 | DDC 813/.6—dc23
LC record available at https://lccn.loc.gov/2017000575

For Sarah, Emma, and Thomas

It is a very human foolishness to insist on the presence of a knife or a gun or a fist in order to recognize the existence of force, when often the most compelling forces on this earth present intangibly, in coercive situations.

—Rachel Moran, *Paid For: My Journey through Prostitution*

It is a terrible thing, this kindness that human beings do not lose. Terrible, because when we are finally naked in the dark and cold, it is all we have. We who are so rich, so full of strength, we end up with that small change. We have nothing else to give.

—Ursula K. LeGuin, *The Left Hand of Darkness*

So I pressed and the lustrous goddess answered me in turn: "Royal son of Laertes, Odysseus, old campaigner, stay on no more in my house against your will. But first another journey calls. . . ."

—Homer, *The Odyssey*, Book X, Robert Fagles translation

Prologue

Through the door, we heard a woman scream.

I stood up from where I'd fallen and used my flashlight to reveal a set of descending stairs leading to a second, open doorway. I brushed the heavily falling snow off my face and walked down a couple of steps before pausing. I yelled her name, but the sound was immediately muffled by the storm, like someone pushing a pillow over my head.

I took a few more steps down the stairs. I hesitated again. Despite how far we'd come, how close we were to ending the hunt, I didn't want to go through that door. Not yet. The man on the other side had a gun and nothing to lose. All bets were off. One decent shot at us and everything we'd worked for was over. I'd already walked straight into one trap this Christmas season. Why repeat history, with the bruises from that mistake still healing?

"Let's go," Theresa hissed, behind me.

"Wait."

Focus, Andy. Focus.

Why repeat history, but why bank on second chances either? I'd already used up enough for a lifetime. Why gamble on somebody else's life?

Focus . . .

"We don't have time," Theresa said.

"Hold on," I said, listening.

"He's going to get—"

She screamed again.

"*Now*," I said, charging down the stairs and through the door.

1

I WAS HAVING ONE OF THOSE DECEMBERS.
Which seemed to happen to me more and more these days.

I sat up straight, trying to ease my aching back, which hurt because of course I'd forgotten to bring stadium seats. It was a couple of weeks earlier, with not that many shopping days left before Christmas. I took a long pull on my beer to compensate, which would have made for a satisfying moment except for the conversation I was having on the phone just then with my ex-wife. I glanced over at Anne and she frowned back, but not in the way that communicates your girlfriend's concern for your well-being. In a way that suggests she's wondering what the hell she and her daughter have been dragged into and is really starting to resent it.

"Stop shouting," my ex-wife said.

"I'm not shouting. It's just that it's loud in here."

"Where's here?"

"I'm at a roller derby match."

"You've got to be kidding me."

"Listen—I told you I'd talk to him."

She'd called about our son, Mike. And it hadn't been to discuss which wrapping paper to use this year.

"But when?" Kym demanded. "You said that last week. And the week before. And then when you went to the hockey game Mike said you spent most of it on the phone and when you weren't on the phone you were complaining about the jumbotron."

"Jumbotrons ruin the experience. People don't watch the actual game anymore—"

"Nobody gives a shit about jumbotrons, Andy. They care about grades. And success that comes from good grades. And right now your son has neither because he's failing three classes. All he cares about is sports. Like his father. Which is pretty damned ironic. Which is why *you* need to talk to him."

"I got that part, believe it or not. I'll speak to him tomorrow afternoon."

"No, you won't," she said angrily. "You aren't coming tomorrow because you were supposed to come last week and you forgot and tomorrow he's going to the movies with his friends. Which puts us at Wednesday, and who knows whether that's too late at this point. What *is* it with you and remembering shit?"

"I didn't forget," I snapped. I knew it was pointless to explain why I'd missed last week's custody visit. To point out that I'd been offered a last-minute job doing backstage security for a second-tier boy band that unexpectedly sold out an Arena District club. A club whose owners were nervous about the liability posed by a thousand drunken twenty-somethings hoping to relive the band's glory days from a decade earlier when the now not-so-young squires could actually sing. When the club manager offered me five hundred dollars and I told him to double it or get lost and he accepted, I knew I had no choice. Because I had no money, as usual. I'd told Kym I couldn't make it, but she said she never got the voice mail.

At least I was pretty sure I'd told her.

"Wednesday, then," I said. "Promise."

"Don't screw this up, Andy. If he has to repeat a grade, it's on you."

"I said I'd be there—"

4

"Heard it before," she said, and hung up.

"Everything OK?" Anne said, frowning as I pocketed my phone and fumed over the retorts caught in my throat. Which is where they needed to stay, since my ex-wife's complaints weren't misplaced. My first ex-wife. I hadn't heard from my second so far today. But it was barely 6 p.m. Plenty of time.

"Peachy. Fine and dandy."

"Great," she said. "So, I don't know how much longer I can stay. My back is killing me."

"Stadium seats. Yes, I know."

Roller derby is not usually a winter sport. The flat-track season starts around March and ends late in the summer. You go a little longer if you make the championships. But this year was different. Columbus's team, the Arch City Roller Girls, had arranged an exhibition bout against their Ann Arbor counterparts, the Tree Town Skirts, on the Saturday after Thanksgiving. The two teams from the college football rival cities were pairing off against each other in a promotion they billed as "Helliday on Wheels." It was both a fund-raiser and a chance to recruit new players, dubbed "fresh meat." The T-shirts and ball caps and coffee mugs at the concession stand all said "Merry Crunchmas."

It had seemed like a good idea at the time. Round up some friends, go see Bonnie skate. Have a couple beers, eat a couple burritos. Make an outing of it. That was before I forgot the stadium seats and Kym called to ask what I was doing about our son and his failing grades. Which was a good question. One I didn't have an answer to at that moment. Or maybe any other time.

Bonnie—Bonnie Deckard—does what I call part-time IT consulting for me because she refuses to be labeled a hacker. In her spare time she plays roller derby, where she skates as a blocker, which is roughly the equivalent of a defensive lineman in football, although they can also be on offense. She goes by the derby name "Bonshell." Her job is helping a player called a jammer break through a scrum of opponents and score points by passing skaters from the other team. The blockers also try to stop the opposing jammer, which was what Bonnie and her teammates were successfully doing at the moment. Ignoring the looks Anne was shooting at me, I clapped and joined the shouts of approval rising up around me in the circular Ohio Building at the State Fairgrounds.

The referee blew her whistle, signaling a foul by one of the Tree Town Skirts. Boos filled the arena. At the break in the action, Lucy, sitting one bleacher below me, pushed her cat's-eye glasses down her nose, leaned over, and whispered something to Roy. He shushed her.

"What?" I said.

"Nothing," Roy said.

"C'mon."

Lowering his voice, Roy said, "She said you and I must be in rear-end heaven, with all that Lycra out there."

"Watch what you say," I said, looking around. The stands were crowded with players' parents, younger siblings, friends, and boyfriends, including Troy, Bonnie's own beau, sitting next to me. If he'd heard Roy, he was ignoring him.

"Do you deny it?" Lucy said, mischief in her eyes.

"Yes," Anne said, glancing at her daughter, Amelia, before glaring at me. "Do you?"

"Pleading the Fifth," I said, and took another pull on my Bud Light.

"Crap," Roy said.

"Nothing of the sort, parson," I said. "It's my constitutional right."

"Not that. *This.*" He held up his phone, which showed an incoming call. Roy's phone rings a lot, which I guess happens when you're a minister. He was mostly immune to the demands on his attention. But I knew Lucy, his long-suffering wife, wouldn't have minded an hour off now and then. Roy listened, putting a finger in his ear to drown out the crowd and the announcer's play-by-play, before getting up and making his way down the stands and over to an exit door. I settled back and watched the match resume, trying to placate Anne. It wasn't easy. Mike wasn't the only person I'd let down recently. I'd missed a long-planned date night with Anne the evening before while staking out two married Ohio State medical school professors meeting up at a Hilton out east. The catch being they weren't married to each other. Like I said, I needed the money. When my efforts to make peace with Anne failed, I turned my attention to the track and tried to focus on the action and not on Lucy's quip. *Rear-end heaven.* Once again, it wasn't easy.

A couple of minutes later Roy walked back inside and signaled me. Suppressing a sigh of gratitude, I hoisted myself off the bleacher and joined him on the floor.

"What's up?"

"What's up is you may need a divorce lawyer, to judge by the way Anne's looking at you right now."

"Excepting the fact we're not married, tell me something I don't already know."

"As if I've got all day. Listen. Guy I think you should talk to," he said, gesturing at the phone.

"What guy?"

"Guy might have a job for you."

"A job?"

"That's what he said."

"But he called you."

"And I'm suggesting you talk to him. You're what, drowning in work?"

I thought about the boy band, about the four or five notes they'd actually hit. "What kind of job?"

"Here," he said, handing me the phone. "I'm going back up. I don't want to miss any Lycra."

"Buy me another beer?" I said to his back.

"I don't buy swill," he replied.

2

I WALKED TO THE EXIT AND STEPPED OUTSIDE.
I didn't need my coat. It was as sunny and mild as an Indian summer afternoon, even though we weren't that far from Christmas.
The temperature had yet to dip below freezing this fall, unusual
for central Ohio. It felt unnatural, whether it was global warming
or El Niño or an approaching asteroid. It ought to be colder this
time of year.

I introduced myself to the caller and asked how I could help.

"My sister's missing," the man said. "I was hoping you could
find her."

"I can try. How long's she been gone?"

"I'm not sure, exactly. A few weeks. Maybe months."

"Months?"

"Maybe." I heard a small boy's voice in the background. My
caller said something indistinct in response.

I said, "Have you talked to the police?"

"Last week."

"Your sister's been missing for months and you just now went
to the police?"

"She disappears a lot."

"Why?"

"She's a prostitute."

I paused. "That's not good."

"I know. That's why I'm calling."

"I'm sorry. I shouldn't have—"

"It's OK."

"Where's she work?"

"Different places. In a motel for a while, but sometimes the streets, too. Bottoms now and then, but east side, mainly."

"OK." Roy's Episcopal church was in the Bottoms, an old and struggling neighborhood west of downtown officially known as Franklinton, which may have explained how he got the call. I said, "What's her name?"

"Jessica. Jessica Byrnes."

"What's yours?"

"Bill Byrnes."

"Where do you live?"

"Whitehall. Off Yearling."

I thought for a moment. "You around tomorrow?" At least I was free, thanks to my screw-up the previous week.

He was. We settled on early afternoon. He gave me his address.

"You think you can find her?"

"I'll do my best. I'm sorry about what I said. The way it came out."

"It's OK. I know it's not good. That's why I called your friend. I saw him quoted in that article. I figured I should try to find her. Even though—"

I waited for him to finish the sentence, but the line went quiet again, the only noise the sound of the child in the background.

"I'll see you tomorrow," I said.

I hung up, pocketed Roy's phone, and went back inside the Ohio Building.

"Doesn't sound good," Roy said, meeting me by the food stand. He traded me a can of Four Strings Skeleton Red Rye IPA for his phone. I nodded my thanks. You can't always drink swill.

"I know," I said, watching the women circle the track. They crouched as they skated, like hunters. Bonnie was having a good match so far. I was happy for her, at least.

"This guy's sister. She'd make, what? Number six?" Roy said.

"God, I hope not," I said. I started to head back to the bleachers when I stopped.

"Where'd Anne go?"

"She left."

"Left?"

"Said her back hurt. And Amelia was getting cranky. And she was tired of waiting for you."

"Jesus," I said. "Could this day get any worse?"

"It will if you take the Lord's name in vain. Remember, when people say 'Jesus,' they usually mean 'Shit.'"

"Thanks for the sermon."

"No need to thank me. It's my job. What's that sound?"

It was my phone. I hadn't recognized my new ring tone, Bon Jovi's "Livin' on a Prayer." I pulled the cell out of my pocket and checked the number.

Crystal. My second ex-wife.

"Guess I answered my own question," I said, turning away to take the call.

3

FIVE BODIES SO FAR. NOT SIX. FIVE THAT they'd found. The actual number? No one knew.

Well, that wasn't strictly true.

One person did.

The first turned up nearly a year ago, on a snowless February morning so cold they canceled school anyway, the woman dumped behind a trash bin in an alley not far from the corner of Main and Champion on the east side. Melissa Loomis. Strangled. "Missy" to her friends and family, what little she had left of either. Twenty-seven. Two kids, though the county had taken them years earlier. Addicted to heroin, a habit she supported by selling the only thing she thought she had left of value, usually on the streets, sometimes, in the better months, out of a rent-by-the-hour motel room. Once upon a time she'd nearly finished a general studies associate's degree at Columbus State, with aspirations to be a teacher. Then she slipped on ice and a friend of a friend offered a pill for the pain and the ensuing addiction ended that dream. The rest was an all too familiar story.

The next, Talanda York, the following April. Body found by a farmer in a ditch in Groveport on the southeast side. Pronounced ligature marks around her neck. Thirty-eight, black, several kids. Also a heroin addict, also a prostitute, although she'd slipped back into the life only recently after what seemed like a couple of good years. It escaped no one's attention, especially the media's, that two prostitutes had been murdered within a few months' time. But the two hadn't known each other and their bodies were miles apart. After a flurry of articles and news segments, people diverted their attention elsewhere.

Then, over the summer, two bodies discovered inside of three weeks. The first, Natasha Rumsey, nineteen, white, last seen by her boyfriend a month earlier after they'd had a fight—his story— and she'd stormed out of his apartment. Taking the missing person report, a Columbus detective needed all of five minutes to figure out that "boyfriend" was a euphemism for a freelance pimp who'd blown his stack at Natasha because he didn't tolerate back-talk and Natasha was, by his account, one mouthy bitch. A homeless man found her in an abandoned house off Bryden Road in late June where he'd hoped to squat. The boyfriend was picked up on unrelated drug charges while they tried to make a case against him. Days went by without a murder indictment. Eventually, it became clear that while he might have consigned Natasha to her death by his actions, he probably wasn't her killer. In a cruel irony, it appeared that in Natasha's short and brutal life, her boyfriend-pimp was the only one who'd cared enough to tell somebody she was gone.

The next body, Lisa Washington, was hooked by fishermen angling for carp at the Scioto reservoir off Greenlawn. Her grandmother had reported the twenty-four-year-old African American woman missing two weeks earlier. She was the same age as Jessica Byrnes and, like her, hadn't been seen for a while by the time the report was filed. People began to get nervous. Fear started to heal estrangements. Family feuds were swept aside. A new reality settled over the city like a chill summer mist.

The headlines surged and then, as they do, faded again. By now it was fall in central Ohio, which meant football season, which meant people had more important things on their minds. Then, just two weeks ago, a kid playing hooky stumbled across the partially decomposed body of Juanita Cowgill in a field along 3C highway between Mound and Alkire, a straight shot south from the Bottoms, the neighborhood served by Roy's church. A part of town where many of the city's most desperate prostitutes plied their trade. Juanita's parents threw her out at eighteen when she accused a family friend of abusing her. She bounced from boyfriend to boyfriend until she landed with one looking for a source of revenue without actually having to work himself. She was two days shy of her twenty-first birthday. After her body was found, the coroner announced at a news conference that each woman had been strangled with a similar cord and each showed signs of sexual assault. There was no disguising it. Columbus had a serial killer on its hands.

Five. Five women raped, strangled, and thrown away like garbage. A task force was assembled. Hands were wrung at City Hall. The FBI got involved. Missing person reports rained down on the police department like parade confetti. Johns grew wary as Columbus vice started running nightly soliciting stings. Right after Juanita's body was discovered, the *Dispatch* and Channel 7 interviewed Roy, whose church worked with trafficking victims. "Being poor and hopeless is not a crime," he said, urging people to put family disagreements aside and account for loved ones.

And then Bill Byrnes called.

IT WAS STILL MILD THE NEXT DAY WHEN I pulled into the parking lot of Byrnes's apartment complex in Whitehall, a working-class suburb just east of Columbus.

"Thanks for coming," he said, opening the door of his spare second-floor unit shortly after two o'clock. We walked into the living room, where a boy sat on the couch watching TV.

"This is Robbie," Byrnes said. "Can you say hi?"

The boy, three or four, grudgingly nodded at me after some additional prodding. My eyes lingered a moment too long on the child, who was dark-complected, unlike Byrnes. "He's Jessica's son," he explained. "I've got custody of him."

So this story got even worse, I thought. We went into the kitchen, where Bill offered me a chair. One leg was shorter than the others, and I braced myself to keep from rocking. I looked around. The cupboards were clean and the counters were spare but tidy. The sink was empty. Robbie's drawings covered the refrigerator.

"So," I said after a couple of moments of silence passed. Byrnes watched me like a patient waiting for the doctor to give it to him straight. "When was the last time you saw your sister?"

"Early July. She called, asked if she could come over."

"OK."

"Her, and that girl Lisa."

"Lisa?"

"Lisa Washington. The one they found in the river."

"They knew each other?"

"They were friends, I guess." He had a corrected harelip and a way of looking just past you when he talked, as if afraid of what he might see. But the worry in his eyes, when you could catch them, looked genuine.

"And did they? Come over?"

Byrnes nodded. "They stayed about an hour. Jessica seemed, I don't know, a little preoccupied or something, but nothing she'd talk about. She played with Robbie. They both did. Seemed to cheer them up. Especially Lisa. Right at the end Jessica asked if she could borrow some money."

"What'd you say?"

"I gave her a hundred bucks. It was all I had."

"And that was it? Last time you saw her?"

"Yeah. But a couple weeks later she called. July 26. I only remember because it was the day after Lisa's body was found. She didn't leave a message. I called back, but there was no answer. That had happened before, so I didn't think much about it."

"But now you've reported her missing."

He shrugged. "I read what that minister said. Everything that's been going on, I thought I better."

"And why'd you call him?"

"See if he'd seen her." He glanced into the living room and lowered his voice. "Since she worked in the Bottoms, for a while. Friend of mine saw her once, on Sullivant, staring at guys in cars. The minister said he didn't know her. But thought maybe you could help."

"Do you have a picture of her?"

He pushed a manila envelope toward me. I opened it and pulled out two photos. The first was of a teenage girl, sixteen or seventeen, laughing at something out of the frame of the picture.

She had a pretty face with freckles marching up her nose, light blue eyes, and brownish hair pulled back off a high forehead into a ponytail. There was something wild in her expression, a gleam in the eyes that hinted at rebellion. But basically hers was no different than the faces of a thousand other girls that age. Girls with nice clothes and straight teeth and futures that didn't include bending their heads into the laps of men with working ATM cards. I put the picture down and examined the second. I almost didn't recognize her. She was heavily made up, her eyes dark with eyeliner and mascara, her lips the red of cheap Christmas ribbon. She was curled on a bed wearing nothing but a scarlet bra and panties, sucking on her right forefinger, glowering at the camera. Glowering a generous word, because the photo was a cruel parody of seduction. She looked sexy the way roadkill looks like taxidermy. Even with the photo's grainy quality, it was clear the light in the eyes of her lively, teenage self had dimmed, replaced by something opaque and exhausted. She looked much older than she should have, weary beyond her years, her face tense, her body strained as if recoiling from a blow. I examined the photo more closely and made out a dark line across her neck, which I first took for a strand of hair but then realized was a name tattooed in cursive. The first letter, B, was all I could decipher.

"When were these taken?"

"First one's from high school," Byrnes said. "Eleventh grade. At a sleepover, I think. Right before she left home. I found the second one on the Internet this summer, looking for her. It was on Reardoor.com. It's a personals site."

I nodded. I'd heard of it. There'd been a lot in the news lately about websites and the trafficking industry. Both Missy Loomis and Natasha Rumsey had advertised themselves that way. A congresswoman was holding hearings on the sites and whether they should be outlawed as facilitating prostitution.

I pointed at the Internet photo. "How recent is that?"

"Not very. Probably a year old."

"The word on her neck. Do you know what that is?"

"Might be her pimp's name. They do that sometimes. It was covered up when she was here last."

"Who's her pimp?"

"I don't know. I asked but she wouldn't tell me. Said it was too dangerous."

Too dangerous for whom? I wondered. I said, "OK if I keep these?"

"Sure."

"You said she left home. Was that here? Whitehall?"

He shook his head. "We grew up in Mount Alexandria."

"I know it. I'm from close by there." The small city was just under an hour east of Columbus. "You have family there still?"

"Just our mom."

"Dad?"

"Died of cancer. My mom remarried."

"When did you move here?"

"Five years ago. After I got out of the army."

"What do you do?"

"I run a forklift at a warehouse, over in Reynoldsburg. But I'm taking classes. I want to do engineering someplace."

"Any chance your mom knows where Jessica is?"

"I doubt it."

"Have you asked her?"

"No."

"Why not?"

Byrnes shifted in his seat. "There's no point. I don't think she would know. They didn't get along."

"Any reason?"

"They argued a lot, especially after my mom remarried."

"How about your stepdad? Would he know?"

"They split up a while ago."

"Do you know when Jessica came to Columbus?"

"After high school. I wasn't around then—I left when I was eighteen."

"Did she come here for work?"

"I think."

"Any idea who she stayed with?"

"No. Like I said, I wasn't around. I maybe wasn't the greatest brother." He looked away, ostensibly to check on Robbie in the other room.

"Don't worry about stuff like that. Things happen no matter what we do, OK?"

"OK, I guess."

"You know how long she's been working the streets?"

"A while. At least since I got back."

"What parts of town?"

"Bunch of places. Bottoms, like I said. East side, more recently. The Rest EZ, a lot of the times."

"Rest EZ?"

"Motel, up there, on East Main." He pointed through the wall behind him. "Where she, you know, met customers. It's a pit. Columbus has been trying to shut it down. Too late now."

"She stayed there?"

"Sometimes. She moved around a lot."

"And you said she called the day after Lisa's body was found?"

"Yeah. But no message, like I said."

"Right." It could mean anything, I thought. A grieving girl looking for comfort after her friend's death. A frightened girl reaching out for help. Or a drug-addled girl looking for more money.

"What'd the police say?"

"They took it seriously. Guy came out and asked me a bunch of questions."

"Do you know who?"

"I don't remember. I've got his card in the other room. So what do you think? About finding her?"

I hesitated. I glanced into the other room at Robbie.

"Any idea who his father is?"

"Not a clue. Jessica just showed up with him. He was nothing but a baby. Said she couldn't handle him. Long story short,

I decided to keep him. Thought it was the right thing to do. Thought maybe, someday, Jessica might, you know—"

"She didn't say anything about the dad?"

"She wasn't around long enough. And to be honest, the guys she was with? I'm not sure I want to know. So can you help me or not?"

"Sure," I said. No idea. "There's just a couple of things—"

"I can pay. That's not a problem. Just tell me how much."

I looked around the spare kitchen. At the worn furniture in the living room. At Robbie, glued to the TV. I wondered if anyone knew who his father was. If even Jessica knew. I quoted Byrnes a number half my usual rate which wouldn't even cover expenses. Even at that, I saw him blanch a moment before pulling out his wallet.

"You have that cop's card?" I said after he'd handed me the cash. "And I'll need your mom's number."

"Why?"

"Standard operating procedure. I talk to lots of people, job like this."

"She hasn't seen Jessica in a lot longer than me."

"I still have to ask."

"OK," he said, doubtfully. He gave me her number, stood up, and went into the living room to hunt the detective's card. When he came back we finished with the part I hate the most. I asked for identifying features in case of. He nodded. There was the pimp's name on her neck. Some roses tattooed on her left shoulder. A broken collarbone from a sledding accident when they were kids. He didn't know about dental records.

"Thanks," he said when we were done and I stood at the door. "You'll stay in touch?"

I told him I would. We shook hands and I walked downstairs to the parking lot. I got in my van, pulled out my phone, and dialed the number for the missing person detective. Larry Schwartzbaum. Name didn't mean anything to me. I left a message, as I figured I would on a Sunday afternoon. I held off calling the mom. Tammy. I needed some more information first.

I drove south on Yearling until it bottomed out at Livingston. I pulled into the parking lot at Resch's, went inside, and ordered a dozen doughnuts to go. I was supposed to have dinner at Anne's that night and figured they might make a decent peace offering. Along with the flowers in the back of my van and a book of sci-fi stories I'd picked up for her at the Book Loft. I was back outside and had just started up the Odyssey when the guitar licks of "Livin' on a Prayer" alerted me to an incoming call. I stared at the caller ID in surprise.

"Shelley?"

"It's Dad," my sister said. "He's had a heart attack. They're not sure he's going to make it."

MOUNT CARMEL EAST WAS LESS THAN FIFTEEN minutes away from Resch's, on the east side of the city, where things are a little more spread out, including the cemetery across from the hospital that I tried to ignore as I parked. Half running into the emergency department, I found my mom sitting in the waiting room and staring at a TV hanging in the corner as if nothing was wrong, as if she were taking a break after a morning of errands. Her eyes widened when she saw me. She stood up. I walked over and put my arms around her. She held me tightly but didn't speak. Then she pulled away. I looked closely at her. I couldn't tell if her short hair seemed grayer and pale blue eyes more exhausted because of what had happened or how long it had been since I'd seen her.

"How is he?"

She shook her head.

"Shelley called," I said. "What happened?"

"I didn't ask her to call you."

"I figured as much. She did anyway. Were you at home?"

She sat down. I took a seat beside her. "We were Christmas shopping," she said. "At Easton." The sprawling Columbus mall was on the far east side of town. "We'd just stopped to look at the kids lined up for Santa Claus. I heard something and looked over and he was slumped against some kid. A teenager, I mean. Then he just fell over. He never said anything." She paused. "His face was absolutely blue."

A splinter of memory. My father exhorting me to throw a football through a tire hanging from a tree branch. I couldn't have been more than three or four. The same age as little Robbie, Jessica's son.

"Had he been . . . Were there any symptoms, or anything?"

"He'd seemed tired recently. He's been working a lot. The hardware store—well, you might not know about that. They've been busy, with Christmas, and they've been giving him a lot of hours. He's good at it. Customers like him. I told him he didn't have to come. He should stay home and rest. But he insisted. Wanted to drive me. He hasn't had any of the usual signs, if that's what you're asking. No pain in his arms, that kind of thing."

Yelling at me to do better. Eye on the tire, Andy! Focus! Wait for it, then throw!

"You're sure?" It would have been just like my dad to hide it. From my mom, but also from himself.

"Yes," she said, sharply. "He's been taking his pills, usually without me nagging."

"Has he been exercising? Walking?"

"Oh, Andy. What kind of question is that?"

"I'm just asking—"

"If he deserved it?"

"*No.*" Yes.

Focus, Andy, focus! You're not listening to me! Swaying as he spoke, but not from excitement or emotion. In the background, the voice of my uncle, chastising my father. Telling him to ease up.

"We walk on the weekends. Sometimes. Satisfied?"

"I'm sorry," I said. "Forget it. I guess it's a good thing you were over here. Close to hospitals."

"There's hospitals near home."

"You know what I mean."

"I don't know what I'm going to do. Nobody's telling me anything. I didn't plan for any of this." She hugged herself as if she were cold, though in truth the room was uncomfortably warm. She was wearing brown shoes and jeans and a red sweater.

"What's happening now?"

"I don't know. They rushed him in. It's been a couple of hours. I called Shelley as soon as I could."

"And then she called me."

"I didn't ask her to do that."

"You already said that."

"I'm surprised you came."

"Of course I'd come. Don't be ridiculous."

"I'm not being ridiculous." After a moment, she said, "If he dies—"

"He's not going to die."

"If he dies," she repeated, "I may sell the house. It's too big for us now as it is. I just want you to know that. They've built some apartments along the Gambier Road. I might move there. It's a little closer to the school, anyway."

"He's not going to die."

She looked at me. "Really, Andy? How do you know that? How could you, of all people, possibly know that?"

I didn't have an answer. There was nothing for me to say. I sat back and locked eyes with a guy sitting across from us wearing a Buckeyes shirt and staring at me like he knew who I was—which was entirely possible. I held his gaze until he looked away. I spent a minute watching four disembodied heads on separate screens yak about something on CNN. I thought about Jessica Byrnes, how similar she looked in her high school picture to the students my mom taught.

"Lynne Hayes?"

My mom looked up. A doctor stood before the double doors to the left of the reception desk. He was frowning.

"Yes," my mother said.

Focus, Andy, focus!

"I need to ask you to come with me."

6

HOPALONG WALKED THE LAST HUNDRED yards of our third circuit around Schiller Park the next morning. I didn't push it. He'd long ago lost that puppyish spring to his step. I could say the same. I patted him on the head and let him pull me over to the cluster of dog walkers in the center of the park. I unclipped his leash for a bout of sniffing and chasing and nipping. It was still dark, sunrise close to an hour away. The mild December air made it feel like the week before a late Easter. I chatted about the Blue Jackets with a guy I'd seen around who had a black lab-collie mix. For the record, he agreed with me about jumbotrons. After a few minutes I called for Hopalong, reattached his leash, and walked up to my house at 837 Mohawk. I opened the door, let the dog inside, and pulled the door shut. I turned around and went back to the park and did three more loops on my own, sprinting for fifteen seconds at every other telephone pole. I'm not *that* old.

When I returned I checked my phone for messages, drank a glass of chocolate milk, and did twenty pull-ups on the bar I'd installed within my kitchen doorframe. I rested and did ten more.

I got on the floor and with Hopalong studying me from under the kitchen table did one hundred sit-ups, a new record. A new age-group record, I corrected myself. I did some core exercises, some planks and some crunches and a back-and-forth thing with my hips that Anne had taught me, and then stretched and lifted some free weights. Anne, who'd texted me three times and called twice when I didn't show for dinner the night before. Whose anger faded when I finally called and explained about my dad, though not without an emotional "Why didn't you call me?" Good question. I tried to think of an answer when I tossed the now-fading flowers I'd bought her into the garbage can out back.

When I was finished exercising I checked my phone again, took a shower, and dressed. I scrambled three eggs and added some shredded Colby-Jack and poured myself the first of three bowls of cereal and sat down at the table with the *Dispatch*. I turned to the sports page and checked my phone again. Still nothing since my sister's text at midnight: Mom finally asleep. Short visit possible in the morning if he's conscious.

I tried to relax. I read the entire paper, even *Marmaduke*. There was nothing new about the serial killings other than a short article about a vigil later in the week for the slain women and those who were still missing. The congresswoman battling the online sites had organized it. Even less than a day after meeting Bill Byrnes I felt an urgency about this assignment. If Jessica was still alive, every moment counted.

When I was finished eating I opened my laptop and searched her name on the Franklin County muni court records page. Soliciting or drug arrests or both going back several years filled a screen. I clicked on the most recent case, from just about a year ago. Her status was listed as "Diversion in lieu of prosecution." I saw that Karen Feinberg had represented her. So that was one good thing. I called Karen on her cell phone. When the connection went through I heard a baby crying, and then Karen's voice.

"This better be an offer to change a diaper."

"A week Thursday work for you?"

"That slot's taken. What's up? I'm on my way out the door."

"I thought you were doing the stay-at-home mom thing."

"Change of plans."

"Gabby's OK?"

"Yes. What do you need?"

I explained why I was calling. Karen, one of the city's top young defense lawyers, and Gabby, her wife, a probate attorney, had bailed me out more than once on difficult cases. The high-profile entanglements I drove their way in return hadn't hurt their own careers either, I supposed.

"She's missing? Shit," she said, over her son's wailing.

"You mean Jesus?"

"What?"

"Never mind. You have time to go over her case today?"

"As if. Four arraignments, and those are just the ones I know about."

"You have to eat. I'm buying. Name your place."

"Usual joint, in that case. High noon. No, make it high noon and a quarter. Gotta go."

After I hung up I shot Bonnie Deckard an e-mail with Jessica's name and date of birth, asking her to poke around on her case online to see if she found anything I might have missed. Then I powered down my laptop, put it in my shoulder bag along with a water bottle, an apple, a notebook, my copy of *James A. Rhodes: Ohio Colossus*, the envelope with the pictures of Jessica, and a phone charger. I didn't need a coat but grabbed it anyway. I went outside, got into my van, and headed to the hospital.

7

"WHY ARE YOU HERE?" MY FATHER SAID, turning his head toward me.

"To see you."

"Make fun of me, more like it." His voice scratchy with fatigue. "Before I die."

"You're not going to die."

"You want me to."

"No, I don't."

Behind me, I heard my mother sigh.

"You think this is my fault," he said. "Because I don't exercise. That's what you said."

Focus, Andy, focus!

I'm trying!

Not hard enough!

"It's not your fault," I said, though I knew I didn't believe it. I glanced at my mom, silently accusing her. She stared back, her face a stone.

"Like you're so high and mighty," my dad said. "My son the security guard. Like you eat vegetables all day long. Like you run marathons."

"Bud," my mother said. "Leave off."

I took a breath and pushed my chair back. We were crowded into his room on the cardiac step-down unit. A tube snaked from his nose down along his side. He had an IV in his left arm. He looked pale and pasty, salt-and-pepper stubble turning the corner into a beard. He'd been stabilized, catheterized, brought back from the dead with the help of stents and angioplasty and some other things I didn't understand. But his blockage was too severe for him to go home before the surgery. Shelley had driven back to Cleveland to gather some things and make arrangements for a longer stay. My mom was driving back to Homer that night, declining an offer to stay with me.

"How are you feeling?" I said.

"How do you think? Like shit on toast."

"Hopalong's favorite snack."

"Who's that?"

"My dog. It was a joke."

A grunt. "What kind of dog?"

"Golden lab."

"Bitch?"

"Male."

He grunted again, gave the slightest nod.

"He's a good dog," I said. "Gets the job done. You'd like—"

"When Bernie died, I thought about telling you. Calling you up. Asked your mother for your number. Then I thought, what the hell. Why? What would you care?"

"Bernie?"

"Yeah."

"That was, like, fifteen years ago."

"I still miss him. That a problem?"

"No. I'm sorry Bernie died. He was a good dog too. And I'm not a security guard."

"What are you?"

"I'm an investigator."

"Of what?"

"People's problems. I help fix things."

"You help people?" He laughed, stopping just short of it turning into a cough.

"What I said."

"Never helped us."

"That's not true."

"All we did for you. Down the toilet." His voice gravel, and low. Though not like when he drank and smoked. "We struggled while you messed everything up. Help people. That's a good one."

"So the fact you couldn't hold down a job is suddenly my fault?"

My mother's sharp intake of breath was audible. "Andy," she said. But it was too late. My father squeezed his hands into fists and rolled his head to the side and shut his eyes. He looked so much like my grandfather in the days before his death that I had to turn away. I met my mother's face, white and drawn. She was shaking with fury.

"I didn't tell Shelley to call you," she said.

"I know you didn't," I said, and turned and walked out of the room.

A FEW HOURS LATER I WAS SITTING AT A table at Jury of Your Pours on Mound near High, just across the street from the courthouse. I spied a brace of judges, a pride of prosecutors, and a drove of defense attorneys, and that was just at the bar. The only thing it lacked was actual jurors. My reconnoitering over, I went back to examining a photo of a fat-cheeked baby with a dark head of hair on Karen's phone. It looked identical to the four other photos of her son I'd just looked at.

"Favors his father," I said.

"So funny."

Giving birth to Noah had swung Gabby's religiously conservative parents around to her marriage to Karen. But I still doubted they'd laugh at sperm bank jokes.

"Tell me about Jessica," Karen said, spearing a forkful of salad.

I went over the call Roy got, my visit with her brother and little Robbie, the Rest EZ, Reardoor.com, and everything else.

"So when's the last time you saw her?" I said.

She reached into her briefcase and pulled out a purple file folder. She opened it and flipped through several pages before finding the one she wanted. "Last December. She was picked up for soliciting near Kelton Street."

"Court records made it look like she was in and out of jail."

"True. Until the last time."

"Oh?"

"She went into a diversion program one of the muni court judges runs. It's like a boot camp for trafficking victims. They spend two years trying to pull their shit together and taking classes and getting off drugs. If they make it all the way through, they graduate and there's a ceremony at the governor's residence and they've got their life back and they aren't prosecuted. It's a good deal."

"Sounds like it. So what happened?"

"She was doing fine as far as I know. I'd sort of lost track of her. This July I got a notice that she didn't show up to the regular Thursday session. They couldn't reach her anywhere. The judge signed an arrest warrant the next day."

"You have the date?"

She took another bite of salad and paged through more papers.

"July 27."

I told her about the call without a message that Bill Byrnes received on the 26th, the day after Lisa Washington's body was discovered.

Karen said, "Makes a little more sense now. She could have been upset, or scared. Which could explain why she went AWOL. Unless . . ."

"Unless she was next, and just hasn't been found."

"We can't discount it. Let's hope we're wrong. Maybe she snapped after her friend's murder and left town. She's not from here, right?"

"Mount Alexandria. Her mom's over there. My impression is they don't exchange Christmas cards."

"Yeah, that's what I remember. She could be anywhere, when it comes down to it. If she's still alive."

I remembered the name tattooed on Jessica's neck. I asked Karen about it. She made a face as if she'd just found half a bug in her salad and had a good idea where the other half was.

"Bronte," she said.

"I'm sorry?"

"Bronte Patterson. His name on her neck is like he branded her. To show who belongs to who. It's a pimp thing."

"He have a brother named Heathcliff?"

"Right. His more evil twin."

"Bronte's his real name?"

She shook her head. "It's Bryan. The joke is he was going for something evoking 'brontosaurus' without realizing they have brains the size of walnuts."

"What's his status?"

"Status?"

"In jail? On the streets? In a management training program?"

"He's out as far as I know. He's a wily guy. Teflon coated, for some reason. Cops can't seem to touch him."

"Wonder if he knows where Jessica is."

"It's a possibility. She was his bottom girl for a while."

"Bottom girl?"

"It's sort of a misnomer. It means his top girl. Best girl. The one he uses to train the new ones."

"Train?"

"What these girls do doesn't come naturally. There's rules. Tips."

"Such as?"

"Such as, get the guys off as quickly as possible so you can move on to the next one. Always carry gum, to get the taste out of your mouth. Lie about your age. The younger they think you are, the faster they—"

"OK. I get it. Did she still turn tricks?"

"Oh, yeah. It's not that important a job."

"Maybe I'll go ask him what he knows."

"I'm not sure that's such a good idea."

"Why not?"

She took a bite of her salad and leaned back in her chair. She picked her phone off the table, fiddled a bit, and handed it to me. I stared at a scowling white guy with blue eyes the color of spilled windshield washer fluid, muscular shoulders bulging through a wife beater, a shaved head, a badly healed nose, a scar on his left cheek, and the letters EWMN tattooed across his forehead.

"I liked the pictures of Noah better."

"I know his name's funny sounding," Karen said. "But don't kid yourself. Bronte's not the kind of guy you want to mess around with. He has a reputation for hurting his girls. He also has a reputation for hurting anyone who hurts his girls."

"And people say chivalry is dead." I took another look at the picture. I'd give Karen this: Bronte Patterson looked like the real deal. Like a guy I'd cross to the other side of the interstate to avoid. "But Jessica wasn't with him anymore, right? If she was in that program?"

"Guys like him have long memories. It's possible he had something to do with her dropping out. Or if he didn't directly, he was trying to find her and she knew that and took off. Which wouldn't be good for you."

"Meaning?"

"Meaning you'd be in a race with Patterson to locate her. And this is not a guy who likes to lose."

9

THERESA SULLIVAN WAS ON THE PHONE
in the office of Zion Episcopal on Grubb Street in the Bottoms
when I walked in. She set the receiver down and looked at me in
that way of hers I'd grown to appreciate. The way people look
when they spy a cockroach on the kitchen counter.

"What?"

"Parson around?"

"Not here. He made a run to the camp."

I nodded. Among Roy's many missions was his street medicine work: checking on the health needs of people in a homeless
shelter tucked in woods along railroad tracks just minutes from
downtown. It was annoying the way he made the rest of us look
so bad.

I said, "Actually, it's you I came to see."

"Me?"

"That's right."

"For what?"

"It's about a case I'm working on."

"What kind of case?"

I gave her the rundown. She frowned when I mentioned Bronte Patterson.

"Hang on," she said, gesturing at the phone.

I left the office, walked down the hall, turned right, and entered the sanctuary. I sat down in the second pew. It was chilly and dark inside, the only light coming in through the stained-glass windows. The air smelled of incense, wood polish, and mildew. The building looked airlifted straight from a small English town, with its stone block exterior, wooden altar, and arched ceiling, as if the architects had stripped a nineteenth-century sailing ship for lumber. Some plaster was coming off the walls here and there, and jigsawed patterns of painted plywood filled in a few stained-glass gaps, but it was in pretty good shape, thanks to the money the diocese had put into it to lure Roy in as priest. Much better shape than the flea market that had operated there most recently. Or the crack house before that. I pulled out my phone and checked my messages. Nothing new from Shelley or my mom. My dad's surgery was scheduled at week's end, and there was nothing to do but wait.

Theresa stepped inside the sanctuary and slipped into the pew beside me.

"Bronte Patterson," Theresa said. "That ain't good."

"So I gather. But maybe not as bad as a serial killer."

"Unless it's one and the same. Is this girl from here?"

"Mount Alexandria."

"Where's that?"

"Little city about an hour east. I grew up in a town near there."

"Always figured you for a country bumpkin. You trust the brother?"

"What do you mean?"

"I mean do you trust him? Is he really worried about his sister? Or does he want her found for some other reason?"

"Like what?"

"Like, maybe did he do something to her when she was younger, and he's feeling bad about it now?"

"Do something?"

"Use your imagination, QB."

"I'm not sure—"

She chuffed in exasperation. "Did he fuck her?"

"Jesus, I don't know. I don't think so."

"It happens."

"Yeah. But he's raising her son. Seems like that counts for something."

"What about Jessica's stepdad?"

"What about him?"

She rolled her eyes. "Did he fuck her?"

"I have no idea. Why are you asking me this?"

She rubbed her hands up and down her thighs, from the cold or from something else, I wasn't sure. She was wearing a long-sleeved yellow patterned dress over brown leggings, and a gray sweater coat over the dress to ward off the chill. In the past couple of years she'd gone from dressing the way you did selling yourself on the streets, which is where Roy found her, to looking like a grown-up Pippi Longstocking.

She said, "She ran away, right?"

"She left Mount Alex to come here after high school. Her brother didn't say if she ran away."

"Girls like her, they're not sucking strangers' dicks at 1 a.m. because they feel like it. They got pushed into it. And most of them got pushed by someone or something at home. Or near home. It's like when you step in dog shit."

"Dog shit?"

"You know how bad it smells? And how the smell don't go away? How hard it is to get it off your shoe?"

"Sure. People say I step in it all the time."

"How about not making it about you for once? That's how these girls live every day. Like their whole life is one big pile of it. I'm just saying for starters it'd be nice to find out who put it on *her* shoes."

I said nothing. The sanctuary was silent except for the sound of traffic up the street on Broad and a mechanical hum coming from someplace near the front. I glanced at Theresa, but she wouldn't make eye contact.

I said, "I get what you're saying. But how does that help us find her?"

"Who knows? She stepped in enough crap, she could be easy to track down."

"Either way, I'm going to need to hit the streets, start asking about her."

She nodded and rubbed her thighs.

"It'd be nice if I had someone to help me. Not exactly my territory."

"That's obvious," Theresa said. I looked up and saw that Roy had entered the sanctuary while we'd been talking.

"So, you available?"

"Me?"

"Yeah. I'll even let you drive the Odyssey."

"No thanks. Those vans look like they have big butts."

I laughed. "You're right. I never thought about it before."

"You gonna pay me?"

"Of course. You'd be on the clock."

"That's all right. I don't want any money. It'll be a freebie." She cackled. "When do we start?"

"How about tonight?"

"What time?"

I did the math. Despite that morning's disastrous visit, I planned to be back at the hospital most of the rest of the day.

"How about I pick you up at nine?"

"That works. I'll check with some girls from that court program. They might know something."

"Like what?"

"Like it's smarter to talk to me than a country bumpkin."

"THERESA'S RIGHT," ROY SAID a few minutes later, walking me outside. "Your van has a big butt. You look dumb driving it."

38

"Says the guy who wears black pajamas to work."

"Be careful, OK? Theresa's got that brusque exterior, but she's still fragile. She's only two years off the streets. One year sober."

"Was she abused? Is that why she was asking me about the brother?"

"I think it was a neighbor. What she always told me. Forced her to give him blowjobs, threatened her if she ever told. No one in the family knew. She started self-medicating with alcohol, and things went downhill from there."

"You're afraid looking for Jessica could be a trigger."

"Maybe. The stuff about dog shit? She didn't read that in a book."

10

"YOU REALLY THINK THIS IS WORTH IT?" I
said, turning onto Main Street off Third a few hours later. The
temperature had dropped into the upper thirties. "Is anybody
going to be around?"

"Cocks need sucked no matter the weather, QB. They'll be
out."

I shook my head at her language. Brusque exterior, indeed.
But sure enough, we saw our first girl just a couple of blocks after
crossing over the highway and across Parsons. She was staring
down a guy dressed like a bad imitation of a bum, one hand on a
shopping cart filled with scrap metal, the other waving at her. He
didn't look like a paying customer. I pulled up to the curb, parked,
and got out. The man took one look at us, laughed out loud, and
rattled down the street.

"Yeah?" she said. I pegged her as late teens, early twenties,
black, wearing tight jeans and an orange sequined blouse with a
tear in the side under a thin, unzipped gray hoodie. She had a face
three degrees from pretty that wasn't helped by dark bruising on
her left cheek. Her eyes were glassy and she swayed as she spoke.

I told her my name and my job and what I needed. I showed her the Reardoor.com picture of Jessica.

"You a cop?"

"I'm private, like I said." I thought of the scene with my father. "Like a security guard." The afternoon visit had gone only marginally better, but at least we hadn't come to blows.

"Bullshit."

"He's true," Theresa said, from the van.

"Who's she?"

"My backup," I said. "In case I get in trouble."

"You gonna need more than her." She studied the photograph for a minute, finally shaking her head and handing it back. She had to take a step to keep her balance. "Don't know her."

"You sure?"

"Not many white girls this side of town. Why you looking for her?"

"Like I said, she's missing."

"Missing from where?"

It was a good question, actually. "People who care about her haven't seen her in a while."

"Ain't that nice. Still don't know her."

"Could you call me if you see her?"

"Not likely. She probably dead, anyway."

"Why do you say that?"

"'Cause of that guy killing the girls. Why else she be missing?"

"Lots of reasons, I hope. How about you? Aren't you worried, being out here?"

"Nah."

"Why not?"

"Because."

"Because why?"

"'Cause the girls he got was stupid. Probably did dumb shit. Went someplace they shouldn't have. Did stuff they didn't need to."

I couldn't help myself. "Like it was their fault?" I said.

41

She laughed, and for the first time I could hear a cold in her chest. "You some big expert on us, huh?"

"I wouldn't say that." I thanked her, gave her my card, and got back in the van. I watched her crumple up the card and toss it in the gutter as I drove away.

"She's lying," Theresa said.

"About what?"

"About the guy. The killer. She's worried."

"How do you know?"

"I know. It's just she's got more important things to think about right now."

"What's more important than a serial killer?"

"How about, her next fix? How about, turning enough tricks to make her daddy happy? Happy enough he don't beat the shit out of her later. All that on your mind, a rope around your throat's the least of your concerns."

"Point taken."

We continued the drive east. A few blocks down I pulled over quickly. Two women were giving us the deadeye from a vacant lot across the street beside an abandoned convenience store. One black, one white. The white woman looked a lot like Jessica.

I got out and crossed over, Theresa following behind me.

"This ain't BYOB," the white one said, looking at Theresa. I studied her more closely and realized I'd been mistaken. She had the same high forehead and cocky purse to her lips as Jessica, and she was about the same height and weight. She even had the same brown hair. The resemblance was real enough. But that's all it was. A cruel similarity that maybe grew from a shared life on the streets.

I gave them my spiel and showed them the photo.

"Know who she is," the look-alike said, taking the photo from me. She was wearing a thin black sweater, red satin shorts, and black stockings with a run all the way down the left leg. "Lisa's friend. Girl who died."

"Lisa Washington," I said.

"Yeah."

I tapped the photo. "Have you seen her around?"

"Not for a while."

"How long a while?"

"Couldn't say. Months, maybe."

"Anybody ever tell you that you look like her?"

"People ain't looking at my face out here, OK?"

"Just asking." But what I was thinking was: in another context, in another world, they might have been. She was pretty underneath the hard set of her mouth and her cold stare. The expressive, intelligent eyes fixed on me didn't fit her current situation. Change a few things and she could easily have been somebody's girlfriend, stepping out to a club or going to a ballgame or strolling through an art museum instead of standing on a street corner in the cold wearing clothes that would barely keep you warm in May, let alone December.

I said, "I heard she was Bronte Patterson's bottom girl."

"You say so."

"You know Bronte?"

"Know of him."

"You know how I can find him? How I could get in touch?"

She laughed nervously. "No."

"Know anybody who does?"

She shook her head, not meeting my eyes.

"How long have you been out here?"

"Couple hours. Why?"

"I meant, how long have you been doing this?"

"Listen, mister. Fuck off, all right? Ain't your business. And you're hurting mine, standing here like this."

"Are you from here?" I persisted. "Columbus?"

"Why do you care?"

"I'm just asking."

"Go to hell." She looked at me with what passed for fire in those expressive eyes. But all she had left was coals after someone pisses on them.

I gave her my card. "You see Jessica, would you call me? I can pay."

"Pay me now."

"For what?"

"Something."

"I'm not interested in—"

"Not that. Something about Jessica."

"What?"

Her eyes moved to the street, where cars were slowing at the corner before moving on when they spied me. She glared at me. I nodded. She wouldn't be the first person to tell me I was bad for their bottom line. I pulled out my wallet and handed her a twenty. It disappeared like a flame snuffed by a sudden breeze.

"She's in trouble."

"What kind of trouble?"

"She's scared of something."

"What?"

"I don't know. Lisa was scared too."

"Like, of him? The guy killing the women?"

"I don't think so. I mean, yeah, shit, they were scared of that. Who isn't? But something else. Something more dire."

"Dire?" I said, pausing at the word, which didn't fit the girl or the situation she was in.

"Lisa had something. Something somebody wanted."

"Something like what?"

"Don't know. It's just what I heard."

"Jessica knew about it?"

"I know Jessica went looking for her, after she disappeared. I know Lisa was scared and then Jessica was scared. And that's all I know. You got another twenty?"

"For more information?"

"For business. We can go in your van. She can wait outside." She sniffed at Theresa.

Theresa said, "How about your friend?" She gestured at the girl next to her, who had yet to speak. She was young, short, stocky, wearing yoga pants and a faded Ohio State sweatshirt. Her matted hair looked as if someone had died midway through an attempt at cornrows. She seemed like a person who'd started with a hard life and gone downhill from there. "You know where Bronte is?"

The girl stared through Theresa. Her friend shrugged. "She doesn't talk much. Why I like her around."

I showed the girl the photograph of Jessica. "Do you know her?" I said.

She shook her head and flipped me off.

"OK," I said. I turned to the first woman. "What's your name?"

"Why?"

"In case I need to find you again."

"Why would you need to do that?"

"I don't know. For business. How about that?"

"That's more like it. Darla. Satisfied?"

"That your real name?" Theresa said.

"Right, bitch."

I said. "You want another twenty?"

"Sure."

I handed her my card. "You see Jessica, positive I.D., call me. I find her, it's all yours."

The card didn't disappear as quickly as the twenty. But at least she hung onto it. We crossed back over. I heard my name called. I turned around. She shouted out the name of a suburb.

"What about it?"

"Where I'm from. Satisfied?"

The small burg she'd named was a destination bedroom community just outside of Columbus. An All-American city. One of those places with good schools and green lawns and subdivisions with no sidewalks and no visible streetwalkers.

I nodded and waved. I got back in my van.

I wasn't satisfied.

11

"THEY CLAMMED UP FAST ABOUT BRONTE,"
I said, a few blocks east.

"Course they did. They don't want to get out of pocket."

"Meaning?"

"Sideways with their daddy. Their pimp. He catches them looking at another pimp, or not crossing the street when one comes by, they're in trouble."

"How'd you know about her name?"

"Nobody uses their real name out here."

"Why not?"

"Same reason you stay high as much as possible. So you can stand the taste of dick."

I grimaced. I was starting to realize how little I knew about what Theresa had gone through in her days on the streets.

"What was yours?"

"My what?"

"Your name."

She hesitated. "Patty."

"Why Patty?"

"Just because." She turned and looked out the window. I didn't press.

We kept it up another hour, driving up and down side streets, pausing at street corners, looking down alleys. I showed the picture and handed out my card at least five more times. A couple other girls knew Jessica; like Darla, no one had seen her in a while. I was getting close to calling it a night as we approached the line dividing Columbus and Bexley, the closest east-side suburb. Above us loomed a complex of abandoned grain silos on the south side of the street. Vandals and the elements had chipped large holes in the base of several silos over the years, and a chain-link fence ran around the perimeter to keep people out. It was the kind of place that might come up in conversations about prostitutes, serial killers, and the quandary of modern urban decay. Right about there I looked in my rearview mirror and saw headlights and thought I'd picked up a tail. I slowed and a minute later lost them as they turned left, just catching a glimpse of a white guy's face I didn't know. It wasn't Bronte, anyway.

I kept a close eye on my mirrors while we drove through downtown Bexley, but the coast was clear. The suburb's sidewalks were empty except for a few Capital University students, a lone jogger, and some late-night dog walkers. Thanks to oddly drawn municipal lines we re-entered Columbus a couple of miles east, just past Johnson's ice cream shop, but we didn't see any other women. It was starting to mist, and even the street corners in that part of Columbus were empty. I figured one more stop would be enough. A couple of minutes later I pulled into the parking lot of the Rest EZ motel.

The one-story L-shaped building fronted Main and a side street, rows of tiny rooms with red doors running along each wing. Its cracked asphalt parking lot was half full. A sign boasted a $39.99 special. It didn't specify daily or hourly. I wondered if the price included clean sheets. Inside a cramped office at the Main Street end of the far unit, a man sat watching a cricket match on a laptop next to a houseplant that looked like it had been left in the microwave too long. The name on his badge was Mr. Patel.

"One night?" he said, without glancing up.

"Is that an ashtray or a fern?" I said.

He looked at me. I explained who I was, placed my card on the counter and the Reardoor.com photo of Jessica next to it, and pushed both toward him. "Have you seen this woman?"

Reluctantly, he pulled himself away from the match. He picked up my card with care, as if he'd seen me fish it out of a diaper bin, examined my information, looked at me, and set it back down. He glanced for a second or two at the photo.

"I do not recognize her."

"She stayed here from time to time."

"Many people stay here."

"Many people dressed like that?"

"How people dress in my rooms is none of my business."

"How about how they undress?" Theresa said.

He frowned. "Was there anything else?"

I said, "It's important that I find her. She's gone missing. Her brother's worried about her because of everything that's going on. All the women who died."

"And as I told you, I have not encountered her."

I pulled my card toward me, turned it over, and wrote down Jessica's name. I pushed it toward Mr. Patel.

I said, "If you see her, I'd appreciate it if you'd call me."

He looked down at the card, and then at his cricket match. A man dressed all in white, like a yacht captain, or a morgue orderly, hurled a ball down a flawless green pitch. Mr. Patel turned away from the match and reached down and picked up the card again. He said, "This is her name? Jessica Byrnes?"

"That's right."

He hesitated. "I don't want any trouble."

"I'm not trying to make any."

"Her parole officer was here. Looking for her."

"When?"

"Several weeks ago."

"What did you tell him?"

"The same thing I told you. That I haven't seen her."

"What was his name?"

"I don't know. He didn't say. And he didn't leave a card," he added quickly.

"What'd he look like?"

"Normal looking."

"Glasses? Beard? Mustache? Distinguishing mole?"

"Normal," he said.

"Black or white?"

"White."

"He must have been her probation officer," I said. "Not parole. That's for prison."

"I do not know anything about that. He said parole. I remember that much. He was very specific about it."

"Specific?"

"As though he thought it would make an impression on me. '*Parole* officer,'" he said, mimicking the visitor's words.

"OK," I said, wondering what it meant. Why would someone calling himself a parole officer be looking for Jessica? "Did he leave a number or anything?"

"I believe he did."

"Do you have it?"

"I threw it away."

"Why?"

"Like I said, I don't want any trouble."

"I can see that," I said.

12

KAREN FEINBERG HAD EVEN LESS TIME FOR me the next morning. But she agreed to find out the name of Jessica's last probation officer. I thanked her, got up from my kitchen table, refilled my McCulloh College mug with more coffee, and called the next number on my list.

"Kevin Harding." The *Dispatch* reporter answered on the second ring.

"It's Andy Hayes. Got a minute?"

There was an uncomfortably long pause before he answered. "Not really. I haven't updated my Twitter feed since I got in."

"Why I auto-schedule mine first thing every morning. Listen." I told him what I wanted. There was another pause.

"You know there's like twenty task forces already looking for this guy?"

"I'm not after the killer. It's a missing person case. At least I hope she's just missing."

"Who is it?"

I told him. I heard the clicking of keys in the background, like several mouthfuls of tiny teeth. "Never heard of her. She's not on our list."

"List?"

"A database we created. Missing women in central Ohio who fit the profile."

"Profile of what?"

"Of our guy's victims."

"Which is?"

"Drug-addicted prostitutes in their twenties and thirties. Your person match up?"

"Unfortunately, yes," I said. "But her brother only reported her missing last week."

"That explains it. We're behind. There's a lot of missing women. Have you talked to Larry Schwartzbaum, at CPD?"

I told him I'd left messages.

"He's the guy you want. So what do you need to know?"

"I'm not sure. Anything classified you can tell me about the killer?"

"Like what?"

"Like, I won't know until you tell me. Like stuff the cops haven't released. It's worth lunch. Name your place."

"Pretty busy. Rain check, OK?"

"OK," I said, but I'd detected something besides busyness in his voice, and I was pretty sure I knew what it was. "Anything you can tell me over the phone?"

"Maybe one thing. I don't know how much it's worth. Except it's mine alone. I see it anywhere, I know it came from you, and this is the last time we talk."

I laughed, but he didn't laugh back. After a second, I said, "I'll keep that in mind. I'll also keep you in mind if Jessica turns into a story."

"Sure you will. So you're not going to burn me?"

"Scout's honor."

"You were never a Scout."

"I swear on a stack of Bibles."

He snorted. "I'll go with the first one. OK. Ever heard of a band called Gätling Gün?"

"Sure. From the eighties. The whole 'umlaut rock' thing. I had a couple albums. Why?"

"You know that song 'Pleasure Prince'?"

"Yeah." Memories surfaced of the raunchy song, background music to several of my romantic encounters as a teen. "What's it got to do with anything?"

"There's a girl, LaVonne Brown. The cops are pretty sure she survived this guy. Sometime in early July, between Natasha Rumsey and Lisa Washington. He picked her up late one night off Bryden Road, wouldn't say where he was going. They'd made a couple of turns when she started to get nervous and tried to back out. Police think he has a lair someplace and Brown realized they were headed that way."

"A lair?"

"Someplace he takes them first. Maybe keeps them there alive, a day or two, before he strangles them."

"I take it she didn't figure out where."

"Sold to the private eye on a fool's errand. Anyway, he pulls around the corner, drives into an alley, drags her out of the car, grabs a rope of some kind, and starts choking her. The whole time he's singing something in this low voice. She's blacking out when a dog wanders by and starts barking and the guy gets scared. He punches her in the face, gets back in the car, and drives off."

"She get a look at him?"

"Vague description. White, thick glasses, mustache, ball cap. Cops figured he's lost the mustache by now."

I thought of Mr. Patel and his parole officer. *Normal looking.*

"Singing something," I said. "'Pleasure Prince'?"

"You got it."

I recalled the song's chorus: *Love my touch, love my push, love my Pleasure Prince.* Things I had done listening to the song were not my finest moments.

"Creepy," I said.

"No shit. No one knows if he sings it every time, mainly because there haven't been any other survivors. He's been thorough that way. Anyway, homicide desk code-named him Prince, just for yuks."

"So why haven't you reported this? The singing."

"Cops asked me not to."

"And you agreed?"

"They made a good case. They're worried it could taint the investigation. Normally, I'd say screw it. If the guy was wearing a *Walking Dead* T-shirt, let's put it out there. Nine times out of ten his girlfriend finds the shirt crumpled in the closet, sneaks around the corner to call 911, and they've got their man. But this is different. The song makes it ripe for copycatters, which is just what they need right now. Couple johns try to be funny, start warbling while they go at it, and the cops are chasing leads all over town."

"I appreciate the tip. And no, I won't burn you. Sure I can't buy you lunch?"

"Some other time."

I said goodbye and cut the connection. It didn't take a genius to figure out what was going on. I had no doubt Harding was busy, but I'd never known him to pass up a free meal. The issue was he didn't want to be seen with me. I guess I couldn't blame him. A reporter who hired me as his bodyguard for a couple of weeks not long ago ended up murdered on my watch. It wasn't my fault, exactly, but plenty of people still blamed me, Harding among them.

Although I recalled that hadn't kept him from running with the inside details of the reporter's death I passed along when the truth came to light. It was OK. We both had jobs to do.

I was mapping out the distance to Mount Alexandria and Jessica Byrnes's mom's house when my phone rang. Caller ID blocked.

"Mr. Hayes? Darlene Bardwell. Have I reached you at a convenient time?"

"Depends what you're trying to sell me." I knew I should recognize the name but was unable to place her. Voice confident, with a tinge of huskiness, as if she talked a lot.

"Very good, very good. I've heard about your sense of humor. Truthfully, I was hoping I could invite you to lunch. To discuss a case you're working on. If it's not too much trouble."

"Case?"

"Jessica Byrnes? Her brother Bill is one of my constituents. He contacted me about his sister. When I talked to him he mentioned you."

Bardwell. Of course. The congresswoman who'd been going after Reardoor.com and the other personals sites.

I cleared my throat. "We talked, yes," I said, in my best imitation of a guy who gets calls from congresspersons any old time. "And I am trying to find Jessica. Without much luck right at the moment."

"I'm sorry to hear that. I understand how difficult these cases can be. Especially now, with everything going on . . ." Her voice trailed off. I couldn't tell if the pause was rehearsed or if she was exuding real emotion.

"As you may know," she continued, when I didn't reply, "I sit on the House Special Committee on Human Trafficking. I wanted to speak to you in that capacity about Jessica. And to see if there's any way my office could assist you. I know it's late notice—any chance you're free this afternoon?"

I thought for a second. I'd intended to head to Mount Alexandria to find Jessica's mom and stepdad. On the other hand, I didn't get calls like this very often.

"That could work. But what do you mean by assist?"

"Anything I can do to help. This hits home, with Bill in my district and all. His sister is a perfect example of the women we're trying to help."

"Have you talked to Columbus police? Or the FBI? They're the ones who really need the help."

"I've interacted with several stakeholders. The mayor, the chief, the sheriff. The special agent in charge for the region. Pretty much everyone."

"I'm not sure what I could tell you that you don't already know. And any assistance should really go to them first."

"I understand that. And you have my word I'm not bigfoot-ing them. But when I get involved in something, this is standard operating procedure. I try to cover all the bases."

Standard operating procedure. The phrase I'd used with Bill By-rnes when he questioned why I needed to call his mother. An interesting coincidence. Maybe her way of calling my bluff. And what was there to lose, anyway? A congresswoman could prob-ably help me, and I'd played fair by checking she wasn't doing an end run around the professionals.

"All right. Where can I meet you?"

"Do you know TAT Ristorante di Famiglia? On James?"

I confessed that I did. We arranged a time.

"Thank you, Mr. Hayes. I look forward to it."

"Call me Andy."

"See you in a bit," she said.

After I hung up I turned to my laptop and Googled Bardwell. I studied the results as I sipped my coffee. She was forty-one, blonde, hair worn in a professional bob, favored dark suits and pearl necklaces. A champion diver in college and a former Miss Ohio. Married, two kids, her husband an ex–TV anchor turned PR consultant. A Republican in her third term, antiabortion but with concerns about climate change. The perfect central Ohio middle-of-the-roader. Also, I noted with interest, on a couple of watch lists for a potential U.S. Senate run next year. Against a Democrat with some semi-serious baggage.

One thing was sure, I thought, clicking on her official bio pic-ture to enlarge it. Whether she could help me or not, I could do worse for a lunch date.

13

I HAD A FEW HOURS BEFORE OUR MEETING and decided to head back to the hospital. It was the best visit so far because my dad was asleep for most of it. My mom barely acknowledged me, and Shelley did all the talking. It was with a sense of guilty relief that I made my excuses to leave for lunch with the congresswoman. The temperature had risen back into the upper forties, and I decided to wait outside the restaurant. Bardwell arrived six minutes late. She shook my hand firmly and thanked me for meeting her. She was as attractive as her bio and picture suggested. The man she was with was not nearly as good-looking.

"John Blanchett," she said, making introductions. "John runs my Columbus office. He's putting together an event we're doing tomorrow night. Something I was hoping you could come to. A vigil for the victims. I thought it might be useful if he joined us today, maybe pick your brain." She was peppy, with a take-charge attitude that went well with her Miss Ohio good looks. A person I was guessing was not used to taking no for an answer.

"Nice to meet you," I said to Blanchett, chastising myself for the slight annoyance I felt at his presence. But in my defense, Bardwell was very pretty.

"You as well," Blanchett said, his handshake strong and professional. "Do you still go by Woody?"

"Not for a long time. Andy's fine."

"And call me John. It's good of you to be here."

Indeed, I thought, casting a glance at the back of the congresswoman's slim figure as we went inside. The maître d' paid appropriate homage to a politician who might be running for the Senate, and we were seated quickly in the closest purple booth. Blanchett beamed. Bardwell unleashed a strategically humble-yet-grateful smile. I tried not to look like a security guard.

"Thanks again for meeting with us," Bardwell said after waters and menus were delivered.

"You're welcome. I'm still not sure how I can help."

"Perhaps you could tell us a little more about your investigation."

"So far there's not much to report." As I spoke, Blanchett pulled a small, black leather notebook from the left breast pocket of his coat, opened it, and looked at me inquiringly. I nodded, and as he took notes I gave them the basics about Jessica, Mount Alexandria, Jessica's record, and her disappearance from the court intervention program. I mentioned my canvassing of East Main and the Rest EZ and the parole/probation officer.

When I finished, Bardwell said, "But still no idea where Jessica could be? Or do you think—"

I waited a moment before replying. "Do I think she's dead? I have no idea. I hope not. For Bill's sake, if nothing else. And her son." Bardwell looked at me quizzically, and I explained about Robbie.

"How sad," she said. "But what a noble gesture by her brother."

"Yes," I said, recalling Theresa's immediate suspicion of Bill and what he might have done to his sister. "The thing is, Jessica's been gone a while. That doesn't bode well. Best case, she's out of town or has a really good hiding place. Worst case, we know. But there's another worst case, which is she died because she's a heroin addict or she froze to death in an alley or she killed herself and no one's found the dark corner of Columbus where her body is yet."

"It's so awful," Bardwell said.

"The pimp, *Bronte* Patterson," Blanchett said after a moment, looking up from his notebook. "I don't mean to make light—"

"You wouldn't be the first." I related the brontosaurus quip. "But if you see his picture. Or read his record. It's another story."

"Sounds like a monster," Blanchett said, shaking his head. He was thick-waisted, in contrast to his celery-stalk-thin boss, and saddled with a weak chin and a receding hairline. But he also had the personable manner of a skilled concierge and a shy smile that bordered on engaging.

"The woman who's helping you," Bardwell said. "Theresa? You said she's a survivor of trafficking herself?"

"That's right."

She and Blanchett traded glances. He said, "Any chance she'd be interested in participating in the vigil? As someone who could speak to the dangers out there? Someone who's experienced them firsthand?"

"I can ask." I recalled Roy's concerns. Thought of Theresa's confrontational comment to Mr. Patel. *How about when they undress?* "But no promises. She didn't sign up for that kind of thing."

"Understood," Blanchett said, nodding. "Only if she's comfortable with it."

"Is there anything specific I could tell her? About the event?"

"I'll let John give you the nitty-gritty, since he's organizing it," Bardwell said. She smiled at him warmly. "But essentially it's a chance to remember the women who died, as a way of keeping a focus on the investigation with Christmas coming. We're holding it at Third Baptist, the church Lisa Washington grew up in. She was the . . ." She stopped and looked at Blanchett.

"The fourth victim," he said. "Found in the Scioto, near Greenlawn."

Bardwell nodded sadly. "I'll also be announcing new initiatives dealing with these personal ad sites. They're open markets for prostitution disguised as online dating. The fear is that many of the girls are underage, though it's hard to prove it. Reardoor. com is one of the worst offenders."

"It's pretty bad," Blanchett agreed, writing something in the notebook.

Our waitress came and took our orders. I asked for wedding soup and lasagna. Bardwell and Blanchett both had chef salads.

"What kind of initiatives?" I asked Bardwell when the waitress was gone.

"Stricter regulations, for starters. The so-called self-policing these sites claim they're doing is a joke. As John says, it's like asking the fox to build the henhouse, then guard it." Blanchett gave a small smile, acknowledging the remark.

"If I had my way," Bardwell continued, "I'd place Reardoor. com and all the rest of them directly under the control of the Federal Communications Commission. That's one of the things I'll be talking about tomorrow night."

A lightbulb went off at her last comment. "This is a news conference as well as a vigil," I said.

"Media have been invited, of course," Blanchett said.

"Of course?"

"The vigil's purpose is keeping this tragedy front and center in the public's mind," he said. "What's the point of yelling fire if no one can hear you?"

"I'm not seeing a lack of attention being paid to this case."

"To the case, maybe," Blanchett said. "The victims? All the missing women out there? That's another story. These are among the most marginalized people in society. Even with this many deaths, it's easy for a certain segment of the population to dismiss the killings as 'just deserts.' Creating awareness is half the battle."

He had a point. Anne had raged over tweets she'd seen along those very lines—#takingoutthegarbage was one of the least offensive hashtags—after Lisa's body was found and the realization that Columbus had a serial killer on the loose began to sink in.

"Exactly right," Bardwell said, casting another warm glance at her aide. "Publicity in the name of a good cause is not a bad thing."

"Still," I said, looking back and forth between the two of them. "A Republican pushing for stronger business regulations. Kind of a man-bites-dog story, not to mention an uphill battle. This kind of publicity can't hurt your efforts."

"There's a difference between overregulation and no regulation at all," Bardwell said sharply. "And we're talking the buying and selling of human beings here, not manufacturing widgets. If that angle is enough to bring out reporters on a cold December evening, so be it. I'm interested in doing the right thing. Not what people think of my motives."

"Point taken," I said, and waited until the lines on her face relaxed. I guessed I'd glimpsed some of the fervor it took to become a congresswoman. Not to mention a Miss Ohio.

I waited to see if Blanchett chimed in, but he merely nodded his agreement with Bardwell and jotted a couple more notes. The two of them had an easy familiarity which made me wonder about the true nature of their relationship. Head of her Columbus office? What exactly did that mean?

"Have you always been based here?" I said to Blanchett, now curious.

"On and off," he said, taking a sip of his water. "I was a producer at Channel 7 when I first got out of college. That's how I got to know Barry." He looked at Bardwell, who nodded enthusiastically. Her husband, I recalled after a moment. Much better-looking than Blanchett. "I joined his PR shop after that gig dried up, and worked in Washington during the congresswoman's first couple of terms. I'd been looking for a way to come home when this job opened up. I've been here now, what?"

"Almost four years," Bardwell said.

I said to Bardwell, "Over the phone, you mentioned helping me somehow. What exactly did you have in mind?"

"Of course we can't force the authorities to tell you anything. But if there's something that might assist you—a file, or a name, or a number, anything like that—I'm offering to use what little influence I have to clear a path."

"And then?"

"What do you mean?"

"Well, let's be optimistic. Assume that I find Jessica alive. What happens next?"

"Then we celebrate. Simple as that."

"Celebrate publicly or privately?"

"I'm not sure I understand." A note of pique crept into her voice.

"I mean, do you hold another news conference? Or meet with Jessica away from the cameras?"

"Probably both, to be honest," Bardwell said. Almost as an afterthought, she added, "I must say, for someone who's in the news quite a lot, you seem to have a negative perception of the power of the media."

"Believe me, I'd be happy never to make another headline. I'm just trying to figure out what I'm agreeing to here. These women are more than public service announcements."

"I never meant—" Bardwell said, her face darkening.

"Let me put it this way," Blanchett interrupted, reaching out to touch Bardwell's arm. She relaxed at the gesture. "Jessica's well-being, and the well-being of all these women, is first and foremost in our minds. But public policy isn't created in a vacuum in Washington. It involves real people. I know what you're asking, because it's something that I—that we—struggle with every day. Are we enlisting your help in the hope that later on, assuming a happy ending, we can use Jessica to advance our cause? Exploit her, to be blunt? In a word, yes." He read the look of surprise on my face before continuing.

"But here's the thing. We're doing this to help Jessica and as many women in her situation as we can over the long run. To help her on the day of a news conference, but the next day too, and the day after that and the day after that. We're not going to just drop her."

"Yes," Bardwell said, with relief in her voice. "That's it exactly."

Our food arrived before I could reply. We ate for a minute in silence. I contemplated my cynicism at their offer. I wondered whether I'd misjudged them, interpreted their obvious passion for this cause for something else altogether. But what if I hadn't, and they were more than just colleagues? Colleagues with benefits. Who cared? Why let that color my willingness to accept their help?

"I appreciate your offer, which I accept," I said at last. "Thank you."

"Thank *you*," Bardwell said. "That means a lot to us."

I nodded, taking another bite of my lasagna. *Us,* she'd said. Not *me.* I reminded myself that I didn't care. I had more important things to worry about than a powerful congresswoman's personal life. I had to hunt down Jessica Byrnes. And if Bardwell, with her obvious political muscle—not to mention her ex–Miss Ohio looks—was offering to help me on my quest, so be it. It's the kind of sacrifice you make in this business.

BY THE TIME WE WERE FINISHED IT WAS TOO
late to head to Mount Alexandria and be back in town in time
for dinner with my boys. Keeping the date wasn't just the right
thing to do; the way things were going with Kym and Crystal,
it was an obligation I'd miss on penalty of death. This brilliant
observation helped me keep my cool that night as Joe and I sat in
the pizza joint we'd selected and listened to Mike complain about
how much he hated nearly all his classes.

"History's stupid. Just a bunch of dates. And my math teacher's an idiot. And why should I learn French? It's not like anybody
speaks it anymore."

"Except for the French," I said. "And Canadians. And half of
Africa."

"Like I'm ever going to any of those places."

"You might. And history can be interesting once you get
into it. And in case you've forgotten, your grandmother's a math
teacher."

My oldest son stared at me. "Who?"

"My mom. Grandma Lynne."

"She is?"

"Yes," I snapped. "You knew that."

"No, I didn't."

"Yes, you did—"

I stopped before I finished my sentence. It was clear from the look on his face that he didn't know. And I knew it wasn't his fault. It had been months since he last saw her, I realized. Since I'd arranged a visit.

"I'm hungry," Joe said, sitting next to his half-brother.

"Me too," I said, craning my neck for the waitress, eager for the food to arrive to break the tension. Both the boys had drained their sodas and devoured the basket of breadsticks we started with when seated in the red booth with cracked vinyl seats. It was a local place off Linworth Road halfway between their houses in the northern suburbs. The long wait was making me think I should have given up standing on ceremony and just gone to a chain.

"Look," I said, and realized my phone was buzzing. I pulled it out and looked at the screen. It was Theresa calling. I looked up, caught Mike's eye, and sent the call to voice mail.

"It's a matter of balance," I said, starting over.

"What is?" Mike said, his face sullen.

"School. Sports. You can't just give up on one to do the other."

A glint came into his eyes. He suddenly looked much older than thirteen, even with the hints of whiskers I'd started to see recently. He said, "Mom said that's what you did. I heard her talking to Steve. She said you never had to study because of how good you were in football."

"That's not true," I said. Even as I scrambled to elaborate, I tamped down a perverse pleasure in hearing him call his stepfather by his first name instead of "Dad," as he had in the past. I glanced at Joe. I wasn't so lucky with him. Joe had two daddies: me and Ben. He was "Dad," I was "Daddy." There was no getting around it. But Joe had been younger when Crystal remarried than Mike was when Kym got hitched again.

"I wasn't the best student in the world," I said, starting over. "That much is true. And I did spend most of my time thinking about sports." And girls, I added, but not aloud. What was the point? I'd already seen how the girls were looking at Mike, even in middle school. And how he looked back. "But I did study. I did what I had to do. My father insisted on it. My mom, too."

"Steve thinks I should play piano. He wants to sign me up for lessons. I told him it's the same time as basketball practice. He won't listen."

It was the first I'd heard of piano lessons. But it was also the first thing I could see myself agreeing with Steve on in a while.

"What if we made a deal?"

"A deal?" Mike said, suspiciously.

"Yeah," I said, and felt my phone buzz. I looked down. Theresa again. For some reason I flashed to Darla, the Jessica lookalike we'd met on the street two nights earlier. I thought of her expressive eyes, and what they must have seen going from life in the suburbs to life on the streets.

"What," I said, answering the call, as Mike rolled his eyes. I watched as Joe tipped the bread basket toward himself hopefully, as if willing it to refill itself.

"Hello to you too. Not a good time?"

"It's fine."

"You sure, QB?"

"Go ahead, please." I tried to soften my voice.

"OK. I heard back from the lady," Theresa said. "With the program."

"Program?"

"The court program. The one Jessica was in. Remember?"

"Yeah. You heard back just now?"

"Supervisor called from home. Doing me a favor. I thought you'd want to know."

"What'd she say?"

"No need to snap."

"Sorry. I'm out with my boys. Been a long day."

"For me too."

"I said I'm sorry. What'd she say? The supervisor?"

The woman had confirmed the story about Jessica getting a call from Lisa Washington shortly before she dropped out of the program. According to her, Jessica said something about going to look for Lisa. That she was worried about her. "She said something about getting a book," Theresa added. "And she mentioned Bronte. And that was the last time anyone saw her."

"A book?"

"What she said."

"A book about what?"

"She wasn't sure. Thought maybe something Lisa had borrowed from Jessica, and she wanted back. She didn't really know. The only book she remembered Jessica reading was one of those vampire ones."

"Did the supervisor think Bronte had the book?"

"She didn't know. My guess, Jessica thought Bronte might know something about Lisa. Or have something Jessica needed to find her."

"Like what?"

"Money, probably. Jessica had to survive somehow."

The waitress was approaching with the pizza. I gestured impatiently for her to set it down and jabbed at the boys' empty soda glasses for refills. She frowned and snapped her gum and looked inquiringly at my half-filled water glass. I shook my head. What I really wanted was a beer. But that wasn't happening on a custody night. I'd learned that lesson the hard way.

"You there?"

"Yeah. I gotta go. Thanks for calling. I'll talk to you tomorrow."

"Lucky me. And also, you're welcome."

"Listen—"

But she'd hung up.

"There's no sausage on this," Mike said. "We ordered sausage."

I looked at the pizza. He was right. I glanced around for the waitress. She'd disappeared into the kitchen. Joe was already halfway through his first two pieces. I've never understood the central Ohio custom of cutting pizza into squares instead of slices. Roy alleged it was an unconscious effort to replicate the angles of a gridiron, which was not out of the question for such a football-crazy place. But it didn't matter at the moment. I was too hungry. I stuffed a piece into my mouth.

"Let's just eat," I said.

But Mike was hanging on. He'd inherited his mother's arguing skills and my stubbornness. It was one of those moments when you cringe inside, seeing the worst of your habits passed on to your kids. "I don't want to take piano," he said, nibbling at a crust, though he had to be as hungry as his brother.

"Back to the deal."

"Which is?"

"Raise your grades and try some piano lessons. Really try. No faking it. In exchange, I'll talk to your mom about an Xbox."

"She already said I couldn't get one," Mike said, trying to keep his voice calm. I could tell I'd caught his attention, and not in a small way, but he wasn't ready to give in yet. "And I'm not missing basketball."

"I'm sure we can work that out. Nobody's asking you to give up one for the other. Plenty of people offer piano lessons. What do you say?"

"Maybe."

"Maybe? An Xbox for what you're supposed to be doing anyway in school? Seems like a good deal to me." Even as I said it, I wondered where I'd find the money for such an extravagance, even if I could persuade Kym. I knew they cost hundreds of dollars, and that wasn't counting the games. And it would have to live at my house: she'd never tolerate it at her home. It was one of the things I'd come to grudgingly admire about her, her refusal to give in to such a ubiquitous entertainment option.

"OK," Mike said, his tone as flat as a kid agreeing to empty the trash. Except his eyes told a different story.

"Real grades, by the way. You're a smart guy. Way smarter than me at your age. You can do better."

"Cs?"

"Give me a break. I'm talking As. B-plus minimum. Xboxes aren't cheap."

"As? C'mon."

"What if they hold the Olympics in France someday? And you're on the basketball team? What then?"

"Everybody speaks English anyway."

"As. Or no deal."

"Fine," he said, and took a real bite of pizza.

"Could I play on it?" Joe said. "On the Xbox?"

"Get your own," Mike said.

I told Joe I'd work it out to let him play too. I felt my phone buzz again and ignored it. I took a long drink of water. Tried not to think about what Theresa had told me, about a book, and Bronte, and concentrate on the boys instead. But as soon as I did, I found myself thinking about the deal I'd just struck. A devil's pact, more like it. A way of warding off the chickens coming home to roost: Mike was more like me than I cared to admit. In sports prowess, and in personality. My only hope in winning over Kym was backing Steve on the piano, which could earn me valuable points. I knew my ex-wife had taken lessons as a girl and always regretted stopping.

Another buzz. I looked and saw I had a text from Anne.

I have a couple free hours tomorrow morning. Want to stop by?

Sure, I texted back, pleasantly surprised.

"No texting at the table," Joe said.

"Sorry." I put the phone away.

"Mom says it's rude. Dad too."

"They're both right," I said. "They're both absolutely right."

I ROLLED ONTO MY BACK THE NEXT MORNING, pulling Anne on top of me. I gasped as she reached down, grabbed me, and slid me inside her.

"*Jesus*," I said.

"Don't say 'Jesus' when you mean 'Shit.'"

"You stole that line from Roy."

"Borrowed, more like it," she said, kissing me as she began to slowly rock her hips.

"*Shit.*"

For the next few minutes, missing women, custodial visits, and even shapely congresswomen were the last things on my mind.

"That was nice," she said, spooning into me afterward.

"Yeah."

"I miss you. You should come around more."

"I'm aware of that, believe me."

"Am I a bitch, for complaining all the time? About us?"

"Not a jury in the world would convict you."

"So how about it?"

"How about what?"

"How about stopping by more often?"

"I just did, in case you hadn't noticed."

"All that noise you made, it was hard not to, believe me. But seriously."

"Seriously, I'm going to do my best. The incentives are strong."

"How flattering. So let's do something."

"Do?"

"Go grab some coffee. Catch a movie."

"A movie? In the morning?"

"What the hell."

Unbidden, thoughts of Jessica Byrnes reentered my mind. The look of concern on her brother's face. The mug shot of her pimp, Bronte Patterson, staring malevolently from Karen Feinberg's phone.

Focus, Andy. Focus.

"I—"

"What?"

"I probably should get back to work." I explained about Mount Alexandria and the mysterious parole officer, and reviewed my lunch with Bardwell, including my suspicions about her and Blanchett.

"Why are you assuming they're lovers?" Anne said. "Just because they have what sounds like regard for each other's opinions?"

"Well, I'm not assuming it automatically. They just seemed overly familiar."

"You'd never say that about two men in an office, just because they agree with one another a lot."

"That's different."

"How?"

I pulled her closer. She tensed, then relaxed into me.

"Two men would have a different work relationship. With men and women, there's always going to be a sexual dynamic, even among colleagues. At least on the surface. I'm just saying this seemed like it crossed a line."

"You're saying men and women can't have a strictly platonic relationship in the workplace?"

"Strictly? No. Mostly? Sure."

"What's that supposed to mean?"

"It means that at some level, almost always superficially, there's going to be a question mark. A 'what if' element. At least for men, but I suspect for some women too. A glance at an ass or an appreciation of a new outfit or whatever. A fleeting conjecture reflecting a basic biological fact, which is then almost always put aside while they get back to preparing that week's TPS report."

Anne sighed and rolled away from me, out of my arms.

"I'm sorry," I ventured. "It was just an observation."

"A sexist one. Your underlying assumption is unfair."

"Sexist" hit home, but I tried to make light of it. "I'm not saying the workplaces of the world are full of male and female colleagues rutting in the storage closet every chance they get. Just the opposite, and not because there's not as many storage closets as there used to be." I waited for her to laugh, but she stayed silent.

I said, "I'm just saying there's an underlying tension that's part of the way the world works."

"What about Bonnie Deckard?"

"What about her?"

"She's your colleague, right? She's young, and attractive. Don't tell me you were focusing on her computer skills at roller derby the other day. I heard what Lucy said."

"Guilty as charged. Bonnie's computer skills look great in Lycra." I smiled to show her I was joking. She looked at me but didn't smile back.

"Is that what this is about?" I said after a moment. "Me and Bonnie?"

"What do you mean? *What this is about?* You make it sound like I'm picking an argument." She sat up, her back to me.

"I'm not sure. You seem angry all of a sudden. I feel like I've done something wrong."

Her shoulders rose defensively, and I braced for her response. Instead she let them fall as she thought about what to say.

"I'm frustrated you're not around when I need you," she said. "It's been a long semester. It seems like it's been getting worse, with you and your jobs. I mean, I get when you're on a stakeout, or whatever, but—"

"I came today."

"And now you have to leave right away. How do you think that makes me feel?"

It was my turn to be quiet. Too late, I was feeling her frustration and realizing more was going on than a reaction to my thick-headed observations about the congresswoman. I knew she was under a lot of stress. She was writing her first book, on women science fiction writers. She'd taken on an extra class to pay for an expensive brake job. Amelia had had difficulty adjusting to her new school, in the Clintonville neighborhood where they'd moved earlier in the year.

I said, "I'm sorry I've screwed up so many dates." But even as I said it, I wondered if it were completely true. I was genuinely sorry I'd let her down. But I couldn't deny I had also appreciated the thrill of the chase at times, even when I knew I was about to break an appointment with her. Appreciated it in ways I hadn't experienced in years. Since—I had to admit it—my playing days.

"Thanks," she said quietly.

"And for the record, you don't have anything to worry about with me and Bonnie." This much was true. I did find Bonnie attractive. But I knew I wasn't alone in that regard, because she was an attractive woman. Especially in Lycra. I also knew that unlike my younger self, I would never have done something to interfere with her and Troy's relationship.

Anne said, "You're the first man who looked at me in years. You know that, right?"

"That's not true," I said, taken aback.

"Yes, it is. Men see me differently."

"No, they don't—"

"Don't deny it." She paused. "So when you're not around, I'm like, well, that's it. I'm losing the one guy who found me halfway attractive."

I kept my mouth shut this time. I knew this wasn't accurate, both from looks I'd seen other men give her and from the fact she was forgetting she'd been with someone when I first met her. But it wasn't the moment to mention any of that. I understood what she was saying. What she was feeling. Anne had a scar as jagged and elongated as a map of Chile on the left side of her face, carved there by her husband as he tried to kill her in a drunken rage several years earlier, right before he killed himself. To me it had become a crack in an otherwise perfect marble bust that often I didn't even notice anymore. But she did, and her fears about how others saw it emerged at random moments like this one.

"This novel I'm reading for my book?" she said. *"The Left Hand of Darkness?* It's about a planet where everyone's androgynous and people are only attracted to each other once a month. Sometimes that seems like the better way to go."

"Sex by a timer? Sounds boring."

"As least you know where you stand."

"So there's no adultery on a planet where everyone's in heat at once?"

"You're a smart-ass, you know that?"

"It's been mentioned." I reached out and pulled her toward me and kissed her neck. When she didn't resist I put my hands around her and caressed her breasts. She turned her head and opened her mouth to me and I felt her relax into me. I moved my right hand down between her legs. But after a minute she stopped kissing me and sat back up.

"I'm sorry," she said. "It got late. I've got some things to do."

"Sure about that?"

She turned to me and smiled sadly. It was an odd fact about her injury that it was less noticeable the more she smiled.

"I'm sure. That was nice. We should do it again some time."

"It's a date," I said.

"I hope so," Anne said.

16

TWENTY MINUTES LATER I WAS IN MY Odyssey and headed toward Mount Alexandria, still trying to process what had just happened while fighting off frustration that I should have been on the road much earlier. The vigil for the slain women was at five o'clock, timed perfectly for the evening news, meaning I had a limited amount of time to track down Jessica's mom and whoever else I might find in the small city. At Shelley's insistence, I was taking a day off from visiting my dad. It was best for both of us, she said, and I couldn't disagree. There'd be time to see him the next morning before the surgery.

I had taken the exit for 661 and was traveling down the two-lane road, back to thinking about Anne and me, when a call interrupted my thoughts.

"It's Detective Schwartzbaum. Columbus Division of Police."

The officer whose card Jessica's brother had given me. I thanked him for calling and explained about trying to find Jessica.

"Her brother hired you?"

I acknowledged it.

"He give you some song-and-dance about how we're not doing our jobs? Not doing enough to find his sister?"

"Not really. He said it seemed like you were taking it seriously."

"So why'd he hire a private guy?"

I thought for a second. I said, "Probably because he's scared, and he's not stupid."

"What's that supposed to mean?"

"In so many words, it means he knows the mayor's got the chief's balls in a vice over these murders. He also knows that shit rolls downhill, and everybody's nuts and tits from the deputy chiefs on down are in the same vice, all the way to guys like you actually trying to solve this thing. I'm also guessing he knows you're staring at a stack of missing person reports getting taller by the minute when your units are understaffed as it is. He knows he's probably not going to get his calls returned unless there's bad news. So he asked someone who has a little more time on his hands to help him. Because it's his sister and he doesn't know what else to do."

There was a long silence on the other end. "I'll give you this, Hayes," Schwartzbaum finally said. "That's some high-quality ass-kissing. Platinum, all the way. And surprisingly on the mark. So what do you want from me? I have like five minutes before my turn in the C-clamp."

I went over what I'd learned so far, and told him where I was driving. He listened without interruption.

"I could see a lot of people wanting a piece of a girl like that," he said when I'd finished. "Even more so if she's scared of something. Starting with Bronte Patterson."

"What I was thinking."

"Anything else?"

"That's it so far. I'll see what her mother says."

"You got time tomorrow, swing by headquarters. I'll dig up her file, see if there's anything else."

I explained about my dad's surgery.

"OK. Just give me a call whenever." He hung up abruptly.

I kept driving, turning what little I knew about Jessica over in my mind. I was interrupted by another call, this time from Karen Feinberg.

"I found Jessica's parole officer. Except you were right. It's probation."

"I figured as much. What's his name?"

"That's the thing. It's Shirley. She's a woman. And she's black."

"Oh?"

"And she checked her files. Jessica's had a couple other probation officers in the past. But none of them was a normal-looking white guy."

17

TAMMY BYRNES LIVED IN ONE OF MOUNT Alex's wearier neighborhoods, a few blocks from downtown. I pulled up in front of a forties-era two-story white house that could have used a new coat of paint a half dozen winters ago. The wraparound porch was missing three and a half rail posts. A gutter hung from the left side of the roof like a dislocated arm. I walked to the door and tried the bell. Nothing. I knocked. Still nothing, but now I could make out a TV. I tried again and a minute later a woman opened the door. I saw the resemblance to Jessica right away in the high forehead and strong chin. The glassy eyes were another matter.

"I tried calling," I said, after she confessed to being Jessica's mom and I explained who I was and why I was there.

"I don't always check the messages," she said. Her voice was almost childlike, assuming the child smoked a couple of packs a day. She let me in reluctantly.

The house smelled of smoke and fried food and cat litter. Baskets of unfolded laundry sat next to two chairs piled with unopened bills. Fox News was on a wide-screen TV opposite the couch, trumpeting the latest terrorism arrest. The TV cast the only light in the room. A can of beer sat sweating on a coffee table.

"I'm trying to figure out why Jessica left home and went to Columbus," I explained, after Tammy cleared a pile of papers off a chair for me. She sat down in the middle of the couch as if it would tip if she positioned herself one inch farther either way. Cats curled up on each side of her.

"Why?"

"I guess I'm hoping that might lead to people who know where she is now."

"She's dead."

"Why do you say that?"

"Because she is."

I wondered if my hunt was already over. "You know that for certain?"

She reached for the can of beer before thinking better of it. She put her hands together in her lap. "A mother knows," she said.

"But just to be clear, you don't know anything specific? Something you might want to tell the police?"

"It's a feeling. I told the minister the same thing."

"Minister?"

"The one that came looking for her."

"A minister was here? Looking for Jessica?"

"What I said."

"What was his name?" Confused, I thought of Roy.

"Father something. I don't remember." Her eyes drifted to the TV. She was wearing faded jeans and a brown blouse missing a button, with the shapeless, slightly heavy body of a woman without means and without hope.

"And he was trying to find Jessica?"

"He said he was worried about her. That he'd tried to help her in Columbus. That he was wondering if I knew where she might be."

I recalled the Rest EZ Motel and the fictional parole officer. "He leave a number?"

She looked around the room, glancing from one pile of paper to another. Eventually she got up with a sigh and sifted through a heap at the end of the couch. "Here," she said. She handed me a scrap of yellow-lined paper with a handwritten Columbus number on it. No name.

"What did he look like?"

"I'm not sure. Ordinary."

"White?"

She nodded. "Mustache, I think. Maybe glasses." That gave me pause. I thought back to my conversation with Kevin Harding, the *Dispatch* reporter. The same description the survivor had given police of the killer. The Pleasure Prince. I shook it off. It fit half the men in any given population.

"When was this?"

"Don't remember. Few weeks back. Could have been summer."

"Bill last heard from her in late July. After that, you think?"

"Could be, yeah." She reached out for the beer can and this time picked it up, though she didn't drink. I couldn't decide if she were lying or really couldn't remember.

"So what'd you tell him? This minister?"

"Same thing I told you. That she's dead."

"What he'd say?"

"Said he hoped that wasn't true."

I looked at the phone number again and tucked the paper into my coat pocket.

I said, "So Jessica left for Columbus after high school?"

"Far as I know."

"You don't know? Wasn't she living with you?"

"She wasn't here."

"Where was she?"

"She moved in with another family, after eleventh grade."

"Why?"

"She and Jimmy didn't get along."

"Jimmy?"

"My husband. Her stepdad. *Ex*-husband."

Theresa's words came back to me: *How about her stepdad? Did he fuck her?*

"Who was it? The family she moved in with?"

"Couple down the street." She waved in a vague direction that could have been the North Pole or North Carolina. "She dog-sat for them a couple times. They got along." She shrugged. "It just kind of happened."

"Do you know their names?"

"Probably, yeah."

"Can you tell me?"

"Why do you want to know?"

"Like I said before. I'm trying to find anybody who might know what happened to her."

She shrugged, her eyes drifting back to the TV. The brash colors of the studio background and flashing red news alerts contrasted with the gray pallor of the living room. After a moment she sighed, got up again, and shuffled toward the kitchen.

"Name's Fischer," she said, returning with another slip of paper. "Mr. and Mrs. That's their address. I don't have a number."

"Do you know where Jessica went in Columbus, after she left here?"

"Not really. We didn't talk much."

"Do you mind if I ask why not?"

"She didn't want nothing to do with us."

"You and Jimmy."

"That's right. He tried to be a dad to her, but . . ."

"Where's he now?"

"We're divorced."

"I meant, where does he live?"

"Here. Mount Alex."

"Any idea if he's heard from Jessica?"

"I wouldn't know. I doubt it. Like I said, they didn't get along."

"I'm sorry to have to ask this. But did he ever, you know, hurt her?"

Her eyes narrowed as if someone had suddenly snapped on a bright light. "What do you mean?"

"Just that, I guess," I said, carefully. "Do anything to her."

"Like what?"

"I'm just wondering if she had a reason to run away."

"She didn't run away."

"You said she moved in with this other family."

"It's not running away if you know where somebody is."

"OK," I said, doubtfully.

"If Jimmy did anything to her, I never knew about it, put it that way." She took a drink of beer, set down the can, lit a cigarette, inhaled deeply, and leaned back. I'd heard stronger denials from half-naked husbands answering the door of their girlfriends' apartments.

"So he could have?"

"Like I said," she said slowly. "The two of them didn't get along. Fought all the time. I hope to hell that's not what it was about."

"You have a number for Jimmy?"

"I sure don't."

"You know where he lives?"

"He moves around a lot."

"Any idea where I could find him?"

She reached out and stroked the cat on her left. It gave a soft "mawk," licked itself, and went back to sleep. "He spends a lot of time in the Parthenon."

I nodded. I knew it. A bar just off the main square. I'd pulled my father out of there more than once, back in the day.

"How about Jessica's friends? Would any of them know anything?"

"She didn't have a lot of friends."

"Do you remember any names?"

"Not really."

I looked at her. She wasn't telling me something, and it didn't take a genius to figure out what. I was guessing it was just as Theresa had suspected.

"Mandie Smith," she said. "They was friends."

"Know how I can reach her?"

She shook her head.

"Is she in town?"

"Wouldn't know. Don't think so."

She looked away, reaching out to stroke the other cat. It stretched in response. It wasn't neutered. Which suggested the sharp smell in the air was something stronger than unchanged cat litter. Which suggested one more reason why a teenage girl being abused by her stepfather would want to move out of such a pit.

"Is there anything else you can tell me? Anything you think might help me find Jessica?"

For a moment Tammy Byrnes looked as if she might change her mind, like a woman deciding she has enough time to cross a busy street before the pedestrian light stops flashing. The moment passed and she stepped back onto the curb. "I'm good," she said. "That's all I know."

I tried to think what else to ask. So far, every question had raised two more. Jessica had run away to this other family— I didn't care what her mother called it—after not getting along with her stepdad, which was consistent with Theresa's theory of abuse. A lack of friends, other than Mandie Smith, spoke to social isolation, which I was guessing made Jessica vulnerable to further abuse once she got to Columbus. To top it off, her mother seemed disinterested in her to the point of not knowing what her own daughter had done after she left town. And then, of course, there was the alleged minister, and the obvious next question: Was he the same person as the fake parole officer?

I stood up. "I'll call you if I find anything."

"When you find her body."

"You don't know that."

"There's no other explanation," she said, reaching for the beer again. "I know what my daughter was doing. I know what was going on. I know what Columbus is like. I'm not stupid."

"I never said—"

"Don't let the cats out when you leave."

18

AFTER I PULLED UP IN FRONT OF THE
Parthenon, I retrieved the number of the minister Tammy gave
me and dialed it.

"Hello?" A man's voice.

I explained who I was and why I was calling. There was a
long pause, nearly a count of ten, before the line went dead. I
called back immediately but it rang until disconnecting. I hung up
and tried again with the same result. I texted the number, asking
for a call back. None came. So one thing was clear: whoever the
minister was, he wasn't keen on any help finding Jessica. Which
probably meant he had his own reasons for hunting her. Which
made me worry about what he would do if he found her first.

THE PARTHENON WASN'T QUITE as I remembered
it: once dark, dilapidated, and rank with the smell of spilled beer, it
now sported actual ferns, brass railings around booths, and a real
live menu instead of bowls of stale bar nuts. It had something else
I didn't recall: a bartender in black jeans, a tight Christmas sweater,
and a smile bordering on saucy who asked me what I was drinking.

She wrinkled her nose when I ordered a Black Label. I asked for a Christmas ale instead, her choice. "That's more like it," she said, taking her time as she moseyed back toward the draft beer tap handles. I followed her progress with interest. I was a detective, after all. My investigation was interrupted by a text from Shelley, informing me surgery had been moved up an hour, meaning I had to be at the hospital by 6 a.m. That was followed by a text from Kym with a list of Christmas present possibilities for Mike. Which meant he hadn't told her about the Xbox yet. A third text popped up from Anne, apologizing for her bad mood that morning. I stared at her message the longest. I was about to reply when the bartender reappeared.

"Here you go." She set down a can of Bud with a green ribbon tied around it. She winked, and put her left hand on her hip in a way that stretched her sweater even tighter.

"Cute," I said, admiring the view. I looked a last time at Anne's text before pocketing the phone without replying. "Good King Wenceslas approves. You, ah, happen to know a guy named Jimmy—?" I paused. I realized I didn't know his last name. Turns out it didn't matter.

"Jimmy Wooding?"

"Used to be married to Tammy Byrnes."

"In the head," she said. "He starts in here around two. Bee-lines for the little boy's room every thirty minutes on the nose. I can set my watch. I'm not kidding."

"I believe you. What's he drinking?"

"7 and 7s."

It was my turn to wrinkle my nose. I told her to bring him a fresh one anyway.

"You're not from around here, are you?" she said, lingering.

I shook my head. "Columbus."

"I love Columbus."

"Me too."

"I bet. So much to do over there." She did that thing again with her hip and her sweater. She was mid-thirties, blonde but not natural, appreciably curvy. No ring, but the faintest line where one might have fit once, and not that long ago. I admired the view again. She watched me admiring her.

"Yes, there is," I replied. I met her eyes briefly. I thought about the scene in Anne's bedroom that morning. I decided to take the moment for what it was. I'd been faithful to Anne since we'd been together, and had no plans to change that arrangement. But I realized with chagrin that I'd missed encounters like this—the tango of possibilities—despite the fact they'd gotten me into endless trouble over the years.

"There's your man," she said.

"Sorry?"

"Jimmy." She nodded. I looked and saw a thin guy emerging from the back. The bartender sent a last glance my way and went off to make his drink. I watched her go. I watched until she came back and placed the drink beside him before I moved down the bar with my beer.

"Already talked to the cops," he said after I'd made my pitch. "Told them everything. Which ain't much."

"You talked to the police? About Jessica?"

"I just said that." He was small and lean, with thinning hair and a distinctive underbite, wearing a red flannel shirt and jeans. I put him anywhere between forty and sixty.

"Who was it?"

"Don't know. Some detective."

"Larry Schwartzbaum?"

"Dunno. Don't think so."

I asked if he'd gotten a card. He shook his head. I realized I didn't know what Schwartzbaum looked like. Wooding couldn't describe the cop anyway, other than saying he was white. And kind of regular looking. There was a lot of that going around.

"When was this?"

"Couple weeks ago. Maybe more."

"Where?"

"Right where you're sitting. 'Cept he bought me a double." He looked at me expectantly.

"Was he in uniform?"

"Street clothes."

"Did he say where he was from? What department?"

He hesitated. He looked up the bar at Christmas Sweater. She had her phone out and was doing a damned good impression of someone minding her own business. Wooding took a gulp of his drink and sucked in two ice cubes. He chewed them loudly, like a dog crunching chicken bones.

"I guess he didn't say."

"Local, maybe."

"Nah. I know all the cops here."

"I bet you do."

"What's that supposed to mean?"

"Skip it. Could he have been from Columbus? Since he was asking about Jessica?"

"Maybe."

"So a cop whose name you don't know, whose department you're not sure of, comes in and asks you about your missing stepdaughter, and you just talk to him, no questions asked?"

"Think you're so smart. Like I even know your name."

I pushed the card I'd offered him at the beginning of the conversation to the edge of his drink. He picked it up, looked at it, folded it in half, and flicked it over the side of the bar.

"Glad we got that taken care of," I said. "So what'd you tell him?"

"Nothing."

"Nothing? After a double 7 and 7?"

"I told him nothing because I don't know nothing. I ain't seen Jessica in years. Since she left for the Fischers." The Fischers—the dog-owning couple whose name his ex-wife gave me.

"Seems odd to leave home like that. Just to watch somebody's dogs."

"Not so odd."

"Why not?"

He turned to me. "She was a brat, is why. Mouthed off to her mom and worse to me. She said she was leaving and she left, and we didn't see any need to stop her."

"Did you know them?"

"Who?"

"The Fischers."

"Little bit. Knew who they were. It's a small town," he said, stating the obvious.

"Ever try to go over there? See if she's OK?"

He shook his head.

"Why not?"

"Why not, because I was sick of her. We both were. And me and her didn't really get along. No point."

How about the stepdad? Did he fuck her? I said, "You give her any reason to be so bratty?"

"What do you mean?" Another gulp of his drink, already on its last legs, followed by more ice-crunching.

"Did you yell at her? Discipline her?"

"I yelled a little. Who doesn't? She yelled back. So what?"

"Ever hit her?"

His head snapped up. "No."

"Ever want to hit her?"

He hesitated. "No."

"Ever say anything to her, or maybe accidentally touch her, in a way that might have made her uncomfortable?"

"That's a hell of question to ask a man."

"I'm just trying to help her."

"Sure doesn't sound like it," he said, and shifted his weight on the barstool. I braced myself. I outweighed Wooding by at least five bottles of Seagram's and had only sipped my can of beer, in contrast to his busy afternoon's work at the bar. But you had to be careful with guys like that. Skinny drunks are like small, rusty nails: they can leave you with surprisingly nasty injuries. Instead of lashing out, though, Wooding relaxed after a moment and shook his head, as if taking the high road after I'd made an ethnic crack.

"Get lost," he said. "I don't have to talk to you."

"Did you?" I persisted.

"I didn't do nothing to Jessica."

"She ran away for some reason."

"Listen," he said, swallowing the last of his drink. "If you're tryin' to rile me up, you're doin' a pretty good job." He stopped, struggling to focus. "But I'm not taking the bait. I told you all there is to know. You want to help Jessica, do your job and find her."

"I'm trying."

"Not trying very hard, you ask me. Like I told that cop, she ain't over here. She's in Columbus. *If* she's alive."

"You got any reason to think she's not?"

"I don't have any reason and I don't have any opinion, be honest with you. How about another drink?"

"How about some other time," I said. I stood up, pulled out a twenty, pulled out another business card and put it on top of Wooding's drink glass, then slapped the bill on the bar beside my nearly full can. "Give me a call, you hear anything about her."

"Fat chance," he said, crunching a mouthful of ice. At least he didn't flip the card away like the first one.

I was on my way out the door when I stopped, turned around, and made eye contact with the bartender. It wasn't hard, since she was watching me watch her. I admired the view one last time, nodded, got a nod and a bit more in return, and walked outside.

19

"WE DID WHAT WE COULD FOR HER," GARRETT Fischer said.

"It sounds like it." I was telling the truth. It was the third time he'd said it to me.

Fischer lived in a town house a couple of miles and a couple of income tax brackets up from Tammy Byrnes. He was overweight, bordering on obese. He used a cane and walked with a limp, though I wouldn't have put him much older than me. He wore white pull-on sneakers and a matching gold-and-black Mount Alexandria Cougars tracksuit that looked new and gave him the demeanor of a coach, albeit one whose best days of eating Wheaties were behind him. He explained he was on disability with diabetes. His daughter, a woman in her early twenties wearing too much eye shadow and a perpetual frown, played with her phone at the kitchen table. Fischer's wife was at work. Two toy poodles festooned with ribbons snoozed in a dog basket between the table and the recliner into which Fischer had sunk after answering the door and agreeing to let me in. The same dogs Jessica had watched and taken for walks, he confirmed, when they were little more than puppies.

"Things must have been bad at home for Jessica to move out," I said.

"We didn't talk too much about that," Fischer said. "We did what we could for her. You said she was a prostitute?" He shook his head.

"That's right."

"Hard to believe. It's not the girl we knew. She was troubled, yeah. But—"

"I can see how it must be a shock."

"You're not kidding." He seemed genuinely upset, his breath coming in gasps as if he'd just climbed a steep hill. "She talked about art school, maybe. She had dreams."

"Did you go to high school with her?" I said to Fischer's daughter.

There was no reaction. I repeated my question. Fischer glared at her. "Lindsay," he said sharply, getting her attention.

"No," she said, not looking up from her phone. "She's older than me."

"Have you heard from her?"

"No."

"Facebook messages? Anything?"

"No," she said, and then, seeing the expression on Fischer's face, said, "I don't really know her that well."

"You know someone named Mandie Smith?"

"Who?"

I explained the connection. She shook her head with an injured look, as if I'd asked her how much she weighed. I looked at Fischer.

"Don't know a Mandie Smith. And haven't heard a word from Jessica. We were a little hurt she never got back in touch with us, tell you the truth. Martha especially."

"I bet." I found myself sympathizing with him, despite the odd circumstances of how he knew Jessica. It was dawning on me how widely the impact of her disappearance—or worse—might spread. "So no idea what she did after she left here?"

Fischer shook his head. "She just took off one day. She was eighteen. We did what we could for her."

"Ever ask her mom? Or her stepdad?"

"Yeah, right."

"Why do you say that?"

"They're the ones she left. Didn't seem likely they'd be in the loop."

"Did you know them before?"

"Before what?"

"Before she came here."

He looked nearly as upset as his daughter had at the question about Mandie Smith.

"It's just that Jimmy seemed to think you knew each other," I said.

"Where'd he tell you that? The Parthenon?"

"He just said he did."

"Guys like him, they'll say anything, I guess."

"So how'd Jessica end up here?"

"Answered an ad. I wasn't doing too great then, and Martha was working a lot. Needed help with the dogs. She did good, and we talked and she just moved in for a while. We had a spare room. We did what we could for her. Lot more than her folks."

I glanced at Lindsay, wondering what had kept her from helping with the dogs. She scowled at me, as if reading my mind.

"It was good of you to help her," I said to Fischer.

"Appreciate you saying that."

"Mmm." I looked around the house. The Fischers' decorating tastes ran to barnyard-scene wallpaper borders, framed paintings of puppies and kittens, and brightly colored crocheted afghans blanketing almost every piece of furniture, as if I'd stepped into the showroom of an acrylic yarn factory. I counted at least four bowls of potpourri on end tables, mantels, and the kitchen counter. "A house is made of walls and beams; a home is built with love and dreams," read the shellacked wooden sign over the fake fireplace. An artificial tree taller than me by a couple of nutcracker soldiers took up most of the living room corner, draped with tinsel and lights and blue and green and red glass ornament balls. The decor was not exactly my style. But everything was clean, and light poured in through the numerous windows, and the potpourri smelled good. It invoked fond memories of similarly neat and cozy homes of various aunts and grandparents and older cousins when I was growing up. It didn't take a private investigator to figure out the appeal of a home like this compared to the dump on Columbus Road where Tammy lived. Especially if Jimmy-the-stepdad was a drunk up to no good. I was surprised Jessica wanted to leave such a refuge right away after high school, but eighteen years old with the world in front of you is what it is, no matter how comfortable your surroundings. Especially if the people you're with aren't your blood relatives.

The doorbell rang, a low, comforting gong. Fischer struggled to his feet.

"Have to excuse me. I've got a client."

"Client?"

"I do some part-time accounting, since I can't work regular. I'm sorry we couldn't help you more. I feel bad for Jessica. We did what we could for her. Maybe you could let me know what you find out."

I told him I would. I got up. I said goodbye to Lindsay. She nodded noncommittally, which was better than the scowl I expected. She reminded me of a lot of girls I'd grown up with, wanting to get the hell out of small-town America but not sure where to start. She looked up as Fischer opened the front door, but quickly returned to her phone. I felt my own phone buzz but didn't take it out of my pocket. Fischer's client was wearing a long, black winter coat and black driving gloves and a worried look that suggested his financials needed some Christmas cheer. He did a double take when he saw me, then walked the rest of the way inside. Fischer didn't introduce us.

At the door, I said, "Anyone else been by recently, looking for Jessica?"

"Like who?" Fischer said.

"I don't know. Her mother said a minister was here a few weeks ago, wondering if she'd seen her. And Jimmy said he talked to a police officer."

"Police? From here?"

"He didn't think so. He was vague on the details."

"Big surprise. Martha might have mentioned somebody coming by."

"She know who?"

He shook his head. "His story didn't make sense, and she didn't let him in. Not like you, with a license and everything. Jimmy and Tammy say anything? To those people?"

"Tammy said she's sure Jessica's dead. Jimmy says he didn't say anything because he doesn't know anything."

"I'm guessing her mom's right. From everything you've told me."

"All right, then," I said when he stayed quiet. "You've got my card. If by any chance you hear from Jessica, or get any information where she might be, you'll let me know?"

"I can't make any promises. She wasn't here all that long. We did what we could for her."

I CHECKED MY PHONE when I got back into the van. There was a text from a number I didn't recognize. I opened the message and found myself staring at a can of Bud with a green ribbon around it. I read the text below the photo.

Picked your card off the floor. I might be in Columbus soon. Let me know if I can buy you a real Christmas ale. ;)

The bartender. *So many things to do there.* I stared at the message for almost a minute, thinking. Finally, knowing I had to get moving, I wrote, Thanks, started the engine, and headed home.

20

IT WAS FOGGY THAT AFTERNOON AS THERESA and I walked up to the knot of people standing in front of Third Baptist. Darlene Bardwell broke away from a conversation with a man I recognized as a city councilman and strode toward us. She was wearing a dark quilted puffer coat that fell to her knees and a red felt cloche hat. I introduced her to Theresa. The congresswoman gripped Theresa's right hand with both of hers.

"Thank you for coming tonight," she said, looking into her eyes. "It means so much to me."

"Well, yeah," Theresa said.

"You know John, of course," Bardwell said, reaching out to tug her aide on the elbow. He turned and smiled and offered greetings to Theresa as warm as his boss's a moment earlier. "And my husband, Barry," the congresswoman said.

"Nice to meet you," I said, shaking his hand.

"The pleasure's all mine," Barry Bardwell said. "Always wanted the opportunity. What a story you've got."

"Let's hope it's got a happy ending," I said, which got a laugh—as the stock line usually did. He had short, dark hair beginning to gray, blue eyes, a cleft chin to do Cary Grant proud, and an authentic dimple in each cheek. Assuming he did dishes and folded laundry now and then, it seemed a stretch that Bardwell would stray too far from such a face.

"And this is Gretchen Osborne," Bardwell said, pirouetting to her left. I shook hands with a woman wearing a black watch cap and a worn-looking black pea coat.

"Gretchen was Jessica's caseworker," Bardwell said. "*Is* her caseworker," she corrected herself. "She has a lot of experience working with trafficked women. She's been a valuable resource."

I nodded and introduced Theresa. They didn't seem to know each other. Before either could say anything, someone called the congresswoman's name and she strode away from us apologetically, her husband following in her wake along with Blanchett, who did everything but hold the end of her train. Gretchen stood uncertainly, hands jammed into her coat pockets. An awkward silence descended.

"She tell you what I was up to?" I said at last.

"Trying to find Jessica. For Bill?"

"That's right. Anything you can, you know, fill me in on?"

"Everything and nothing." I'd seen happier faces at children's funerals.

"Meaning?"

She shifted back and forth in a pair of lived-in hiking boots with faded red laces. "Jessica's one of those women that got let down at every stage of her life. Even by her brother. It's no wonder she ended up on the streets."

"Her brother?"

"He walked away from the family as soon as he could. Joined the army, right? Lost touch with everybody, including Jessica. Now, all of a sudden, he's interested?"

"Better late than never? Plus, he did take in her son."

"Sure. Except that's kind of convenient, isn't it? Gives him an incentive to get her back in the picture."

"That's a cold way to look at it."

"I'm just telling you how I feel. My loyalty's with Jessica, not her family."

"As it should be, I guess. When's the last time you saw her?"

"I couldn't even say. A while."

"Apparently she was scared of something. Her and Lisa Washington. Any idea what?" I told her what Theresa had heard about the book, and about the theory Jessica had gone looking for Lisa and maybe re-encountered Bronte in the process.

That seemed to catch her attention. "Where'd you hear that?"

"Couple people." I mentioned Darla, the woman who'd fallen from grace, or at least the suburbs.

Gretchen frowned. "I know her. Hope you didn't pay for that information. She'd make anything up if it got her some business."

"You're saying I wasted my money?" I thought about how quickly Darla had taken my twenty. Money that another girl her age might have used for Friday night drinks with girlfriends.

"I'm saying I could tell you what they're scared of for free."

"I'm all ears."

"They're scared of getting raped, that's what. Scared of getting robbed. Scared of getting beaten up, infected, strung out with no fix in sight. That good enough for you?"

I took a small step backward as I experienced the near-palpable anger emanating from her, like heat off midsummer asphalt. "Enough to make me feel bad, sure," I said. "But I got the impression it was something more than that."

"Like what?"

"This book, or whatever. Something that might help me find Jessica if I figure out what it was."

"I wouldn't hold your breath on that front."

"Why?"

She turned and glanced toward a small crowd of reporters by the curb. I made out Kevin Harding with the *Dispatch* and Suzanne Gregory from Channel 7, among others.

Gretchen said, "You know the paper has a database of missing women?"

"I'd heard that."

"Jessica fits every single indicator for this guy's victims. Every one."

"You think she's dead."

"I think you could save her brother a lot of money and just wait for the inevitable."

I struggled for a response but came up empty. Gretchen Osborne struck me as a furious and unhappy person. But not necessarily an untruthful or naive one. I had to concede her point, which came with far more authority than the same, vague pronouncement by Jessica's mother. The chances were much better than even that Jessica was dead and my hunt was nothing more than a gritty wild-goose chase. I looked at Theresa for help. Before she could speak, the vigil began with a request from the church's minister that we close the circle and bow our heads. We stood in silence for the next few minutes as he prayed for the slain women, speaking each of their names aloud, then prayed for the women who were still missing.

"These deaths were preventable tragedies," Bardwell said when her turn came at the microphone. "For too long we've blamed women like them for their situations without acknowledging an uncomfortable truth: they're the victims here. No one turns their body into a commodity for abuse willingly. We should be helping them, not treating them like criminals. Our brave law enforcement officials"—a nod to the left to the police chief—"and our local public servants"—a nod to the right to the mayor—"are doing all they can in this fight. But we have to do more. Targeting the supply isn't the answer. We have to cut off the demand. That's why I've introduced legislation that will end the ability of online sites to advertise these women like chattel. It's not going to stop the problem. But it's an important first step."

She paused for clapping that seemed more dutiful than heartfelt, like cold rain on a cold sidewalk. After a moment, the minister returned and introduced Gloria Washington, the mother of the last victim—and Jessica's friend—Lisa Washington. Washington led the group in a chorus of "Amazing Grace." When we were finished singing, I watched as the congresswoman's husband leaned over to her aide to say something. Blanchett nodded solemnly. If there was enmity between the two, some tension over Blanchett's cozy relationship with Bardwell, I couldn't detect it. I recalled Anne's frustration at my view of men and women in the workplace. Was I assuming something amiss simply because I found Bardwell so attractive? It wouldn't be the first time I'd let my baser instincts overrule logic.

Bardwell, the mayor, and the police chief moved to the edge of the crowd, where the reporters waited. I caught Kevin Harding's eye, but he turned away without acknowledging me. I looked in vain for Theresa, before seeing to my amazement she was standing next to Harding while a couple videographers attached mikes to her coat in preparation for an interview.

"There you are," the congresswoman said afterward, as the lights from the cameras dimmed. "I wanted to introduce someone. Andy, Marc Copeland."

I acknowledged the man at her side. He didn't offer a hand.

"Marc's a Columbus vice lieutenant," Bardwell said. "He was good enough to come by tonight."

"Sergeant," Copeland said.

"Of course, of course," Bardwell said. "I've told him about your work with Jessica. I'm sure you'll compare notes at some point."

I nodded, trying to figure out where I'd seen him before. Copeland nodded back. He looked like the kind of cop who'd rather toss on a pink dress, feather boa, and stiletto heels, and then jump off a cliff, before he'd compare notes with a private investigator. He was stocky, with thinning hair and protuberant ears; his build that of a former wrestler or small school lineman. *Parole officer? Minister? Cop?* But, as with Bronte Patterson's distinctive mug, I didn't think Mr. Patel, Jimmy Wooding, or even Tammy Byrnes, who seemed to care more for her cats than her missing daughter, would have failed to register this guy's description.

"Let me know if I can do anything to help," he said between clenched teeth.

"Ditto," I said, seeing his clench and raising him a white lie.

Bardwell kept us chatting about nothing for a few minutes before saying her goodbyes, after which Copeland and I walked away from each other faster than estranged relatives on *Jerry Springer*.

"So how'd it go?" I said to Theresa as we headed back to the van. "The interview, I mean."

"Fine. Their questions were stupid."

"Like what?"

"Like how did I *feel*."

"Feel?"

"About the dead girls. 'Because of your own *experiences*.'"

"Everybody has a job to do, I guess," I said, although in truth I was wondering the same thing about her. "What'd you think of the social worker?" I turned and nodded toward Gretchen, now deep in conversation with the vice sergeant.

"I liked her. No bullshit. Not touchy-feely. She told me she'd have coffee with you. Talk more about the case."

"Really? She didn't seem like she wanted anything to do with me."

"She doesn't. Who can blame her? But I talked her into it. Said you were sucking air and could use some help."

"Thanks for the vote of confidence."

"Don't thank me. Just take me home." She shivered.

"Are you cold? It's barely in the forties."

"I ain't cold. Too many memories."

"Right," I said, and wondered if it had been such a good idea to bring her along after all. How had Roy put it? Only two years off the streets, and one year sober?

We walked half a block to my van. I was fumbling for the keys when I heard a rattle of wheels on concrete behind me. I turned and saw the guy with the shopping cart we'd seen the other night when we were canvassing the neighborhood. A bum's bum. He was black, with a street beard, wearing a grimy beige coverall with holes in the elbows and knees, running shoes with one of the heels flopping loose, and an orange hunter's hat that looked as if someone had pulled it out of a campfire at the last second.

"Cigarette?" he said, coming to a stop.

"Don't smoke," I replied.

"Smart man. It's a cover-up, you know."

"I'm sorry?"

"The guy. The dude. The *killer.*"

"Killer?"

"The one that did the women. They're covering it up. The *government* knows. He's one of *them.*"

I tried to decide if he was high or crazy. Or both. But at least his eyes were clear. "The serial killer?" I said, palming my keys. "He works for the government?"

He nodded, looking at Theresa, then back at me. "The mayor knows. But they'll kill him if he tells. The police know too. But what are they supposed to do? Comes out, shit's gonna hit the *fan.*" He lowered his voice. *"Goes all the way up to the White House."*

"There a grassy knoll involved too?"

"Don't believe me, do you?"

"Not sure I have an opinion."

"That's what they're counting on."

"Who?"

"Them. They don't want you to know. To think about it. Until it's too late." He pulled his hand across his throat.

"I also heard they're building concentration camps for gun owners out west," I said. "Just F your I."

"You a joker, ain't you?"

"Hey." A raised voice, behind us. I turned and saw Copeland, the vice sergeant, striding toward us.

"Everything OK?"

"I think so." I looked at the man. "Right?"

But he was looking at Copeland. *"The government,"* he said. "They *know.*"

"Beat it," Copeland said. He stared hard at the man, who waved his hands in front of his face and backed off, rattling down the sidewalk.

"Dumb ass," Copeland said to no one in particular, and turned to go. Then he stopped and added something that surprised me. "I probably can't tell you much. But call me if something comes up." He handed me a card.

"Thanks."

He pointed his finger at the retreating conspiracy theorist before shaking his head and walking back to the church parking lot.

"*They know,*" the man said to Copeland's back. "*They know the truth.*"

21

INSTEAD OF HEADING HOME WE DROVE
farther east, figuring we might as well see who was on the streets.
Along the way I briefed Theresa on my interviews in Mount Alexandria before the vigil.

"Stepdad," she said.

"What about him?"

"He's the guy."

"The guy?"

"The one that hurt Jessica. What she was running from."

"Could be. He got pretty upset when I suggested the possibility. And her mom didn't fight the idea very hard."

"Yes, she did. She fucking blew her top."

I looked at her, confused. "What did you say?"

She shook her head and rubbed her hands on her thighs.
Under a thrift store parka she was wearing a denim dress with
sparkles on the pockets over orange woolen tights. "Nothing."

"You OK?"

"I'm fine."

"You sure?"

"Leave it, QB."

I left it. I went back to my conversation with Garrett Fischer. "That town house would've been tough to leave, considering where Jessica came from. It must have been bad, whatever Jimmy did."

"It was bad," Theresa said.

Something in her voice caught my attention. Something in her eyes warned me not to ask. Instead, I said, "Our friend back there. Mr. Truth Teller?"

"What about him?"

"Makes you wonder if he's the one."

"The one what?"

"The killer."

"Him? You gotta be kidding." She rubbed her thighs extra-vigorously. "He wasn't even half there."

"Or even thirty-three and a third. But a decent disguise, if you think about it. Crazy dude wandering the streets with a shopping cart. Hidden in plain sight?"

"And he what, stuffs the bodies under all that junk?"

"How about, lures them someplace? Cops say the killer's got a lair of some kind." I paused. "Someplace he might keep them a couple of days, before, you know . . ."

She breathed out her dissatisfaction. "Your head must have bounced around in your helmet a lot harder than I thought, way back when."

"I guess it does sound far-fetched."

"Sounds like something even the cat wouldn't throw up."

Two blocks farther down, just before the giant silhouette of the abandoned grain silos, we came across a girl wearing sweatpants and a blue sweatshirt with paint stains on the front. I recognized her. It was the same girl we'd seen with "Darla" the other night. But tonight she was alone. She was pacing back and forth and hugging herself. I pulled over and Theresa got out. While they talked I checked my messages. Shelley had texted me some last-minute instructions for the next morning. Anne wished me and my dad well. Bill Byrnes wondered how it was going.

The side door of the van opened. I turned and saw the girl climb in, followed by Theresa.

"This is 'Mary,'" Theresa said. "She's coming with us. I'll take her to see Pastor Roy tomorrow. See what we can do for her. Maybe find her a program. She ain't got any place to go home to."

"OK," I said, taken aback.

"She's a little scared, after the other night. After we talked to her."

"Scared of the guy?"

"Scared of Bronte. Bad things happen, he finds out they were talking about him."

"But she didn't say anything," I said. I offered the girl a smile. I got a thousand-yard stare in return.

"He don't know that," Theresa said. "Let's go."

"Where's her friend?"

"Who?"

"Darla."

Theresa looked at the girl, but the girl's expression was as blank as the street she'd been selling herself on. Theresa looked at me and shook her head. I pulled a U-turn and headed back west toward downtown. A minute later we passed the bum pushing his cart and talking to himself. Someone else hunting Jessica? Theresa was right. I couldn't see it. I looked in my rearview mirror. Mary and Theresa were holding hands. So the night hadn't been a complete waste. I'd found one person, anyway.

22

SHELLEY, MY MOM, AND I HAD LESS THAN
twenty minutes with my dad the next day, the morning of the
surgery. He was breathing a little better, but his color was off. He
looked pasty and wan, as if recovering from the flu. He looked as
bad as one of the last times I'd pulled him out of the Parthenon,
where he sat boasting that he'd never watched a down I played in
my short stint with the Browns, so ashamed he was of me. It was
a lie, just like his boast he'd seen every one of my college games
in person. He'd watched a lot of both on a barstool, in a joint he
wouldn't recognize now. It was OK. I would have lied about me
too. I looked at him carefully, as if seeing him for the first time in
years. His doctor had made it clear that while the bypass surgery
would improve his condition immensely, some irreparable damage had been done because he'd ignored his symptoms too long
before keeling over at the mall. His ejection fraction number was
just too low, whatever that meant. That was the bad news. The
good news was had it happened twenty-five years ago, he probably wouldn't have left the emergency room alive.

When the orderly came to wheel him to the operating room,
my mother leaned over and kissed him on the cheek and told him

she loved him. He grunted something I couldn't hear. Shelley kissed him too. I reached out and took his right hand and squeezed it. Nothing happened. At the last moment, he squeezed back.

"HE'S OK," I TOLD Anne over the phone as I drove home several hours later. Between the unusually long operation and the hours spent waiting to see him afterward, I was there almost the whole day. I'd arrived in the dark of morning and walked out as the sun was setting. "It was a success, as these things go." I told her what the doctor had told us, about the worrisome EF number.

"I've heard of lower," she said. "My grandfather was a cripple after his heart attack. Three steps was like a marathon. Sounds like your dad has plenty of years ahead of him."

We talked until I pulled into Happy Dragon on Livingston. It was the most stress-free conversation I'd had with her in weeks. Even though, I reflected as I went inside the restaurant, she'd demurred when I raised the possibility of stopping by. So what was going on, exactly? I had no idea, I decided, as I paid for a large Hunan beef with two egg rolls, got back in the van, and juddered along the brick streets of German Village until I pulled up in front of my house on Mohawk. I was pleased to see an open parking space, especially now that it was dark. I parked, grabbed my food, and walked to the front door. I set the bag down, collected the mail, and put the key in the lock. I paused, realizing with a twinge of guilt that it was a relief to be walking into my own place, despite another missed opportunity with Anne. Right now I just needed my feet on the table and a beer or two. Satisfied, I turned the key and felt something cold and hard against my neck.

"Smells good, Woody. Hope you brought enough for two."

I opened the door and stepped slowly into the dining room. The pressure went off my neck. I set down the bag, took a step forward, and turned around. I'd only seen him once, and then only in a photograph on Karen Feinberg's phone, but there was no question about his identity. You don't forget a face like that.

"Hello, Bronte," I said.

23

"I LIKE THEIR PAD THAI BETTER," PATTERSON said. "How come you didn't get that?"

"I have a thing about ordering Thai at a Chinese place."

"You talking food or girls?" His smile was a wide gash of white teeth and red tongue.

"Is that supposed to be funny?"

"I thought so."

"Maybe try not to think so much."

"Maybe be careful what you say."

"I am. I'm using small Anglo-Saxon words so I don't confuse you. What do you want?"

We were in the living room. Patterson sat on the couch, working his way through my Hunan beef. His gun was on the coffee table within easy reach. He was chewing with his mouth open, but I think he was doing it on purpose. He'd helped himself to one of my Black Labels, though not without a disparaging remark about swill. I was in my armchair gnawing on the egg roll he'd left me. I looked at the letters on his forehead and tried to figure out what they stood for. EWMN. Hopalong, loyal companion to the end, lay at my feet, ready to leap into action the moment Patterson accidentally dropped a morsel on the floor.

"I want you to talk less," Patterson said, his mouth full. He was staring at me, but his eyes didn't read malice. They read genuine curiosity, which felt scarier.

"Fine. Then answer my question."

"I want to know where Jessica's at."

"Is."

"What?"

"Where Jessica is. 'At' sounds ignorant. I have no idea."

"Bullshit."

"Bullshit yourself. If I'd found her there'd have been a press conference and a proclamation and probably fireworks. Her congresswoman's involved now. Don't you watch the news?"

"Do I look like I watch the news?"

"You look like you dropped out of TV after *SpongeBob*."

"Woody, I'm getting tired of your lip."

"Feeling's ever so mutual, believe me." But I was thinking the fact he knew my old nickname meant he knew a little about me. Which wasn't a good sign.

Patterson smiled like a boy the first time he figures out the wings come off flies. He said, "Why you looking for her?"

"Her brother asked me to."

"How come?"

"He's worried about her."

"Why?"

"She's his sister. You know how that works, right? Worrying about someone you love?"

"I know all about love, Woody. Got the best bitches in town. Looking to buy?"

"Not on your life."

"Ain't my life we're talking about." He chewed some more, spittle flying. I could make out little specks of beef on my coffee table.

He said, "I'm worried about her too. How about that?"

"Give me a break. She was your bottom girl. You're worried about her like a trap losing sleep over a mouse. Let me guess. She owes you money."

He blinked in a way that made me realize he'd be a lousy poker player. "That's more like it," I said. "How much?"

"None of your business."

"I'd say it's my business with you parked on my couch belching up what was supposed to be my dinner. But I'm not sure I get it. She left the streets months ago. Went into a delousing program after all that time with you. You're just trying to find her now?"

"I said, it ain't your business." He drained the can of Black Label and crushed it in his left hand like a Dixie cup. The sound helped jump start my brain. I added up numbers and divided by clues.

"Jessica disappeared from her program after getting a call from a friend."

"What friend?"

"Lisa Washington."

"Girl in the river."

"So you do watch the news. Seems Jessica may have gone looking for her. Was it you she found instead?"

"You ain't asking questions tonight, Woody."

"I'll take that as a yes. So if you saw her then, and she owes you money, maybe you didn't exactly loan it to her. Maybe she took it and now you want it back. How'm I doing?"

"I didn't say I seen her."

"Or maybe I've got it wrong. Maybe you killed Lisa Washington and Jessica found out. Maybe you want to have a little chat with her that ends with her in the river too. Bet the cops would be happy to put that together."

"I didn't kill that girl. And it's none of your business why I'm trying to find Jessica. And the cops ain't got squat on me. Nobody's coming after Bronte."

"You wish."

"I know."

"Listen," I said, starting to lose my patience. "I don't know where she is or at. But I'm not optimistic she's alive, OK? My top suspects are that guy killing these poor women, followed by you. And that's it. That's all I've got."

"That ain't nothing."

"I didn't say it was. But it's the truth."

As casually as a man checking his watch at a wedding, he picked up the gun and pointed it at Hopalong. "How about I shoot your dog?" Patterson said. "You tell me something then?"

The room went still. I willed my heart to slow down. I looked at Hopalong. Exhausted from staking out the possibility of dropped food, he'd fallen asleep, snout parked on his paws. Stupid dog.

"You could do that," I said. "But here's how it would play out. I'm not quite as fast as I used to be, but I guarantee I work out more than you. You look soft as a bunny on crutches. I'd be halfway to you after the first shot. You might or might not get a round off at me, but either way I'd be on top of you quick and because I happen to love my dog and hate fat-ass white boy gangster wannabes like yourself, I'd do some serious damage. Since you're armed and I'm not, which by the way is a chickenshit way to do business, I'd still probably end up dead, while you'd walk out of here as big an asshole as when you walked in. And the thing is, you'd still know squat about Jessica and now you'd have people looking for you, and I don't mean the cops. I mean people not interested in arresting you, let alone reading you your rights. I don't care how safe you think you are. So it's up to you. You can believe what I'm telling you, or you can be a brave man and shoot a dog and pay the consequences. Honestly, I couldn't care less."

"Pretty speech for a—"

"Also, close your fucking mouth when you chew."

He didn't close his mouth, but at least he stayed quiet for a second. He stared at me with renewed curiosity. I held his gaze. I swallowed. I'd been lying about how soft he looked. His face was lean and his neck bulgy with muscles on muscles, and his upper body, even under his oversized Cavaliers shirt, exuded the strength and power of a perpetually coiled snake. And then there was the gun. I tried to persuade myself there was something to my idle threat, that someone would come after him if I died. But who? Roy? He was a crack shot with the Beretta he'd brought back from Iraq, but he was an Episcopal priest now, all respectable and stuff. Theresa? Probably a better bet, but I had a hard time believing even she could handle Patterson. After that, I was out of options. I had friends the way some people have kidneys: barely enough to get by on.

"Think you so smart," Patterson said at last.

"I'm light years from smart. And believe it or not, I want the same thing as you. I want to find Jessica. But like I've been trying to tell you, I don't know where she is."

"You find her, you bring that bitch to me."

"What if she has different plans?"

"What if I don't care?"

"I work for her brother, not you."

"You already told me that. But ain't nothing can't be renegotiated. Because here's something you didn't tell me. You didn't mention that little black boy he's got living with him." Patterson proceeded to recite Bill Byrnes's address, the make of car he drove, the name of the day care where he dropped little Robbie off every day. He said it in the voice of a guy reading baseball standings to his dad. I felt my insides go cold. When he was finished he shoved the last of my Hunan beef into his mouth and chewed loudly and sloppily.

"We're both hunting that bitch," Patterson said. "Only difference is who gets hurt if you find her first and don't call me."

I said nothing. He stood up and turned the Styrofoam box upside down on the couch. The brown liquid dribbled all over the center pillow and down either side. He'd used every extra soy sauce packet they'd dropped into the bag. I got up. Hopalong scrambled and stood up too. Patterson and I locked stares as he passed, and for a moment I thought we'd reached some kind of mutual tough-guy standoff.

I said, "Extra Wide Monkey Neck."

"What?"

"Your tattoo. Those letters on your forehead. I've been trying to figure out what they stand for. How'd I do?"

"Not so good, Woody," he said. Too late I saw the shiny butt end of his gun out of the corner of my left eye. The next moment I was sprawled on the floor, my vision rapidly narrowing like the picture on an old TV collapsing into a tiny, white dot.

"You find that bitch, you call me first," Patterson said.

24

TWO HOURS LATER I WAS SITTING IN A
curtained treatment room at Grant Hospital downtown, across
the street from the main library. I'd been there before. Two different nurses cracked frequent flyer jokes. I'd been poisoned with
iodine and tortured with stitches, but was told I was going to live,
despite the goose egg on top of an ostrich egg wreaking havoc
with my hat size.

I was lying on my back, fighting sleep, when the curtain
opened. I sat up, prepared to go. I was not prepared to see Vice
Sergeant Marc Copeland step inside.

"You OK?"

"I guess. What brings you here? I take it it's not the food."

"Word gets around. I heard Bronte Patterson did a number
on you."

"Feels that way."

He leaned toward me. "Looks that way, too. Any idea why?"

"Possibly." I gave him the short version of the encounter. He
shook his head. I was still thinking he looked familiar.

"Evil, wicked, mean, nasty," he said.

"What?"

"The tattoo you made fun of. That's what it stands for. Lotta guys in prison get 'em. No wonder he clocked you. You think Jessica took cash off him?"

"That's the working theory. Cash or drugs or both. Dropped in on him when she went looking for Lisa Washington, maybe. And I could see him being the kind of personal banker who refuses to forgive a loan."

"You run this theory past him?"

"SparkNotes version."

"And?"

"The suggestion appeared to aggrieve him."

"Thanks, professor. So what'd you tell him? About Jessica?"

"Same thing I've told everyone. That I can't find her, and I'm not optimistic."

"Why not?"

"Wounded animals get killed or crawl off to die alone. Short of a better explanation, that's why."

"I hope you're wrong. Meantime, we'll find Patterson. Assuming you're pressing charges."

"He said he didn't have anything to worry about. Seems to think he's untouchable."

"He said that?"

"More or less."

"What a dipshit. Don't worry. We'll get him."

"Be sure to wash your hands afterward."

BACK HOME, CHECKING MY phone, I saw two more messages from Bill Byrnes looking for updates on Jessica, on top of three missed calls from Kym. I texted Byrnes back, promising him news soon, trying not to think about Patterson's threat against Robbie. If Jessica was alive, I had to find her first. And soon. I looked again at the text from the Parthenon's bartender. Then I called my ex-wife.

"What the hell," she said.

"I'm sorry. I know it's late."

"Nice try. Mike says you're buying him an Xbox. If he gets his grades up. Just like that. Without asking me."

"I told him I'd talk to you about it first. And it's *if* he gets his grades up, and takes piano lessons. He tell you that part?"

"Like that makes it any better. How dare you? You know how I feel about those things. They're so violent. And what am I supposed to tell his brother?" I knew she meant her and Steve's son, not Joe.

"There's nonviolent games."

"Right. And boxing's safe because they wear gloves. Honestly, Andy. I don't even know what to say. Where to start."

"How about, Thank you?"

"Thank you? I ask you to talk to him about his grades and this is your response? I mean—"

"You don't mean anything," I interrupted.

"I beg your pardon?"

"You don't own this issue, Kym. He's my son, too. I'm as worried about his grades as you are, believe me. Because I'm the tree his apple fell close to. Not you. We all know about your good grades in school."

"You didn't just say that—"

"I did. And this is why. This is how I'm doing it, with Mike. This is the only way I know how, since I'm down to Wednesdays and odd weekends. And before you remind me, yes, I know that's my fault, too. But he's going to raise his grades, and take piano along with basketball, and in return he's going to play on the Xbox when he's at my house. And if he fucks up, the box goes in the closet. That's how it's going to be. You understand?"

"Are you threatening me?"

"No." Yes. "I'm sorry. I didn't mean it like that. But I've got a say in this, too."

"It's not right. It's setting such a bad example for him. He's already begging us for a phone day and night. Now this?"

"I've got to go," I said, abruptly. "Been a long day. I'll call you with the names of some piano teachers in a couple days."

After we mutually disconnected, and not in a nice way, I texted Roy and told him I needed recommendations on teachers, and soon. His girls had all taken lessons. Then I went into the kitchen, opened the bottle of Vicodin the hospital had sent me home with, dumped the pills into the sink, and ran water until they dissolved down the drain. I pulled a bottle of extra-strength Tylenol from my spice cabinet—I keep it between turmeric and vanilla—popped three, and opened a Black Label, draining almost all of it as I stood there. I grabbed a second beer, went into the living room, sat down, and watched Jimmy Fallon until I dozed off, which lasted only until the ache in my head woke up me. After that, I went to bed.

25

I SPENT A LOT OF THE NEXT DAY AT THE hospital with my dad. We kept it to Cavs basketball and Bengals prospects, with Shelley refereeing, and bloodshed was averted. Late in the afternoon I left to keep an appointment with Lisa Washington's grandmother. Theresa arrived a minute behind in the beater Honda Civic Roy had helped her buy. She didn't mind the car's age or condition. It was the first vehicle she'd ever owned.

At first Gloria Washington refused to meet with me. Told me over the phone she wasn't ready yet; even six months after her granddaughter's death, she was still having difficulty talking about it. In a coincidence annoying because of its usefulness, John Blanchett called a few minutes later to see how I was doing and if there was anything he could help with. Without asking for any favors I told him about Gloria. Fifteen minutes later he called back and said she was expecting me that night. I had to concede his powers of persuasion.

When Gloria answered the door of her Dutch Colonial in the city's Eastgate neighborhood that night, she was dressed formally, even though it was Saturday, wearing a dark pantsuit with a white blouse and purple scarf for color. I told her she looked young to be a grandmother.

"I'll be seventy-two in a week," she said, showing us into the living room. "I've no interest in retiring. Three of my friends stopped working at sixty-five and were dead a year later. It's not for me."

"Where do you work?"

"Defense supply center. Going on forty years."

I nodded. The massive office complex handling logistics and finances for the military was down the road on the east side.

"You have a beautiful house," I said, admiring the room's tasteful furniture and large Oriental rug.

"Thank you. Normally, I decorate for Christmas. But not this year . . ."

She excused herself and walked out of the room. While Theresa settled herself in a chair, I studied a mantel full of family photos. Gloria's resemblance to Lisa, and to other men and women of various ages and shapes and sizes, was easy to see. There was a set to the eyes and mouth they all shared. She returned a minute later with a tray with a teapot and cups and a plate of biscotti.

"Lots of days I still can't believe she's gone," she said after serving us. She handed me a framed photo of Lisa. I recognized it from looking up her case in the paper. An attractive, smiling girl wearing a cheerleader's uniform. She looked, as teens do in such pictures, as if she had her whole life ahead of her with nothing to slow her down. Just like the picture of Jessica at about the same age. And Darla, the girl from the suburbs. I handed the photo to Theresa.

"She never really knew her father," Gloria said. "He took off when she was two. He was living in West Virginia for a while, and then he was in prison. I'm not sure where he is now. Her mother, Jackie, and I raised her. They were close."

"Where's Jackie now?"

"She's dead. A car ran into the bus stop where she was waiting to go to work. Two months after that picture was taken." She sighed. "That was the beginning of everything. Lisa never got over it. Her grades started to suffer. She hurt her knee in practice one day and a friend gave her a pill he said would help with the pain. Three months after that I realized all my spoons were missing. She was a full-blown heroin addict at nineteen. I did everything I could to help. But before I knew it she was on the streets. She came home from time to time, but she was never the same again."

I said, "And that's where she met Jessica?"

"I'm not sure. Lisa worked out of a house for a while, off and on. She tried to tell me it was safer. Maybe she was right. I think they knew each other there."

"A house?"

"A brothel. You know what I mean."

"Do you know where?"

"She wouldn't tell me. Said it was better I didn't know. Someplace on the east side. She still tried to see me. She'd drop by, take me grocery shopping, take my vacuum cleaner to be fixed, sometimes even go to church with me. As if everything was normal. Then something happened and she left and then she was gone for good. And then . . ."

"When did she leave?"

"Last summer sometime."

I told her about the call Jessica got from Lisa.

"First I've heard of it," she said.

"One of the girls I talked to, one of the girls on the street, said Lisa was scared of something. She had something that someone wanted. Did you ever hear anything like that?"

Gloria sat up a little straighter in her chair. "No," she said, cautiously. "Something like what?"

I glanced at Theresa. She explained what the supervisor had told her about a book. "Other than that, we don't know anything more," I added. "The girl either didn't know herself or didn't want to tell us. I don't know if it was drugs or money or what."

Gloria was quiet, holding her cup in her lap. Theresa and I waited. After a few moments, Gloria said, "The day of Lisa's funeral, somebody broke in. It was hard to fathom. But you hear of such things."

"I'm sorry to hear that," I said, and meant it. It had happened to my mother's mother, the day my grandfather was buried. She was cleaned out.

"It was horrible," Gloria continued. "I was an emotional wreck, and then to come home to that."

It got quiet enough to hear the clock in the hallway. The tick-tick-tick played on my fears that time was running out.

"The funny thing was, nothing much was taken. Some money I keep in a drawer in my bedroom and some jewelry, but nothing fancy or even that expensive. A pearl necklace my husband gave me was right where I left it. Same with my computer and TV. It was more the shock of it. You feel so violated. The police said it was probably a drug addict who got scared off before he could take much."

"Your husband . . . ?"

"Robert," she said, with a sad smile. "Died five years ago." She paused. "Right after he retired."

"That sounds plausible, about the break-in," I said after a moment. Petty crime was up across the city, and police placed the blame squarely on heroin. Once upon a time Columbus was a second- or third-cut city when it came to the drug, far down the pipeline. Now we were a first-cut city, heroin arriving directly from Mexico. The price of progress. And that meant the drug was everywhere, including the veins of the richest kids from the fattest suburbs. But the east side had also been hit hard, and nobody seemed able to stop it. People like Bronte sold girls and dealt drugs with impunity.

Gloria said, "I haven't thought about the break-in since then. I had the door repaired and I cleaned everything up. But now you've got me thinking."

"Somebody might have been looking for whatever it was Lisa had," I said. "They stole a few things to make it seem like a real burglary."

"Maybe so," Gloria said.

I glanced at the mantel, at all the pictures. I said, "Did Lisa ever bring Jessica by?"

"Once or twice."

"Any impressions?"

She sipped her tea. "Angry. Angry and hurt."

"Hurt?"

"Like she'd gone through something bad. I mean, besides what she went through every day."

I glanced at Theresa. She was rubbing her thighs nervously. Sweat had broken out on her upper lip.

"She was only here a couple of times," Gloria said. "I didn't pay a lot of attention to her because I knew, you know, who she was. What she did." She looked at Theresa curiously. Theresa lowered her eyes. She was wearing purple wool leggings under a red corduroy dress, looking as out place in Gloria's elegant living room as a Raggedy Ann doll on a church altar.

I said, "Did Jessica ever have a baby with her?"

"A baby?"

I explained about her son.

"Not here. But it doesn't surprise me. I was terrified the same thing would happen to Lisa. You just don't know, out there." She glanced again at Theresa.

"Did Lisa ever talk about Jessica?"

"About what?"

"I'm not sure. People Jessica might have been afraid of. Enemies she might have. Places she might have gone."

She shook her head. "I just knew they were close. A couple times she'd say something like, 'I don't know what I'd do without her.' It was touching, if you hadn't known what they were up to. Like they worked in an office and had a demanding boss." She frowned. "That's what made it so much harder when Lisa died. If that were even possible."

"What do you mean?"

"There Lisa was, saying she didn't know what'd she do without Jessica. And yet it was Lisa who died and left Jessica alone."

"I DON'T THINK SHE liked me," Theresa said as I walked her to her car.

"I think she wondered about you. There's a difference."

"She knew I'd been on the streets."

"She could tell you seemed upset. I'm sorry if you were uncomfortable."

"It's OK. Been uncomfortable my whole life."

"Mind if I ask you something?"

"No." But her eyes said yes.

"When you were, you know, younger. Anybody ever held accountable for what happened to you?"

"What do you mean?"

"The person who did, you know, what they did. The, ah, neighbor."

"Neighbor?"

"I'm just going on what the parson told me," I said, quickly. "Whoever it was that hurt you."

"What about them?"

"Were they ever arrested?"

"Why you asking me this?" She looked away from me, across the street.

"I'm not sure. I want to know if you're OK, is all. With all this."

"I'm fine."

"You sure?"

"Yes." But her eyes said no.

26

SUNDAY CAME AND WENT. I SLEPT IN THAT morning, now that the ache from Patterson's beating was starting to fade. After coffee and breakfast I thought about jogging, but instead felt my eyes droop and fell back asleep on the couch. That meant I was nearly an hour late picking up Joe, but, as I tried to explain to Crystal, at least I hadn't forgotten. I offered to take him to a movie, but he just wanted to drag Hopalong through the Park of Roses off North High and play fetch. We walked around the casting ponds afterward, and I regretted not bringing my ancient fishing pole, despite the fact it was December. We dropped by Anne's in the late afternoon so Joe could hang out with Amelia; the two of them were getting along better these days than Anne and me. My conversation with her was muted and flat, pleasant but without depth. We weren't invited for dinner. After I dropped Joe off, I called Roy. He said he thought he could find it in his heart to meet me down the street at O'Reilly's.

"What the hell's wrong with me?" I said, draining a glass of PBR.

"Besides drinking swill?" Roy said, taking a sip of a Great Lakes Brewing Company Christmas Ale. As far from a can of Bud with a green ribbon around it as you could get. We were sitting in a corner booth. I was eating a burger topped with mushrooms and cheese, suddenly famished, and thinking about ordering a second one.

"I think that's been established," I said between mouthfuls. "I mean when it comes to Anne. I feel like I'm blowing it big time." I explained about the missed dates and her frustration with me.

"You're not winning boyfriend of the year," he agreed.

"I'm supposed to be the uxorious type now. You told me that. Remember? But things keep getting in the way."

"Just because you're uxorious doesn't mean you can pull it off, you know."

"What the hell's that supposed to mean?"

"Well, ever consider the fact that the very thing that makes you attractive to women is the thing that makes long-term commitment impossible? Your, *je ne sais quoi,* predilection for gunfire and brass knuckles? Or, in the olden days, all the work it took to throw those damn touchdowns every week? Christ, that was annoying, how good you were."

"Gosh, parson. Never dawned on me, and I think you mean 'fuck,' not 'Christ.' No, I've never considered that, other than every single day on my uncle's pig farm one summer." It was the manual labor beating I took under his watchful gaze that finally got me out of a decades-old funk and on the track to a semi-respectable life.

"Must not have dawned very hard," Roy said. "Since you don't seem to have accepted the fact."

"Accepted it? I'm trying to overcome it."

"Why?"

"Why?" I stared at him. "Because it's aberrant behavior, that's why. The handsome rogue and all that bullshit. I hurt people, you know. Hurt them badly. And I'm not talking just physically."

"Ah," he said. "Maybe that's what you've got wrong."

"How could I have that wrong?"

"I think you've figured out the aberrant behavior stuff by now. The part about not treating the women you hook up with like doormats. At least that's my impression."

"I sure as hell hope so."

"But listen to what you said a minute ago. 'Things keep getting in the way.'"

"What about it?"

"You make it sound like you're an office worker getting crapped on by too much e-mail. If you really wanted to make that date with Anne, or not blow your time with your boys, wouldn't you have bagged those jobs? I mean, you're not telling me there's only two unfaithful medical school professors in town. Always more where that came from."

"Would you please put your point out of its misery?" I said, signaling for another beer.

"My point is, you might be frustrated at the wrong thing."

"Meaning?"

"You make it seem like you're angry you can't settle down properly. That you can't be home in time for dinner and a pipe every night. You ask me, factoring in the part about not being a raging asshole any more, you've got it backwards."

"I still don't get it."

"Listen, QB," he said, pulling off a not bad imitation of Theresa. "You weren't the best college quarterback in America by mistake. You accomplished that because you were chasing something. Glory, the thrill of it all, dreams, whatever. And all that got taken away from you. For good reason, maybe—" he said, warding off my objection.

"For damned good reason."

"Shut up and use your ears for something besides listening to that crappy eighties music for a change, why don't you? My point is, all of a sudden you're back in the game. You're feeling it again. You're the man, even if sometimes you get manhandled a bit on the way to the goal line. You're fixing problems, not scoring touchdowns, but what's the diff? Seems to me that's what you're frustrated about."

I looked closely at him, something finally starting to burrow its way into my thick skull. "Go on."

"That's about it. I don't think you're frustrated because you can't achieve domestication. I think you're frustrated because domestication ain't you. You're not mad because you missed a date. You're mad because you realized keeping the date would have made you miss the stakeout."

My second beer arrived. I decided to let it breathe.

"Some people have clean garages and keep the lawn nice and always remember to buy milk," Roy continued. "Some people save the day going down these mean streets. A few, a very few, can do both. But I don't think that includes you. And that's not necessarily a bad thing."

"So—"

"So you've got to decide which it's going to be. True to others or, to quote ol' what's his name, true to yourself."

"You make it sound so easy. And by the way, I always remember to get milk."

"Good for you. But to your point, sometimes it is easy," Roy said. "Sometimes 'no pain no gain' only gets you so far."

"Is that so?"

"'Tis. It's like me sainted grandmother used to say."

"Oh?"

"Sometimes the hard way is not the best way."

I MET GRETCHEN OSBORNE AT BLOCK'S ON
East Broad Monday morning. She worked for a drug and alcohol
outreach center called Lilyhaven farther down the street, close to
Hamilton Road. I offered to meet her there, but she said it was
easier and more private to find a restaurant. We went through the
line together and ordered bagels with cream cheese and coffee. I'd
asked Theresa if she wanted to come, but she was busy trying to
find a placement for the girl we met the night of the vigil. "Mary."
Theresa was also hoping she'd tell us where Bronte stayed. She
wasn't optimistic. Girls snitching on pimps had short life spans.
Girls snitching on Bronte made mayflies look long-lived.

"Thanks for meeting with me," I said when we found a booth.

"Your girlfriend said I should."

"Theresa's not my girlfriend."

"What is she?"

"Someone helping me look for Jessica. I figured, with her
background, she knows a lot."

"How's that working out?"

"It's working out just fine. Except we can't find her."

"Of course you can't. Because she's dead."

"Her mother said the same thing."

"Then her mother's a smart lady."

"I wouldn't bank on it. Why do you think she's dead?"

"Because I know."

"How?"

"Because Jessica told me."

THE LADY AT THE counter called out our orders. I got up and retrieved them. I grabbed a fistful of napkins and came back and handed Gretchen her bagel and sat down.

"What did you mean by that?"

"Exactly what I said. She predicted this would happen."

"How?"

She took a bite of her bagel. Unlike some people I know, she kept her mouth shut until she swallowed. She said, "We stayed in touch. Even after she dropped out of the court program. She'd call or text every day. Usually after she was done working."

"Working?"

"She was back on the streets. She had to support herself. She didn't know what else to do."

"Wasn't that risky? Wasn't there a warrant out on her?"

"These girls don't think that way, OK? She had to survive. I told her she needed to just turn herself in. But I also didn't want to scare her off. So she'd call and I'd ask how she was and she'd tell me, and that was that. Like clockwork. It was like I was her one connection to normalcy."

"Any idea where she was living?"

"I'm not sure. The Rest EZ was probably on the high end, I'm guessing. But here's the thing that matters. She used to say I shouldn't worry if a day came when I didn't hear from her. Because it wouldn't mean she was in trouble. It would mean she was dead."

I filled in the blank. "And that day came."

"Yeah."

"When?"

"A week ago."

Right after I took the case. "No call."

She nodded. I said, "How about the day before?"

"Same as always."

"Did you tell the police this?"

"No."

"Why not?"

"I'm not sure. No one asked. Plus, I was holding out hope. I told myself something happened to her phone. I waited. Another night passed, then another. I kept making excuses. I started to look for her, but by then . . ."

"By then you figured she was dead."

"That's right. And what was I supposed to tell the cops at that point?"

It was the worst news I'd gotten yet. It was as sure a sign as any that my hunt was over. *Like clockwork.* No news would be very bad news. Worst of all—I'd been so close. Just a couple days too late. I thought of the trip I'd postponed to Mount Alexandria in order to lunch with the congresswoman. The hours I'd spent—wasted?—at Anne's apartment the next morning trying to revive the old spark.

"I'm sorry," Gretchen said. "I almost didn't tell you. I know it's not what you wanted to hear."

"I'm glad you did. I needed to know."

"I figured."

I took a bite of my bagel. I went ahead and talked with my mouth full. I said, "How long did you work with Jessica?"

"A few months. She came to Lilyhaven after one of her arrests. It was an alternative to jail time. We're an addictions center, but I specialize in human trafficking victims."

"How'd she do?"

"Up and down. She got sober. Talked about taking a college class. But she also had a lot of, I don't know, demons. Things she was working through. And she was tight-lipped. Wouldn't give a lot of stuff up, from her past. Same shit a lot of them struggle with. The crap these men put them through."

I told her my suspicions about Jessica's stepfather.

"It sounds right. She was hiding something she didn't want to talk about. Even though she knew I could sympathize, she couldn't tell me."

"Knew you could sympathize how?"

She gave me a funny look. "I thought you knew. I thought that's why Darlene Bardwell introduced us."

"I'm sorry. I'm not following."

"I've been there. I was an escort for five years."

"Ah," I said, feeling myself color. "I didn't realize."

"It's OK. It's not like I shout it from the rooftops."

"Was that here?"

"Mostly. Online bookings around town. Reardoor.com, and a few others."

"Where did you . . ." I stopped. "I mean, if I can ask." I told her what Gloria Washington had said, about the brothel where Lisa and Jessica worked.

"It was guys' houses, mostly. The ones that were single, which usually meant divorced or separated. If they were married we'd meet at a hotel. I was a seventy-niner."

"Sorry?"

"Price of a room. I wasn't down at Motel 6 level, but I wasn't good enough for the Hilton, either. I worked the middle of the spectrum. Places where rooms run $79.99."

"That sounds—"

"You can say it. It sounds shitty. But I had it better than most. Lot of guys who called me just wanted the GFE. The Girlfriend Experience," she added, seeing my face.

"Which is?"

"Somebody they could talk to, with benefits. Especially the married ones. People think it's all about the sex. But a lot of my clients would spend most of their time telling me things they couldn't tell anybody else. Not their wives, for sure. I don't mean

kinky stuff. Personal shit. Things about their childhood. Unful-
filled dreams. Poems they wished they'd written. Yeah, right at
the end I'd be on my back, or whatever. But sometimes that was
the quickest part of the deal. And sometimes, I'd have to remind
them what I was there for."

"How'd you, you know, get out?"

"A guy I arranged to meet one night picked me up and took
me back to this house. Nice place in New Albany. He was a doctor. His wife and kids were out of town and his buddy let him use
the place when he wasn't around. He had this idea we were going
to snort some coke together. I told him I didn't do drugs and he
got upset. Slapped me a couple times. I got scared and ran into
the bathroom and called the cops. Of course, I was the one who
ended up in jail. But at least I was alive. I just kind of stopped
after that. I had a little money. I knew some people at Lilyhaven
and asked for help. Took me a while. I always blamed it on me,
you know? Like I put myself in that position. Had to get over that
first. I finally finished my degree and ended up working there."

I nibbled at my bagel and didn't reply. I'd never paid for sex, although whether you believed that depended on what you thought
of money shelled out for drinks and dinner and flowers in antici-
pation of a "nightcap" afterward. I had also told girlfriends things
I couldn't tell my wives. I'd never gotten to the point of forgetting
the reason I was in bed with them. But it had almost slipped my
mind a couple of times.

"Sorry to get so heavy," she said.

"Believe me, it's OK. I appreciate the insights. Listen—there's
one other thing." I told her about the man—men?—looking for
Jessica. The parole officer. The minister. The cop.

"Could be a former client. Some guys get these ideas about
helping girls leave the business."

"Leave?"

"Like they think they're in love with them. Or they get this
creepy sugar daddy complex. Thinking they can make everything
all better. Usually it's bullshit—they just want the cow and the

milk for free. Every so often, they're truly guilty about our lives and their participation and want to make it right. But that's rare."

"Think that could be this guy's story?"

"It's how they operate. They get real focused on 'helping,'" she said, making air quotes.

I considered the idea. It was comforting if only because it meant the person didn't intend to do bodily harm to Jessica. Harm of another kind? That was a different question. But in the end, based on what Gretchen had told me about the lack of phone contact, it was probably moot.

"I need to get going," she said. "Was there anything else?"

"I don't think so. I appreciate your help. Can I call you if I have any more questions?"

She nodding, taking a card out of her backpack. She crossed something out on the front, turned it over, and scribbled on the back. "Use my cell. Sometimes it's hard to track me down at work. Plus people at the office are skeptical when guys call. No offense."

"None taken."

She scooted out of the booth and stood up. We walked outside. We shook hands formally.

"I'm sorry Jessica's dead. I really am," she said, and walked away.

I WAS SITTING IN MY VAN CHECKING MESSAGES when the strains of "Livin' on a Prayer" signaled an incoming call. It was Bonnie. An image of her in green Arch City Roller Derby Lycra tights and satin shorts and tank top popped into my head. I served the picture as quick an eviction notice as possible and answered.

"Got a second?"

"Sure," I said, gruffly.

"Everything OK?"

"It's fine. What's that noise?"

"Noise?"

"It sounds like a moose with appendicitis."

"Oh, that. It's Troy's new dog. He moans when he hears sirens. Selling point for his last owner. Troy's trying to wean him off it."

"Who was the owner?"

"A drug dealer who liked to hear cops coming. The dog's protective, at least. He just needs an owner on the right side of the law."

Bonnie's boyfriend had been working at a dog training center on the northeast side for almost six months now, and often brought problem animals home overnight. Animals not seized from drug dealers came from dogfighting rings. It was the first job he'd held down in a while, since Bonnie's dad hired me to find out why Troy had stopped talking to the world and I untangled a dark family secret of sexual abuse. Troy was good at what he was doing. He said he could identify with what the animals had gone through, and they sensed that. I was just glad he was on his feet again.

Once the moaning died down I filled Bonnie in on my conversation with Gretchen.

There was silence on the other end. "That may make this call pointless," she said.

"What do you mean?"

"You know how you asked me to double-check court records on that girl? Jessica Byrnes?"

"Right."

"It's just that I found something interesting. Somebody. Somebody it looks like knew her."

"Who?"

"Guy named Leonard Lortz."

"Who is he?"

"He bailed her out of jail last year, after she got arrested for soliciting."

"Bailed her out? Like he's a bail bondsman?"

"I don't think so. It's just his name on the court docket."

"How much was the bond?"

"Five hundred dollars."

"When was this?"

"December of last year."

I ran through the timeline of Jessica's arrests as well as I could remember. That might have been the one that led to her entering the diversion program. The one she'd dropped out of suddenly after getting the call from Lisa. The one that led her once again to Bronte, if only long enough to take something he now wanted returned, badly.

"Any idea who he is?"

"I couldn't find much about him. Except get this. He also has a soliciting arrest. A month earlier."

"Where?"

"You can't tell online. We'd have to go to the court to find the file."

"Just one?"

"That's it."

"Interesting," I said.

"That's what I thought." She stopped, waiting for me to respond. After a couple seconds she said, "So did you want me to look a little further? I mean on this guy."

"Sure."

"I just thought, you know, it might be somebody who'd know something about her."

"Listen. It's a good find. Don't mind my mood. I'm just feeling deflated. After what Gretchen told me."

"I don't blame you. So how about Mandie Smith? The girl who knew Jessica? Should I keep trying with her?"

"Why not?" I said, though I knew I didn't sound convincing. "We've made it this far. If you've got time."

She said she did. We talked for another couple minutes, pausing midway as Troy's dog let loose again. I could tell Bonnie was still disappointed by my initial reaction. I didn't blame her. But honestly, was there much point pushing this any further?

ON MY WAY BACK downtown I called Larry Schwartzbaum and related my conversation with Gretchen. I told him where I was. He said he could meet me at Cafe Brioso up the street from headquarters in twenty minutes.

The coffee shop at High and Gay was crowded when I walked in. He recognized me and called my name. I'm used to it by now. It's why I have a hard time going undercover or minding my own business in bars. I bought us both coffees. We sat in a pair of up-holstered leather chairs at the rear, underneath a bicycle wheel rim hanging from the ceiling. He set down a manila folder on the table in front of us.

"The thing the caseworker told you," Schwartzbaum said. "That could mean anything. She wants to believe she had this strong connection with Jessica, so the radio silence is the worst-case scenario. But maybe Jessica just decided to ghost her. Didn't need her anymore. Happens all the time."

"Gretchen claims she has a feeling. That it's more than that."

"If she had such a strong feeling about it, she should have reported it."

"I asked her about that." I gave him Gretchen's explanation.

"Lame," he said. He had a thick black mustache that would have done an outfielder from the seventies proud, and equally black eyebrows that rose and fell like seismograph squiggles. "She say anything else? Last known location? Anything like that?"

"No. She seemed as much in the dark about that as we are. The only difference is she'd heard from her more recently."

"She sure it was her? Her as opposed to Bronte Patterson's newest bottom girl trying to pull a fast one?"

"She seems sure." I told him about Gretchen's former occu-pation. Said it seemed like that would give her insight into a scam. "Besides," I continued, "what would be the point of Bronte doing something like that? If anyone was pulling a fast one it'd be the Prince."

"The who?"

I realized I'd slipped. But did it matter? "The serial killer. Isn't that his nickname with you guys? The Pleasure Prince? After that song from Gätling Gün?"

"Who told you that?"

"Word gets around. It's not important because I'm not doing anything with it."

"You better hope that's true. You got a number for Gretchen?"

I wrote down her cell and handed it to him.

"So what are you going to do now?" Schwartzbaum said.

"Do?"

"About Jessica."

"Depends. You think there's any hope?"

"I have to. It's my job. But this table's running out of legs to stand on. You knock one more off, I'm afraid that's it for her."

29

DARLENE BARDWELL CALLED ME THAT afternoon. Wondered what I knew. Said she was headed to Washington for the last few days before Christmas. Her husband had already flown back with their kids. If I needed anything right away I could call Blanchett. I told her what I'd told everyone so far, that it wasn't looking good because of Jessica's apparent disappearance a week ago. She told me how sorry she was and she'd try to find out what she could. I thanked her and hung up and took Third Street down to 70 and headed east to Mount Carmel to see my dad. But all the way there, the only thing I could think about was the least important thing the congresswoman thought she'd told me. Her husband had already flown back to D.C. Which left her alone in Columbus with Blanchett, at least for a couple of days.

BILL BYRNES CALLED ME late that afternoon. I was in the family waiting room in the heart center with my mom and Shelley. I excused myself to take the call and walked to the other side of the room.

"So she's dead," he said when I finished.

"No, no. Not necessarily."

"Really? She calls or texts this caseworker every night for months, and then just stops for good? What else could it mean?"

"Her phone died. She went out of town. She got sick." I wasn't convincing and I knew it. I was like a siding salesman short on his quota on his last call of the night.

"Do you really believe any of that?"

"I know it doesn't sound good. But she was living on the margins. Is," I said quickly. "We already know that. Even more so if she's hiding from someone or something. Maybe she thought it was too risky to keep communicating with Gretchen. It's a stretch, I know. But I'm not ready to give up."

"I am."

"Why?"

"What's the point? I mean, I don't really have the money to keep paying you. You've done what I asked you to, which is find out what happened to her. It's not the answer I wanted. But I'm not seeing any reason to keep looking. It seems like a waiting game now."

"It doesn't have to be that way. We could change our arrangement. I want her found as much as you do."

"No, you don't."

"You know what I mean. It's important to me to keep looking."

"It can't be that important. I mean, you could have found her. According to that caseworker, she was still alive when you started. You had the chance."

"I didn't know—"

"Of course you didn't know. That's what I'm saying. If you'd known, maybe she wouldn't be dead."

THE HOUSE FELT CHILLY WHEN I GOT UP THE
next morning. I stumped into the kitchen, let the dog out, made
coffee, let the dog in, and went into the bathroom. I brushed my
teeth. I stood before the mirror, hands on the sink. I turned and
took a washcloth from the shower and soaped and rinsed my
face. I picked up my can of shaving cream and put it down again. I
stared at the man looking back at me. Short, wiry dark hair, receding a scratch on top, with hints of gray at the temples; more gray
than my father had at my age. Lean face, though not as lean as it
once was. Eyes so light blue they might as well be gray. Crow's-
feet making themselves at home, like relatives planning for a long
stay. A nose bent at different times by fists and weaponry. Hair
starting to grow from my ears. I touched the lump on my head
left by Bronte Patterson's gun. Still tender, but the swelling was
down considerably. Fun fact: it's hard to stare at other people for
very long without feeling awkward or blinking or averting your
gaze. But it's easy to stare at yourself. Another fun fact: I was
almost certainly chasing a dead woman. And had I chased just a
little bit harder, she might be alive.

AFTER A JOG AND breakfast, I decided to take a second look at what Bonnie had sent me about the guy who bailed Jessica out. It was either that or e-mail her brother the official notification that our contract was terminated, and I wasn't quite ready for that yet. There was only one Leonard Lortz listed in Columbus. He lived on the far east side. A strained male voice told me to leave a message at the tone. I got as far as my name and three digits of my cell when a woman's voice interrupted.

"Who is this?"

I repeated my name and told her I was looking for Lortz.

"He's at work. Can I take a message?"

"That's OK. Is he still at Buckeye Steel? On the South End?"

"Buckeye Steel?" She laughed dismissively. "He works at Dollar & Done. You sure you have the right number?"

"My bad. The store on South High, right? By Lou Berliner Park?"

"Main and Nelson. Does he know what this is about?"

"I imagine so. Thank you, Mrs. . . . . Lortz?"

"Buchanan. I'm his mother."

"Thank you," I said again, and cut the call. I thought for a minute, looked up Theresa's cell, and dialed.

"HOW'S IT GOING WITH Mary?" I said half an hour later as we walked out of Roy's church and headed to my van.

"Shitty," Theresa said. "She's barely talking. We found out she just turned eighteen. She's already been on the streets a year or two."

"Is she from the east side?"

"Yeah. Of Cleveland."

"How'd she get here?"

"Some guy dumped her downtown by the Statehouse after screwing her for a week in motels between here and there."

"How'd she end up with Darla?"

"Not exactly sure. Like I said, she ain't talking much. Stuff about Cleveland took me a whole day."

"It's good you're with her. You're the best person to be around her right now."

"I guess."

"I mean it." When she didn't reply, I said, "What's the parson have to say about it?"

"He said he's tired of guys who can't keep their dicks where they belong."

"Always the Goody Two-shoes, that fella."

We drove in silence for a minute, passing the remnants of the old Clippers baseball stadium on the right.

"I've been thinking," Theresa said.

"OK."

"That thing Lisa's grandmother said about a brothel. Where Lisa worked. We hadn't heard that before."

"Yeah," I said, eager to keep her talking. "Plus the fact she may have met Jessica there." I explained that I'd been wondering if that's where Jessica first ended up when she left Mount Alexandria. But how would that have happened? Recruited straight from the bus station to a brothel? It seemed unlikely somehow.

"Then there's that thing about a book," Theresa said.

"OK."

"So you're a john, you go to a place like that because you're banking on privacy. That's the whole point. You're not worried the girl you're bargaining with is a cop, or that you might get beat up by her pimp, or robbed, or all three."

"Cops don't visit cathouses?"

"Yeah, they do. And most of the time to bust them. But it's harder to fake your way in if the owner's doing her job right. Which is why it costs so much."

"How much?"

"Enough for a few Christmas presents your kids aren't going to get. Hundred bucks to walk in the door. Two hundred to the girl. But it's worth it because nobody's gonna find out you're spending your lunch hour prone."

"What's this have to do with Lisa?"

"I'm just thinking about that privacy. And what it means to those johns."

"Keep going."

"Their names get out, that's bad. Like that Dolly Madison thing."

"Now I lost you."

"That website, lets married couples sign up for affairs. Always thought it was kind of stupid, like ain't that what the office or the church choir is for? You know. The place that got hacked."

"*Ashley* Madison," I said. The hacking of the hook-up website a couple of years back had no doubt ruined countless marriages as the names of affairs-seeking husbands and wives went online for all to see. It made my storage closet skepticism seem quaint by comparison. I wasn't sure what Theresa was getting at. Then it dawned on me. "Are you suggesting—"

"I'm saying maybe Lisa got ahold of something like that."

"Like a list of names. Of customers."

"Yeah. A book of names."

"A book that whoever ran the brothel would have a strong incentive to recover."

"Them, yeah. But not as strong as one of the people in it."

"That would definitely be worth going out on a limb for."

"Like breaking into somebody's house the day of a funeral," Theresa said. "Maybe that's what Lisa had. Maybe that's what her and Jessica was so scared about. Maybe somebody was after them because they had a list of customers for that house."

"And Lisa's dead."

"So that leaves Jessica to hunt down," Theresa said.

31

A FEW MINUTES LATER THERESA AND I pulled into the parking lot at Dollar & Done on East Main, not far from the old grain silos near Bexley. The blue-and-red cut-rate grocery and house supplies stores had found a niche in the city's poorest neighborhoods during and after the recession. Inside, a heavyset woman restocking generic toilet paper with her ear buds in pointed us to the far side of the store.

"Leonard Lortz?" I said to the man staring at a computer screen inside a cubbyhole of an office.

"Yeah?"

I glanced at Theresa. I could tell we were thinking the same thing. Lortz looked like that guy you walk past on the street or in the mall or in the airport without a second glance, and not much of a first one either. Average height, a bit overweight, brown, thinning hair, a scratchy-looking beard. *Normal looking*. It could easily be him. The guy always two steps ahead of me, hunting for Jessica. *The parole officer. The minister. The cop.*

I handed him my card. I said, "I'm looking for someone named Jessica Byrnes. I thought you might have some information about her."

He started, as if I'd just identified the skin rash he thought he was hiding from everyone. "How'd you get my name?"

I explained about the court docket.

"What do you want to know?"

"Anything you can tell us about Jessica. For starters, where she is."

"I have no idea." He looked at Theresa, taking in today's outfit: red tights, orange dress, and a recently added nose ring. She looked like Pippi Longstocking on the way to a college humanities seminar.

I said, "Could we ask you a couple questions anyway?"

"No. I'm sorry. I don't have time and I don't want to get involved."

"You should probably know the police are looking for Jessica too. You won't mind if I pass your name onto them?"

"Of course I'd mind. Why would you do that?"

"Because it's my civic duty. Unless of course you'd rather just talk to me and get it over with."

I wouldn't have wanted to meet the angry look that Lortz shot me in a dark alley, even in the middle of the day.

"I can't talk here," he said. "There's a Wendy's across the street. Meet me there in ten minutes. And whatever you do, don't tell anyone here who you are."

"Why not?"

"Because Jessica Byrnes already cost me one job. I can't afford to lose this one, too."

"I'M NOT TOO HAPPY about this," Lortz said after we were seated and I'd brought us each a black coffee. "Not happy at all." He looked at Theresa for the third time since he'd come in. She was busy texting someone; likely Roy, dealing with Mary, the girl she'd rescued.

"What's the problem?"

"Are you kidding me? After what I've been through?"

"I'm only interested in finding Jessica. I'm not trying to cause trouble for you or anybody else."

"Easy for you to say."

"It is because I'm being honest. And if you really want to know, I'd say things don't look good for her. But I figured it couldn't hurt, talking to you."

"It could hurt a lot. But go ahead. Ask your question. Just promise me one thing. You're not from the cops, right? Or you're not undercover reporters or something, trying to screw with me?"

"Cross my heart and hope my warranty expires." I gave him the short version of my quest, how Roy's work with trafficked women had led me to Bill Byrnes. How we'd canvassed the streets for Jessica. About "Darla" and "Mary" and Bronte Patterson.

"So tell us why you helped her. Helped Jessica," I said when I was done.

"Bailed her out, you mean?"

"Sure."

"I was trying to make amends."

"For what?"

"For exploiting her?" Theresa said before he could respond.

He stared at her warily. He said, "You know what John School is?"

I shook my head. Theresa said, "For guys that get caught."

"That's right," Lortz said, keeping his eyes on her. "An alternative to jail time if you're nailed for soliciting. You attend mandatory classes downtown where former prostitutes tell you about their lives and what drove them to it and the risks they ran and the diseases they caught and the toll the life took on them. It's not a pleasant experience. It makes three days in lock-up sound appealing."

"Try sucking somebody's cock when they haven't bathed in a week," Theresa said. "That ain't pleasant either."

He looked at her, speechless. I nudged her foot with mine. She kicked back before glancing away, out the window.

"John School," I said.

Lortz stared at Theresa a moment longer before replying. "Anyway, it's meant to educate you, but it's basically total humiliation.

Was for me, anyway. And this is after my behavior already cost me big time. My wife. My kid. My job. Talk about a Scarlet A. You'd think I raped a kid, the way society treated me."

I could feel Theresa tense up beside me. Quickly, I said, "What'd you do, that got you sent there?"

"What happened was I solicited an undercover Columbus cop. I had a problem, OK? And once I got arrested it all came out. It was too much for my wife. I don't blame her. But afterward, I decided to try to help the girls"—he caught Theresa's eye—"the women I'd hurt. I knew who Jessica was, all right? I'd been with her. When I saw in the news there'd been a sweep, I decided to try to make it right. I emptied my savings. I got her out and told her I'd give her anything she needed. Help any way I could."

I remembered what Gretchen told me about customers trying to help women they'd been with. The sugar daddies.

"What'd she say?" Theresa said, locking eyes with Lortz.

"Like you can't figure it out. She wanted nothing to do with me. Flipped me off, right in the jail lobby. Got in somebody's car and left. And that's the last I saw of her."

"Would you really have helped her?" Theresa said.

"Yes, damn it. And I did, starting with her bond. I was trying to make things right. I can see you don't believe me"—this, aimed at Theresa—"but it's the truth."

"You're sure about that?" I said. "I mean, sure that's the last time you saw her?"

"Very sure. Frankly, after her reaction at the jail, I didn't want anything to do with her."

"The reason I ask is someone's been looking for her."

"Wasn't me," he said, looking out the window at Dollar & Done across the street. "I told you, I haven't seen her since last year."

"Any idea who it might be?"

"None."

"Thing is, you sort of match the description of the person."

"According to who?"

"According to people this person talked to."

"Good for them. It's not me."

"I don't care if you're looking for her," I persisted. "I care if you find her."

"I'm not going to find her because I'm not looking for her."

I let it go. I blew on my coffee. Theresa was back on her phone. I nodded at the convenience store through the window and said, "How long have you worked there?"

"Since my arrest. I used to be a regional sales manager for National Way Insurance. That was a good place to work. It wasn't a place interested in having employee names in the paper next to the word 'soliciting.' At this point I'm lucky to have anything at all."

"You paid for sex with Jessica Byrnes. That's what you said?"

He grimaced as if he'd stepped on something cold and wet on the kitchen floor.

"Yes."

"Blow job? Or something more?"

"Jesus. I don't see what—"

"Answer the question," Theresa said.

A long pause while they stared at each other. "I paid for oral sex, yes," Lortz said.

"When?" I said. "How long before your soliciting arrest?"

"I don't know. A week, maybe. Two."

"Where?"

"Where what?"

"In what part of town did you pay Jessica for oral sex?"

He shook his head. After a moment he pointed down the street. "I picked her up a few blocks west, and we pulled behind there."

"Behind the silos?"

"It's secluded back there."

"And you haven't seen her since you bailed her out."

"I already answered that question."

"But if you see her. Can you call me?"

"I'm not going to see her."

"Hypothetically. Driving down the street at night and she's on a corner."

"And what, you call the police as soon as you hear from me? And I'm back behind bars? No thanks."

"Not unless you break the law. Otherwise, we come pick her up and there's a good chance you never see us again."

"That'd be one good thing, anyway."

"Unless we need something at Dollar & Done," I added.

32

WE STOPPED AT B & K SMOKE HOUSE ON East Main on the way back into downtown. I was suddenly starving. I also wanted to treat Theresa to something, anything, to make up for what we'd just gone through. We ordered two beef brisket sandwiches with collard greens on the side and sat down.

"I think he's lying," Theresa said.

"About what?"

"About not trying to find her. You don't bail somebody out like that and just walk away. I think he's mad about that little scene in the jail lobby after he forked over his savings, and he wants to do something about it."

"Hurt her?"

"Or get his money back. Or get more 'oral sex,' or I don't know what else."

"The what else is what worries me."

"He also knows I think he's lying. The way he kept looking at me."

"Hard to blame him. You pissed him off."

"It served him right. Equating John School with life on the streets. Give me a break, QB."

Something occurred to me. "He wasn't anyone that you, you know—"

"Gave a blow job to?" she said, her eyes flashing. "Ten, twelve guys a night, it all kind of blurs together, you know? But I don't think so. I think I'd remember him."

"I wish I'd taken his picture. Be nice to show it to the guy at the motel and Jessica's mom and stepdad."

"Like this?" she said, and handed me her phone. She'd taken a good profile shot of him as he looked out the window at Wendy's.

"How'd you get that?"

"I pretended I was texting."

"Ain't technology grand," I said. Our food arrived and I had her message me the photo. I took my first bite and the door opened and I looked up and saw Marc Copeland, the vice sergeant. He did a double take.

"We gotta stop meeting like this," he said.

"Beats the emergency room."

"I'll give you that," he said, shaking his head with a smile. He walked to the counter and picked up a carry-out box that was waiting for him. After he paid he came over. He shook my hand and said hello to Theresa.

"What are you doing over here?" he said.

I explained about Leonard Lortz and then what Gretchen Osborne told me about Jessica's radio silence.

"I don't remember Lortz," he said. "But we got a lot of guys around that time. Gretchen told me the same thing at the vigil. I wasn't sure if I believed her. But maybe that's really what happened. How's your head?"

"Better. Any luck on Bronte?"

"Not yet. It's only a matter of time. There's only so many rat holes a guy like him can crawl into. We'll find him. I'll see you later?"

"You know they're taking this seriously," Theresa said after he left. "Sergeant patrolling like that, middle of the day. What?" She was looking at me.

"I just remembered something."

"What?"

"The first night we went out looking for Jessica. The car I thought was tailing us, by the silos. That was him."

"Him?"

"Copeland."

"You sure?"

"Pretty sure. I kept thinking I'd seen him someplace. I wonder what he was doing out there."

"Doing? He's vice. He was probably undercover. They're blanketing the streets right now."

"Yeah. But a sergeant?"

"They're pulling out all the stops. What's it matter who's out there?"

"I suppose. I guess we're lucky we didn't get pulled over."

"You guess right, QB. White guy driving an Odyssey down East Main at night? You might as well put a sign in your window. 'Got Pussy?' Good thing I was with you."

"Unless they thought I'd just picked you up."

"Don't flatter yourself," she said.

OUTSIDE THE RESTAURANT WE were hit up for money by none other than the shopping cart conspiracy theorist. I stared at him carefully, measuring my notion that he could be the Prince. I had to give Theresa credit; it was a stretch. Though his eyes were clear, he was too disheveled, too arthritic looking, and frankly, too odiferous to seem like he could get anywhere close to a prostitute, at least long enough to do much beyond drooling on her. I told him politely to get lost, but Theresa gave him two bucks.

"Do-gooder," I said, as we got into the van.

"Wait till you've been there. Two bucks looks different on that end."

We were getting back into my van when my phone buzzed. The area code was outside Columbus, the swath of Ohio to the east and northeast of the city.

"Detective Mullan, Mount Alexandria police department," the voice on the other end said. "Were you over here recently, sir?"

"Yes."

"You acquainted with a Jimmy Wooding?"

I thought of Jessica's stepdad, swimming in 7 and 7s at the Parthenon as he angrily denied abusing her. "I know who he is."

"When was the last time you saw him?"

"Last Wednesday. No, Thursday. Why?"

"There's a problem I need to talk to you about."

"What kind of problem?"

"Sir, how soon can you get over here?"

"However long it takes to get there. An hour tops, I guess. What's the situation?"

"The situation is he's dead and he's got your business card in his back pocket."

33

I HADN'T EXPECTED TO BE BACK IN MOUNT Alexandria so soon, and certainly not in an interview room inside the tired red-brick police station two blocks off the main square. Which also happened to be two blocks from the Parthenon, where I'd last seen Wooding. I sat across a small conference table from Mullan, who was writing on a yellow legal pad. I was by myself. I'd dropped Theresa back at the church and told her I'd be in touch. Checking my phone, I glanced at the headline on the *Mount Alexandria News* website: *Local man found shot to death in home.*

"A source close to the investigation," I said, reading a couple paragraphs. "That you?"

"License," Mullan said, without responding. I dug out both my driver's license and my investigating license and handed them over. He called for someone in the next room to retrieve them and make copies. In the meantime he kept writing. I watched him, fascinated. He had one of those rectangular cop faces that look hewn from granite, with a squared-off crewcut on top, a chin that looked perfect for breaking your knuckles against and shoulders so straight you could balance glasses of water on them.

Copies in hand a minute later, Mullan handed my licenses back to me. He said, "How's your dad doing?"

"My dad?"

"Heard he had a heart attack."

"He's back home, thanks," I said, hesitantly. "He's OK. Long road. You know him?"

"A little. That's good to hear. Especially after everything you put him through." He looked up at me. "So, did you kill Jimmy Wooding?"

"That what passes for small talk around here?"

"That's what passes for a direct question."

"The state of Ohio has a thing about licensing investigators who shoot people on the job. So, no. Also, I don't carry a gun, as you probably know since you know who I am. And who my dad is."

"Why did Wooding have your business card?"

"I gave it to him."

"Believe it or not, I puzzled that part out. Why were you talking to him?"

"For a case I'm working on."

"What kind of case."

"Missing person."

"Who's missing?"

I decided it wasn't going to jeopardize national security to tell him the basics. When I finished, he said, "So long and short, you're looking for a dead Columbus prostitute an hour away in Mount Alex."

"First of all, I don't know if she's dead. Not for sure. Secondly, since she's from here, I was asking her mother and ex-stepdad if they had any ideas about her whereabouts. Like you do. When you're detecting."

"What'd they tell you?"

"Not much, like I said. It didn't seem as if Jessica was too happy with either of them. She moved out before twelfth grade."

"Where she'd go?"

I told him about Garrett Fischer. I left out the potpourri.

"She answered a dog-sitting ad?"

"From what I gather. It seems a little weird, frankly. But they've got a nice place. Comfortable. Miles beyond where she was. It's hard to blame her. And it may have saved her from some really bad stuff."

"Bad stuff like what?"

"Like maybe her stepdad was doing things to her he shouldn't have."

He stopped taking notes and looked at me. Even his eyes seemed to sit in bony, rectangular sockets. "You know that?"

"I'm strongly inferring it. Her mom did a bad job denying the possibility. So did Wooding. And girls like her who end up on the streets usually have a history of child or teenage sexual abuse." I thought of Theresa, of the neighbor who'd violated her. "You don't just become a prostitute, is what I'm trying to say."

"Thanks for the sociology lesson. So if this place she ran away to was so nice, why'd she leave?"

"She was eighteen. It wasn't home. Columbus was a bigger city with brighter lights. Your guess."

He frowned. "Can anybody verify you were at the Parthenon?"

I thought for a second. "Bartender. Buys sweaters one size too small. Decent sense of humor."

"Mary Beth. My wife's second cousin. Nice lady. I won't mention the crack about sweaters. So if it wasn't you, who do you think killed Wooding?"

"Who do *I* think?"

"I look like I'm talking to someone else?"

"It's just I'm not used to police officers asking me my opinion."

"Is that so? Well we do things just a little bit different out here in the country," he said, affecting an exaggerated drawl.

"Well, pickle my pig trotters. I have no idea who killed him. But there's one thing. Someone was over here, looking for her, before I was."

"Who?"

I explained about the parole officer who visited the motel, the minister who came to Tammy Byrnes's house, the cop who Wooding said he talked to. The man—had to be the same—Fischer wouldn't let into the town house.

"No idea who?"

"There's a guy, over in Columbus, who has a history with Jessica. I've got my suspicions." I laid out what I knew about Leonard Lortz.

"You believe his story?"

"Yes and no. He doesn't seem like he's flat-out lying, but something feels funny. He swears it wasn't him."

I gave him Lortz's address and told him where the Dollar & Done was and texted him the picture Theresa took. When he'd written everything down, Mullan said, "Can you think of any reason this guy would have to kill Wooding? I mean, if he's lying and he really was over here?"

"None," I said, truthfully. "Unless Wooding said something to piss him off or threatened to expose him somehow. But that wouldn't make sense. It's no secret Lortz got arrested for soliciting. He went through the system. His name was in the paper. He was booted from his big insurance company job. He's angry about what happened to him, for sure. But it's not like he had any secrets left."

"We'll contact him," Mullan said. "So let me ask you. You think she's dead? This girl?"

"I don't think it looks good."

"You think the serial killer got her?"

"It's a strong possibility. Unfortunately."

"How about Wooding? Could he have done it?"

"Killed his own stepdaughter?"

"Why not? You show up at the Parthenon, accuse him of abusing her. Maybe he did. Maybe he thinks she's been talking. Maybe he knows where she is. Maybe he's not as drunk as you thought he was."

"Good theory," I said. "But then who killed him? Especially if Leonard Lortz is telling the truth?"

"I don't know. Somebody who wanted to find Jessica first and was ticked off he got beat to the punch?"

"Sounds plausible. Only one problem."

"Which is?"

"You might need a bigger paddy wagon. That describes a lot of people right now."

I RESISTED THE URGE TO RETURN TO THE
Parthenon to ask the bartender a couple of questions. Purely for
investigative purposes. I was probably off limits anyway, being a
person of interest in Wooding's death and all. Instead, I headed
out of town, cutting across a gray country road that bisected
miles of fields like a tape measure until I ran into 661. I headed
north, toward Homer. I slowed for the minute needed to take in
what remained of the tiny downtown. For a long time, the town's
only claim to fame was being the birthplace of Victoria Wood-
hull, the first female candidate for president way back in 1872.
Then I came along and there was talk of a second plaque. Then I
caught a mild case of point shaving and disgraced myself and the
university and apparently most of the western hemisphere and
sank to the level of other infamous Ohioans like Jeffrey Dahmer,
and that talk faded fast.

Focus, Andy, focus. Indeed.

The road to my parents' house sat a quarter mile north of
Quarry Chapel High School, just inside the Knox County line.
Their lawn, still partly green with the mild weather, was trim as a

golf course at tournament time; my dad's pre–heart attack work, no doubt. When I walked in, he was sitting in his recliner in the living room, watching TV. Guys on ESPN were yapping about the college football playoffs. My mother was on the couch, using a laptop desk to grade papers.

"How are you feeling?" I said, sinking into the couch. Some of my mom's papers shifted off her desk and slid onto the floor. She sighed. I reached over and retrieved them.

"Everything hurts," my dad said. "Satisfied?"

"I'm sorry to hear that. Can I get you something?"

"I'm fine."

"How about some coffee?"

"I said I'm fine."

I stood up carefully, went into the kitchen, and found the can of Maxwell House grounds in the refrigerator. I put a filter in the coffee machine basket, ladled in five spoonfuls, poured the water in, and pushed the start button. I checked my e-mail and text messages while it brewed. A couple TV stations were reporting a husband and wife had died of a heroin overdose in a car parked outside a suburban McDonald's with their two-year-old daughter in her car seat in the back. A detective was promising to go after their dealer on homicide charges. I thought of Bronte, seemingly untouchable, his carefree dealing and pimping. When the coffee was finished I set out three cups and filled them, adding milk to my mom's. I went back into the living room, delivered the cups, and sat down again.

"You don't need to visit me like this," my dad said.

"I guess you're right." I didn't feel like getting into it with him. "To be honest, I was just in the neighborhood. Over in Mount Alex."

"Not really the neighborhood. What's going on over there?"

"A guy I talked to for a case got killed. Shot to death. He had my card in his wallet when they found him. The police interviewed me about it. He knew you. The detective. Elliot Mullan?"

My dad leaned forward, pulled the remote from its pocket in his chair, and muted the TV. He made me repeat what I said. My mom stopped what she was doing and listened. I explained about the hunt for Jessica and the serial killer and my visit to Mount Alexandria looking for background information. It all sort of spilled out.

"They think you killed this guy?" my dad said.

"Not really. Mullan's just dotting his i's. He doesn't like the fact I was snooping around. Not a lot of murders in Mount Alex, so he's on high alert. It's hard to say what happened. Wooding was living on the margins, as far as I could tell. He'd be lucky to graduate up to barfly. He might have been shot over five dollars and a bottle of Percocet. Or maybe it is about Jessica."

My dad picked up his cup of coffee and took a sip. "Mullan's ex–state police. Nailed me for drunk driving. I yelled at him. Told him I was Woody Hayes's dad. That he didn't know who he was dealing with. Never blinked an eye. He tell you that?"

"He just asked how you were doing."

"Like he cares."

"Seemed like he did."

"So did you kill that guy?"

"Bud," my mom said.

"Do you think I did?"

"I guess not," he said. "I guess you wouldn't talk to the police if you had. You'd probably leave town, hightail it or something. That's what usually happens, isn't it? You always know right away who did it. It's not like in the movies."

"You don't say."

"I also don't think that guy getting shot was random. Not some drug thing. I think it had something to do with the girl. His daughter. The prostitute."

"Stepdaughter. Why do you say that?"

"Just feels that way. Too much of a coincidence. You're over here, asking questions, talking to him, then he gets shot? I mean, c'mon."

"So you're back to thinking I killed him?"

He shook his head. He took another sip of his coffee. He picked up the remote and unmuted the TV.

"I don't think you killed him. But it sounds like you're responsible for his death."

IT WAS DARK OUT AS I PULLED IN FRONT OF my house two hours later. I heard my phone ping on the seat beside me. I put the van in park, killed the engine, glanced around for psychopathic pimps lurking in the shadows, and looked at the screen. My stomach fell as I read the Channel 4 news alert:

Police suspect serial killer in discovery of woman's body on east side.

I went inside and let Hopalong out and fired up my laptop and surfed news websites. No one had much more, but everyone had the only detail that mattered: the killer may have struck again. I called Larry Schwartzbaum and left a message. Same with Gretchen Osborne, Jessica's caseworker. I even tried Marc Copeland, the omnipresent vice sergeant. But when my phone rang next it was Bill Byrnes.

"Are you hearing this, on the news? They found Jessica's body?"

"Are they saying that? Using her name?"

"They haven't said it yet. But it's her, right? That guy from the congresswoman's office just called me, to see if I was OK. Why else would he do that?"

Good question, I thought. "Did he say he knew it was Jessica?"

"No." I heard little Robbie in the background.

"I'm making some calls. Don't assume anything. There's a lot of missing women out there. It could be anyone."

"It's her. You don't have to sugarcoat it. I've sort of known all along. I just want it to be over with. And I want the guy caught. This isn't right."

"Bill, listen—"

He hung up. I considered calling back, but dialed the number I had for John Blanchett, the congresswoman's aide, instead. If he knew something, it was irresponsible to call Jessica's brother and not tell him the truth. If he didn't know anything, it seemed a little—I wasn't sure; overly solicitous?—to check up on him when the news was just breaking. Either way, he wasn't answering.

I didn't get much done the rest of the night. Schwartzbaum returned my call close to midnight, but only to tell me homicide was handling it and he knew what the reporters knew, which wasn't much. Gretchen picked up on my third attempt but also said she didn't know anything and couldn't talk just then. She sounded exhausted and distant, as if she'd only recently come inside after spending the day in the cold. I was starting to think about turning in when the phone rang yet again. It was Darlene Bardwell.

"John said you called. We don't know anything. But we're doing everything we can. He's been on the phone since the news broke. He's talking to everyone we can think of. If we hear anything, anything at all, I'll let you know. Immediately."

"I appreciate that," I said, though I guessed investigators trying to deal with another body wouldn't be jumping with joy to get a call from a congresswoman's aide in the middle of everything. "But maybe you could go easy on Bill Byrnes. He's a bit of a wreck at the moment."

"What do you mean?"

"He was one of the people John got ahold of. Bill assumes it was more than a courtesy call. He thinks your office knows more than you're saying."

"John was checking in with him, nothing more. And if Bill had heard anything, it was a chance for us to offer our support."

And line up morning talk show interview slots, I thought.

I said, "I just think we need to be careful with Bill. Every call could be the one he's dreading."

"I understand that, Andy. I have a little experience making hard phone calls. Many of my constituents have family members serving overseas."

"But you don't have pending legislation dealing with the war on terrorism that you're pushing. Like your websites bill."

"I beg your pardon?"

"Forget I said that. Thanks for calling. I'll let you know if I hear anything."

I CALLED GEORGE HUNTINGTON at the Franklin County Coroner's Office at eight o'clock and five seconds the next morning. The deputy investigator passed on information from time to time. In exchange I kept him supplied with growlers of beer from Barley's in the Short North. "Beer for bodies," he liked to call it, though I asked him to keep it out of e-mails.

"I can't help you," he said when I got through. "Autopsy's this morning. We might know more after that. We're looking at a couple indicators. She had a few tattoos that might tell us something. But she's not in great shape."

"What kind of tattoos?"

"Little hard to tell. Flowers, maybe."

Same as Jessica. I described her to him, including the "Bronte" tattoo. "She also had a broken collarbone, from a sledding accident. If that helps."

"I'll let the pathologist know." A pause. "I'm not going to bullshit you. It sounds like the person you just described."

"Any idea when she was killed?"

"Not really. Not yesterday, not the day before. Maybe last week? Beyond that, hard to say. She could have been outside for a while."

"Cause of death?"

"Off the record, it's looking like the same M.O. But have to wait for the autopsy to be sure. When did you say your person went missing?"

I explained the timeline I had for Jessica, from her brother's last sighting a few months back to the day the calls to Gretchen stopped.

"So more than a week since anybody last heard from her? That could be about right. You have a phone number for the brother? We can try fast-tracking DNA with the state. It's as solid a lead as any we've got right now."

"Let me call him and have him get ahold of you, if that's OK. He already thinks it's her. I'd rather he not hear from you out of the blue."

"That's fine. The sooner the better."

I hung up and called Bill Byrnes. His voice mail picked up. I left him as tactful a message as possible under the circumstances, concluding with Huntington's number. I hung up, fighting gloom. It was irrational, but it felt as if by putting Byrnes in touch with the investigator I had consigned Jessica to certain death.

My phone buzzed. It was Theresa. I told her what I knew about the latest victim.

"Thanks," she said when I finished. "But that ain't why I was calling. You know Mary?"

"Yeah. Is she OK?"

"Not really. Got the lab results back from the doctor. She's HIV positive and full of STDs and pretty strung out. Also, Mary ain't her real name. It's Deborah. Good news is Pastor Roy found her a place at a treatment center."

"Is she any closer to giving up Bronte's address?"

"Not likely, assuming she even knows it. Her face gets kind of dead looking every time I mention it. But here's the thing. She told me something interesting. About Lisa Washington."

"Which was?"

"She knew someone who was in a house with her."

"A house?"

"A brothel. Like Lisa's grandmother said. Some guy runs it out of the back of his business. It's a vacuum cleaner store. The johns come through the front, the girls go through the back. And get this. You want a girl, you have to bring an actual vacuum cleaner to get repaired."

"The list of client names. That could be the place."

"If that's what Lisa had, what she was scared of."

"Deborah tell you who it was knew this? Who was with Lisa?"

"She wouldn't say. But she said the place is on Cleveland, between Fifth and Eleventh, someplace in that stretch. Said you can't miss it."

She was right. Forty-five minutes later I parked outside Saunders & Sons, a plain, two-story tan brick building on the east side of the street with vacuums lined up across the building's wide, store-length windows. "American Made Vacuums!" declared a sign in big plastic letters. "Over 200 Different Bags And Belts!" said another. I grabbed the ancient Hoover I'd dug out of my closet and walked in.

The shop was empty. To the right, dozens of hoses were draped over a panel wall, leaving me with the uneasy impression of an army of octopuses making a break from an aquarium. Cleaning machines that would have been old the day my parents got married were collecting dust along a ledge on the wall behind the store's front counter. Below and to the right, cubbyholes in a floor-to-ceiling set of shelves were jammed full of what looked like order slips and invoices. What little space in the shop that new and used machines didn't fill was taken up with cans of spray cleaner and bottles of carpet soap. A computer monitor big enough to double as a yacht anchor was in danger of falling off the counter. The place felt weary and dated, the repair shop equivalent of a ten-year-old hunting and fishing calendar that nobody's ever bothered to take down.

A man emerged from a door in the far rear of the shop behind the counter. "Help you?" he said, setting down a black composition notebook and casting a glance at my Hoover.

"You think you could you repair this?" I said, raising the machine with my right hand. I was oddly fond of it. Kym brought it to her divorce attorney's office the day we split as a reminder of how I could never be bothered to do any housework. I'd hung onto it over the years as a reminder of a chapter in my life I hoped I'd left behind, as if Captain Edward Smith had survived the sinking of the *Titanic* and kept a loose rivet on the mantel as a keepsake. In that moment I found myself thinking of my conversation with Roy at the bar. Hopefully, I'd given up being the kind of cad I was around Kym. And Crystal. And—well, I got the point. But, as Roy suggested, had I given too much else up in the process?

"What's wrong with it?" the man said.

"I'm not sure. It doesn't have the same pull it used to."

"Let me take a look." He raised a panel in the counter and walked through. He took the Hoover, pushed it onto a square of carpet remnant, unraveled the cord, plugged it in, and turned it on. He rolled it back and forth. He stopped, went over to a shelf, grabbed a coffee canister, and spooned grounds onto the carpet. He tried again. A sprinkling of black specks stayed behind like tiny grains of gunpowder.

"Tell you what. I can take a look at it. But the repair's probably more than it's worth at this point. We've got some new Orecks that are really reasonable." He gestured at the store window.

"I'm attached to this one," I said. "How long would it take?"

"Maybe a week. I can give you a call."

"Sounds good. Does anything come with that?"

"What do you mean?"

"Just that, I guess. Anything else you might sell?"

He looked puzzled, as if I'd asked him for directions to someplace in western Indiana. I put him late fifties, maybe sixty, short, gray hair, tired-looking and thin as an upright Kirby. He said, "You mean like bags or something?"

"Yeah. Or something."

"I'm not sure I follow."

"I don't know. Anything you might have in the back?" I pointed across the counter.

"There's the repair shop and inventory. That's about it."

"Could I take a peek?"

"Like go back there? I don't think so."

"That's fine. I was just asking. You said a week?"

"That's right." He looked at me suspiciously. I smiled and said a week would be great. After a couple moments' hesitation he pulled out an order pad from below the counter, set it beside his notebook, and took my particulars. As I walked out two minutes later, receipt in hand, I turned and saw he was staring at me. I gave him a little wave. I felt bad about leaving the Hoover there, as if it were an old friend I'd sent on a dangerous mission across enemy lines. Of course, Mary—Deborah—might have been wrong about what a vacuum cleaner got you, at least for a first-timer. Or maybe you needed some kind of introduction from an existing client. Or maybe I had the wrong store. There might not have been anything in the back but a repair shop and inventory.

Still, it was hard not to notice the way Mr. Saunders continued staring at me until I pulled away from the store and drove down the street.

36

I MADE A FRUITLESS ROUND OF CALLS IN the afternoon, looking for information about the latest victim. I was losing hope. I felt my pulse quicken late in the day when the phone rang, then saw it was just Bonnie calling. But it turned out that like Theresa with her vacuum shop tip, she had news too.

"I think I found that girl. Mandie Smith. The high school friend of Jessica's?"

"Great," I said, mustering as much enthusiasm as I could. I still felt bad about my muted response to her discovery of Leonard Lortz.

"It took me a while. You know how many Mandie Smiths there are out there?"

"I'm guessing it gives grains of sand on a beach a run for their money."

"A *lot*. But I think this is the one. She lives over by Dayton. I've got a number for her. And an e-mail. And I sent her a Facebook friend request."

"Nice job," I said, trying to keep it positive, despite the fact I knew that any second now George Huntington from the

THE HUNT

coroner's office or the congresswoman or Dr. Phil or just about anybody else could alert me that they'd positively IDed Jessica Byrnes's body.

"But listen to this," Bonnie continued. "If it's her, she does roller derby. Can you believe it? She's on Dayton's team. The Fembot Flyers. We played them three seasons ago."

"That's handy."

"That's what I was thinking. It might persuade her to talk to us. More than just a random friend request."

"That's really good. Let me know as soon as you hear back."

When we were finished I checked in with my mom. I talked myself out of driving over to see my dad. He needed recovery time more than he needed to see me right now. Besides, it was a custody night. I was practically giddy that I'd remembered. As I picked Mike up he presented me with a French quiz he'd gotten an A on, along with a list of Xbox games he wanted.

"You said."

"Yes, I did," I replied, stuffing the papers into my jacket. We retrieved Joe and went to the Christmas lights display at the zoo. Mike was bored but Joe liked it. Par for the course. We stopped for burgers on the way back, and everyone was home by nine-thirty.

I was pulling in front of my house, still trying to figure out where I was going to get the money to make good on my Xbox promise, when my cell phone went off.

"Is this Mister Andy Hayes?"

"Yes."

"This is Ramesh Patel. At the Rest EZ Motel on East Main."

My heart sped up. "Of course. What can I do for you?"

"The man who was looking for that girl whose picture you showed me. The parole officer I told you about."

"Yes. I don't think he's a parole officer, though."

"I don't know about that. But you said to call. If I saw anything."

"And?"

"And that man was just here, looking for Jessica Byrnes."

THE MOTEL MANAGER HADN'T gotten a name. But he did have security cameras trained on the parking lot, and he thought they might have seen something. I texted him the photo of Leonard Lortz that Theresa took and told him I'd see him soon.

"That's not him," Mr. Patel said when I rushed into the office twenty minutes later.

"What did he look like?"

"Difficult to say. He was wearing a dust mask this time. Like in China, with all that pollution. Said something about bronchitis. And he had sunglasses on."

"Very convenient."

"He wasn't that man in the picture. I'm sure of that. But perhaps he's on the security tape?"

He let me come around the counter. With a hint of reluctance, he closed the cricket match he was watching on his laptop. He clicked on a security camera icon on his desktop and pulled up a series of files. He clicked on the top one, opened it, and used the mouse to scroll forward in time. Cars zoomed in and out of the parking lot like images in a flip book. The Rest EZ seemed to do a lot of business, even on a weekday Wednesday night. At last Mr. Patel stopped the footage at just over an hour earlier. A car pulled up in front of the office. The camera was badly angled, so only the person's torso was visible as he crossed the camera's field and entered.

"That doesn't help much," I said.

"Wait a minute," Mr. Patel said.

And that's about how long it took before the man exited the office, walked around to the car and drove off.

"Can you stop that?" He froze the picture. The car was a new-looking white Toyota Corolla with a Florida plate. I retrieved my phone from my back pocket and took a screen shot.

"I hope that helps," Mr. Patel said.

"Did he say anything about her?"

"He just asked if I'd seen her recently. Just like before. He was very polite."

"Did you tell him about me? That I'd been by?"

He looked surprised. "Did you want me to?"

"No, of course not. Did he leave a number?"

"Yes. I kept it this time."

He handed me a slip of paper. I recognized it immediately. It was the same number that Jessica's mom got from the man calling himself a minister. Bonnie had done her best to find a name to go with it, but had determined only that it was a prepaid phone and it would probably take a subpoena to learn more than that.

"Thanks again," I said, pushing a twenty-dollar bill across the table.

"You're welcome," he said, pushing the money back. "I hope she's not the girl on the news. I hope you find her."

"Me too."

37

THERESA WASN'T ANSWERING AS I DROVE
back down East Main. I was disappointed I couldn't reach her, because I was finally excited about something. I could run the plate
as soon as I got home. It was a solid lead. Even if the worst came
to pass, it was still a chance to trace what Jessica had been up to.
Above all, to find out who'd been looking for her.

I was driving down Mohawk, almost back to my house, when
Roy called. Late for him.

"How'd it go? I'm dying to hear."

"With Mr. Patel? How'd you know about that?"

"I mean with Jessica Byrnes. Is she OK?"

"What are you talking about?"

"I'm talking about Jessica. I've been waiting for the good news."

"Waiting since when? I'm sorry. I'm not following."

There was a pause on Roy's end. "Where are you?"

"Nearly home." As I pulled in front of my house I told him
about the Rest EZ and the stranger's license plate.

"So you're not out on the east side?"

"I just told you that."

"And Theresa's not with you."

"No. What's going on?"

"Theresa got a call about an hour ago. Actually, I got the call first. Somebody from the police. Larry something."

"Larry Schwartzbaum?"

"That's it. Said you had found Jessica but there was a problem getting her to talk and could Theresa get out there and help. The guy said you'd asked him to call. You're telling me that's not true?"

My stomach hollowed out. "Do you know where she went?"

"She didn't tell me the address. Just said off East Main someplace. She was in a hurry to get there. I've been worried about her doing this job but it really seems to have been good for her. And I thought, with this—"

"This is all wrong. Does she have her phone with her?"

"As far as I know."

"Don't go anywhere." I hung up and tried Theresa's number, but it went straight to voice mail again. I thought about what to do. I only had Schwartzbaum's office number. I called it anyway and left a message. I phoned Bonnie and told her what was going on. Troy's foster dog was winding up in the background.

"Can you ping her phone?" she said when she'd removed herself to the quiet of their kitchen. "That could tell you where she is."

"How would I do that?"

I called Roy back two minutes later. "Do you have Theresa's account information?"

"I have no idea."

"Did she pay for the phone?"

"The church did. It's part of her benefits package."

"Get to your computer and keep your phone free."

I hung up and called Bonnie back. I gave her Roy's number. I started the van, performed the world's worst K turn, and drove back up Mohawk to Livingston. I turned right, gunned it up to Parsons, turned left, and went up to Main. I turned right and started driving slowly down the street, willing Theresa to magically appear. I called Bonnie back. It went to voice mail. She called me back five minutes later.

"Anything?"

"Almost. He had the wrong e-mail. Then we had to reset the password because he had no idea what it was."

The connection went quiet. Main Street was nearly deserted as I drove east, past the city Health Department, the only people out a couple of guys in hoodies trudging along, heads lowered, and a tired-looking woman waiting for a bus. No sign of "Darla" or any other street women. Even our conspiracy theorist was MIA. Perhaps no surprise, since the temperature had started to drop in the past couple of days to something resembling actual winter. I tried to think who could have called Theresa. Who would have wanted to pull such a prank? Who, and why?

"Got it," Bonnie said. "It's by Kelton Avenue. Near Mooberry Street. Where are you?"

I slowed, coming to an intersection. "Main and Linwood."

"Turn right." I put her on speaker and followed her block-by-block instructions. After two minutes that felt like two hours, I parked along a row of dark houses, most of them boarded up except for one burned-out hulk. Empty malt liquor 40s littered the front yards.

"Looks like it's inside No. 383," Bonnie said. "Do you see that?"

"Yes. I see her Honda too. The house looks abandoned. Call Roy and give him the address. Tell him I'm going inside."

"Andy, be careful—"

"And Bonnie?"

"Yes?"

"Tell him to bring his Beretta."

I HUNG UP, OPENED the glove compartment, and pulled out a flashlight I use for sensitive investigations and for hunting change under the van's seats. I reached behind me and grabbed my Louisville Slugger. I got out and pushed my phone into the front right pocket of my coat and snapped the pocket shut. I didn't want it falling out in case Bonnie needed to perform the same search-and-rescue on me. I jogged up to Theresa's car, tried the door, and shone the flashlight inside till I was sure it was empty. Hoisting the bat in my right hand, I walked up to 383 and mounted the porch steps. The front door wouldn't budge.

I ran back down the stairs and around to the side. I found another door, but that was locked too. At the rear of the house a metal chain-link fence surrounded a yard grown over with weeds and tall grass like a prairie. Or an abandoned cemetery. A gate was open, pushed inward. I went through. Cracked concrete steps climbed up to a rear door. I tried it. It pushed open easily. I raised the bat and stepped inside.

"Theresa?" I yelled. I clicked on the flashlight and moved the beam around the room. I was in the kitchen. I smelled rotted food and feces and burned plastic. Something skittered on the far side and I started back, my heart drumming. I flashed the light in that direction but caught empty wall. As I swung the beam back something glinted on the floor. I stepped forward and picked it up. It was Theresa's Zion Episcopal medallion, given to her by Roy at the church's christening ceremony. I swore. Had it come off in a struggle? Or had she dropped it as a clue? I moved farther into the room. I called Theresa's name again. No response. To the left a doorway opened into the rest of the house. To the right a closed door. To the basement? I turned the handle and pushed. Nothing. I tried again, using my shoulder. Still nothing. Locked, or blocked from the inside.

I went the other way, into a dining room that opened into a living room. The house was a shambles. Someone had been squatting. A bad feeling came over me. I thought about what Kevin Harding at the *Dispatch* had told me, the day he'd given me the Pleasure Prince tip. That the cops were looking for a lair. Had I found it? Almost all the furniture was gone, replaced by piles of trash, papers, boxes, and lots and lots of balled-up food wrappers. The smell was nearly as bad as in the kitchen.

Something skittered again. I swung the flashlight in time to catch a streak of brown fur racing past a fireplace and disappearing around the corner. I walked across the room, looked around, satisfied myself it was empty, and headed upstairs two steps at a time. I paused at the landing, holding myself still as I listened. I heard nothing yet everything: the myriad complaints of an old, abandoned house with loose windows and gaps in boards and holes in the roof. I turned and went up the remaining stairs to the second floor. The smell was even worse up here. I stepped inside the bathroom and stepped out just as quickly, gagging. I cast the flashlight beam over a toilet bowl overflowing onto the tiled floor with waste. I turned and walked into an open bedroom. A bare mattress lay on the floor, stained with something I didn't want to think about, a green blanket crumpled beside it. Through the curtainless cracked window I could just make out the peeling paint of the house next door. I stepped out of that room, called Theresa's name again, and explored the next two bedrooms. One was completely empty, the other filled with an assortment of metal junk: copper tubing, dented appliances, wire clothes hangers, and what looked like pieces of dismantled grills. The deposits of a scrap-metal thief. Standing in the doorway to the room, I thought of the conspiracy theorist who prowled these streets. *The government knows.* Was it possible? Him? I heard the skittering sound again, raised the baseball bat, and started to turn around.

Too late. I felt myself jerked back and off balance as something tightened around my throat, pulling me swiftly backward into the hall. I dropped the bat and the flashlight and clawed at my neck, fingers brushing against a cord as I gasped, already losing air. There was no purchase, not the slightest gap that would let me penetrate the tight band and find traction to ease the pain, to take in oxygen. I tried to turn around, to face my assailant, but he was bearing down with enormous strength, backing me up and bending me over as I struggled and spit out choked, guttural coughs. Even in my panic I understood that if he reached the wall behind him I was finished; he'd have all the leverage he'd need to bring my garroting to its ugly conclusion. My vision narrowed as black dots swam in the air before me, and I heard an odd humming sound, a familiar noise coming from the attacker. Something I'd listened to before. I thought of Theresa, and Jessica, and my complicity in Jimmy Wooding's death, and my father's accusatory words . . .

Focus, Andy, focus!

With my last bit of strength I put all my weight on my right leg, pushed down, and swiveled to my left as I pressed myself backward against the attacker, using his motion against him. I felt him stumble and heard the humming stop, replaced by an angry grunt. The cord loosened as he lost his grip for a moment, and I took an enormous, sucking breath and swiveled again and backed up, hard and fast. A moment passed while I stood motionless as if suspended at the edge of a precipice, and then I felt myself fall backward, felt both of us fall, dropping like a teenage game of trust gone horribly wrong as we tumbled down the stairs, landing with a crash on the lower landing. He groaned at the impact of my weight coming down on him. I pushed myself up to turn and grab him, and as I did felt a new stab of pain as a fist connected with my throat and he scrambled free and took off down the remaining stairs.

I raised myself onto my knees, caught my breath, stood up, and hurled myself after him. I gave chase through the living room and dining room and into the kitchen, saw his back disappear through the outside door, started to follow, and then stopped. The basement door, the one I hadn't been able to budge when I first came inside, was open. I hesitated, went a step or two farther toward the door he'd fled through, and stopped.

I found her on the far side of the basement, which was cold and damp and smelled of mold and decay, like an abandoned meat locker that hadn't been properly cleaned out. She was lying on her side, hands and feet bound, with a cord around her neck. Her eyes were shut. Her skin was clammy and she didn't respond when I called her name.

I stumbled around the basement, cursing, until at last I found a discarded file with a still sharp edge sitting in a pile of tools on a rear counter. I used it to carefully cut the cord around her throat.

"Theresa!"

I pulled out my cell phone and dialed 911. As I spoke to the operator I cut through the cords binding her hands and legs. I turned her onto her back. Her face was pale and I could see a large bruise on her right cheek. I reached out to put my hand on her neck to check for a pulse. She raised her left hand and wrapped it around my wrist and opened her eyes.

"QB," she whispered. "I'm sorry."

"Thank God."

"It was him. I'm so sorry."

"It's OK. You're safe now. Are you—"

"Doing better than him. Almost clawed his eyes out, before . . ."

"Good girl. Do you know who it was?"

"I'm sorry. He had us both fooled."

"Who?"

"Lortz," she said. "It was Leonard Lortz."

WITHIN A FEW MINUTES WE WERE SITTING in the back of a Columbus Fire Department medical squad. A paramedic was examining Theresa's cheek and neck. Larry Schwartzbaum was with us, along with a Columbus homicide detective. Outside, patrol officers were still securing the scene. Inside, more detectives were searching room to room.

"I knew it wasn't right as soon as I got here and didn't see any other cars," Theresa said. "Then he just, like, appeared, as soon as I opened the door. He told me he had a girl inside and she'd die if I tried anything. He took me to the basement. I figured I was dead when he pushed me down the stairs and there wasn't nobody else down there." I cursed at myself for giving up on that door as I'd entered the house.

"What did he say?" Schwartzbaum asked.

"He kept asking what I knew about the missing girls. And what I knew about Andy. And . . ."

We waited.

"And he sang," she said, and just for a moment her voice cracked. "He sang this song. These same words, over and over. *Love the touch, love the push. Love the touch, love the push—*"

"—*Of the good-time Pleasure Prince,*" I said.

"Yeah," she said, and hugged herself. "That's it."

The humming as he'd pulled the cord tight around my throat. It had been the same song. I felt my insides freeze up a little.

I said, "So now there's no question."

"No question about what?" Schwartzbaum said.

"Lortz is the guy. He's the killer. He's the Pleasure Prince. And now we've found his lair."

IT WAS AFTER 1 a.m. when I got home. I opened a can of beer, sat on the couch beside the dog without turning on any lights, and thought about the evening. From time to time I rubbed my neck. I thought for a long time. Eventually, after I started awake at the sound of the empty can dropping from my hand and hitting the floor, I got up and went to bed.

I should have tossed and turned; instead I slept without dreaming until past seven. The first thing I did when I rolled over was check my phone. Alerts and messages crowded the screen, taking me several seconds to scroll through all of them. Columbus's serial killer had been identified. His rat hole was found. A woman had been rescued. *An ex-prostitute!* Twitter feeds and news websites were chockablock with breathless live shots in front of Lortz's house and outside the Dollar & Done and even—I'm sure they were pleased as punch—National Way Insurance's headquarters on East Broad, catty-corner from the art museum. People had everything they needed from a story this big except for Lortz himself. He'd vanished into the night.

At ten o'clock I accompanied Theresa to a new round of questioning at Division of Police headquarters downtown. I took along Burke Cunningham, the defense lawyer I work for periodically, to make it a real party. It took a while. When we were finished I drove Theresa to Roy and Lucy's house in Clintonville, where she'd be staying for the foreseeable future.

I took a short nap back at home, exhausted from the previous night. When I woke up and looked at my phone again, I saw another long scrolling mess of text messages, news alerts, and missed calls. One of the callers had tried me three times. I called him back first.

"Just give it to me straight," I said when he answered. "I don't have time for any bullshit."

"Are you OK? I was worried, all the stories out there," George Huntington said. The coroner's investigator could be annoyingly attentive when he wanted.

"Just tell me, goddamn it. It's not like this day can get any worse."

"Suit yourself. We don't have a positive ID on the body. On the sixth victim."

"That's why you're calling me? To tell me nothing?"

"No. That was a courtesy clue, which is going to cost you an extra growler of Christmas ale, seeing as you're so grumpy. What I was calling to tell you was that it's not her."

"What?" I said, confused.

"It's not her. Whoever that poor girl is, it's not Jessica Byrnes."

39

I HUNG UP, LEANED MY HEAD AGAINST the back of the couch, and stared at the ceiling. Relief flooded through me. *Not Jessica.* There was a chance, probably a slight one, but a chance nonetheless, that she was still alive. That there was hope. I nearly laughed out loud before the bigger picture dawned on me. There was still a sixth victim. My happiness, even if it was only temporary, was the flipside of some family's continued despair. And even though we knew who the killer was, he was gone with hardly a trace. The fact Lortz hadn't been arrested yet was a bad sign. A sign he may have prepared for the eventuality of being flushed from his hiding place. An indication he might have another rat hole lined up—

A loud knock on my front door. I rubbed the lump on my head, still tender to the touch, thinking of Bronte Patterson. Another guy specializing in hiding places. I tried to remember where I'd left my baseball bat. In my van, of course, retrieved from the abandoned house where it had proved as useless as always. I stood up slowly, massaged my neck, palmed my phone, and walked to the door. I looked out the window and sighed.

"Hello, Suzanne," I said, opening the door to the Channel 7 reporter. Who in addition to being my ex-fiancée happened right at the moment to be the alpha journalist standing in front of a throng of at least ten other people with notebooks and microphones and cameras. I saw Kevin Harding at the edge of the pack, trying to avoid eye contact. I called to him by name and said hello.

I gave them ten minutes. It was the least I could do after Theresa braved the cameras at the vigil. I said as much as I thought I could without pissing off a lot of people with badges. I played dumb when someone asked about Gätling Gün and the Pleasure Prince. I told them there was no chance Theresa would be talking. I played along when someone spied Hopalong standing in the open door and asked me to bring him out for some B-roll shots. I even told them how I was feeling.

"You're looking well," I said to Suzanne when the klieg lights had dimmed and the crews were packing up.

"Thanks," she said, tucking her microphone into the pocket of her oversized red parka with real fake fur. "I feel pretty good too. Finally."

"Finally? Are you OK?"

"I'm fine," she said, shooting me a surprised look with those stomach-flipping blue eyes of hers. "I'm pregnant. Where've you been?"

"Nowhere, I guess. Congratulations."

"Sorry. I thought I'd told you. I'm just past four months. Glen's a little apprehensive, starting over. His kids are almost out of high school. But he's excited, too. Gotta run. We're live at five at the courthouse."

"Thanks for stopping by," I said.

I went inside and sat back on the couch and thought some more. Realized that I'd been wrong when I barked at George Huntington that the day couldn't have gotten any worse. I shut my eyes, processing everything from my blown opportunities with Suzanne to my rapidly cooling relationship with Anne to the obvious fact that despite the good news from the coroner's office, I still had no idea where Jessica Byrnes was.

When I opened my eyes again it was close to midnight. I was wide awake. I thought about reading and was looking for *Ohio Colossus* when I remembered the Rest EZ Motel and Mr. Patel and the license plate. Theresa's near-fatal encounter with Leonard Lortz had blasted it clean out of my memory. I realized it wasn't too late to do something with the information, to find out who was hunting Jessica. My mood brightened. I felt like Scrooge on Christmas Day. *I haven't missed it. The Spirits have done it all in one night.* I powered up my laptop and opened a browser and went to TrackerTracer.com. I logged in with my username and password, found the field for auto searches, and typed in the make of the car and the license plate. I had my answer in less than sixty seconds. The Toyota was a rental. The plate came back to Car Rite. I did some Googling and determined the only Columbus location was at the airport. I tried the number but got a recording; no surprise given the hour. It would have to wait until the morning.

THE PHONE AT CAR Rite Rental rang busy until past eight-thirty. Finally a young-sounding woman named Morgan answered and asked if she could tell me about their winter weekend special.

"Maybe some other time," I said. "Name's Mike DiSalle. Hoping you can help me out with something."

"I'd be happy to try, sir. Does it involve a past or current reservation?"

"Little of both, I guess. Thing is, I'm over at"—I paused, brain scrambling—"Columbus Amalgamated Insurance, and I've got a claim involving one of your vehicles."

"Oh, geez. What happened?"

"Far as we can tell, looks like it was stolen. Somebody left it parked kind of funny on a side street yesterday morning over in Merion Place, by German Village? One of our policy holders who was headed out of town early didn't see it in the dark and clipped it. Police said the plate came back to Car Rite. So what I'm wondering is, any chance you've got the driver info? Or should I be talking to your claims people?"

"You don't have a name?"

"Just the plate, sorry."

"That's OK. What is it?"

I read the number to her. "Just a minute, please," she said. She put me on hold. A wobbly jingle instructed me that Car Rite was the Right Choice for Right Now. At least five times.

"Mr. DiSalle?"

"Yes, ma'am."

"I've got it for you. He went with our coverage. You have something you can write on?"

"Sure," I said, notebook at hand.

She told me the name. I hesitated. I said, "Would you mind repeating that?"

"Not at all."

I pushed the notebook aside. There was no reason to record a name I already knew.

"Thank you, Morgan. You've been very helpful."

"No problem. Hope it works out. Hey, could I ask you a question?"

"Fire away."

"Are you related to the Mike DiSalle who was Ohio governor, by any chance? I did a paper on him in college. Pretty interesting guy."

"Is that so? Not that I know of. I get that all the time, though."

"I bet," she said with a laugh. "Have a good one."

"You too," I said, cutting the call.

I knew I had to reach the person who'd rented the Toyota, and quickly. But then the morning got complicated. Kym rang to say the principal at Mike's school had phoned to say Mike had been in a shoving match with another student first thing that morning and was being held after school, and what was I—that was Kym's question—intending to do about it? I told her I'd call the school. Forty-five minutes later I finally hung up after talking to the principal and a guidance counselor and promising I'd speak to Mike about his behavior. I called Kym back and filled her in, and that took another fifteen minutes, very few of which were spent on my virtues as a parent. I was still fuming when my phone rang with an unfamiliar number.

"Yeah. You the guy dropped this Hoover off a couple days ago?"

"That's me."

"There's nothing wrong with it. You need to come get it."

"OK. I can be by this afternoon—"

"You got an hour or I'm stripping it for parts. I saw you on the news, OK? Private investigator? I'm not sure what you're up to. But it's now or nothing."

He hung up before I could reply. I tried to decipher his anger. Had my questions about the back of the store struck the wrong note for the right reasons? Or was he just annoyed at me for wasting his time by trying to coax a little more life out of such an old machine? Either way, despite everything that had happened, I wanted it back. There's a reason they call them keepsakes.

I pulled into the store's parking lot twenty minutes later. It was almost eleven. As I walked inside a guy was coming out, holding a beat-up machine that looked even older than mine. He kept his eyes on the ground as if hoping to spy a lucky penny and walked past me. Inside, Mr. Saunders charged me twenty bucks for the going over he said he gave it and told me to get lost. I didn't complain, though I did ask for a receipt.

Something about the guy walking out who wouldn't make eye contact didn't sit right. I turned left out of the parking lot onto Cleveland and turned left again into the parking lot of a strip mall next door. I drove all the way to the far end, turned left, took another left, and drove back up the rear of the mall along a service road. The back of the long building was deserted except for a guy outside the rear of a Somali coffee shop talking on his cell phone. I parked at the end of the drive. I had a decent view of the back of the vacuum shop and the small parking lot behind it.

After about ten minutes the shop's rear door opened and Saunders stepped out carrying a large black plastic garbage bag. He used his foot to shift a wedge of wood in place to keep the door from locking behind him, walked coatless to a metal trash bin, glanced in both directions, threw the garbage inside, looked around again, and went back into the store. I waited another fifteen minutes and was about to call it a stakeout and get back to my Car Rite renter when the door opened again. A young woman walked out. Black leather jacket, short red skirt, high— very high—red heels. She click-clacked into the parking lot and glanced around before checking her phone. A minute later a car pulled up. She opened the door and got in. The driver pulled away quickly, like a kid warned against meeting his date's parents. I couldn't see who was behind the wheel. It didn't matter. I could guess. Because I'd seen the girl before. And as I realized who it was, my heart sank almost more than the night I'd realized Theresa was in danger. The young woman was Garrett Fischer's daughter, Lindsay. The woman I'd seen sitting at his dining room table the day I'd gone to ask about Jessica.

As I sat there, I realized the girl's relationship to Fischer had never been delineated. I was the one who'd assumed he was her father. I thought about the accounting client who came to the door while I was there. Fischer's apology as the man arrived, that he had to excuse himself to get to work. Work he did at home because of a disability. I thought of the guy passing me on the way out of Saunders & Sons just now. I had a sick feeling in my stomach as the pieces clicked into place.

It wasn't Fischer who'd needed to get to work the day his client arrived at the cozy town house.

It was Lindsay.

40

THE SMELL OF POTPOURRI HAD BEEN A comforting accent when I was at the Fischers' place the first time. When I'd envisioned the home as a stable refuge for Jessica Byrnes after the abuse she suffered at stepdad's hands. Now, as I stood at the open door a couple of hours later, the odor struck me as sickly sweet, like flowers disguising the smell in a hospice room.

"Garrett's not feeling too well," Mrs. Fischer said after I introduced myself and reminded her of my previous visit. "Maybe I could let him know you stopped by?"

"How about your daughter, Lindsay. She around?"

"Daughter?" she said faintly. She was pleasantly plump, with frosted upswept hair, wearing comfortable brown slacks and a Mrs. Claus Christmas sweater. She looked like a person who made a lot of cookies with sprinkles on them.

I described the young woman I'd seen leaving Saunders & Sons.

"Lindsay's not here," she said after a slight pause. "Was there something I could help you with?"

A noise from upstairs interrupted her. It reminded me vaguely of Troy's foster dog.

"What was that?" I said.

"One of the pipes, probably. Perhaps I could have Garrett call when he—"

"Sounds like you need a plumber," I said, brushing past her and heading to the stairs.

"What are you doing?" she called after me. "You need to stop. Right now. I'm going to call the police."

"More the merrier," I said over my shoulder.

A soft, light-butterscotch carpet covered the upstairs hallway. Another bowl of potpourri sat on an antiquey-looking wooden end table by the back wall. Doors to two bedrooms were open, revealing beds made up pretty as a Currier & Ives print with Christmas quilts. A third door was closed. On it hung a painted wooden Christmas cutout of a dog with a red bow on its head nestled beneath a decorated tree. I stood close and listened for a moment. I heard a familiar sound that wasn't made by a pipe. Or a dog, though in truth the moaning of Troy's foster animal did come close. I looked at my watch. It had taken me a while to figure out what to do after seeing Lindsay leave Saunders & Sons and get on to the road to Mount Alex. But even so, Fischer hadn't been that far ahead. Which made it even more impressive how fast he'd gotten back in time for Lindsay's next appointment. I tried the door handle. It was locked. I pounded. Mercifully, the sound stopped.

"Who is it?" A man's voice, gruff and petulant.

"Santa Claus. Open the door."

"Garrett?"

"Open the door. I'll explain everything."

A long moment passed during which the only sound in the house was Mrs. Fischer's voice downstairs, speaking to someone. Something clicked on the other side of the bedroom door. I grabbed the knob and turned and pushed my way inside.

"Hey," said a man, stumbling backward. He was wearing nothing but striped boxer shorts. He had a billowy, hairy stomach that looked like someone had rolled bread dough around the floor of a barber shop. He stared at me in shock as he realized I wasn't Garrett Fischer. Or Santa Claus. I stepped farther in and glanced at the person in the bed. It was the same woman I'd seen at the table downstairs as well as leaving the vacuum store. She was sitting up, back against the wall and eyes wide, gripping a comforter that covered everything but a bare left shoulder. The comforter was printed with a repeating design of an elf going down a snow-covered hill on an old-style Flexible Flyer sled with red runners.

"Play time's over," I told the man. "Get dressed."

"Who the hell are you?"

"You've heard of the Grinch?"

"Get out of here." He called out for Fischer, then Fischer's wife, before starting to move toward me.

"It's you who's leaving, not me," I said.

"I don't think so," he said, and took a flimsy swing at me. I responded by punching him in the nose, but not in a bad way. He yelped as blood began pouring from his nostrils.

"Are you all right?" I said to Lindsay.

"Get the fuck out of here," she said.

Holding his left hand over his face, the man balled up his right fist and headed back in my direction. I waited a moment, dipped my right shoulder, and hit him in the stomach. It was like punching a freshly filled water bed. It shook like a bowlful of jelly. He doubled over. I looked around the room until I found his pants, lying crumpled on the floor. I picked them up, removed his wallet, and pulled out his license. Stewart Rehner, forty-eight years old, with a Mount Alexandria address. I took out my phone and snapped a picture of the license. I put the license back in the wallet and dropped it on the pants. I turned to the girl.

"What's your name?"

She swore at me.

"I'm guessing Lindsay's fake?"

She simultaneously flipped me off and started to cry.

"I can help you, if you want. Get you out of here."

She swore again. I said, "I know I asked you this before. But things are different now. Do you know where Jessica Byrnes is?"

She shook her head.

"She's still in danger. Anything you tell me could help."

She shook her head again. There was something familiar about the cast of her eyes. It took me a moment. I'd seen the same look at the Franklin County animal shelter a few years back the day I adopted Hopalong. The look of someone whose short life of violence has been rewarded by living in a cage.

"You broke my fucking nose," the man said, still hunched over.

I swiveled toward him. I said, "Between us, it's an improvement."

"I'm going to sue your ass. Have you arrested."

"Say cheese," I said. He looked up and I took a picture of him with my phone.

"What the hell—"

"I ever hear a peep from you, I'll post that side by side with your driver's license on every social media site in the world, including Weibo in China, which is very large, I'm told. Understood? And you come near her again"—I nodded at Lindsay—"and you'll have a lot more to worry about than pictures."

Defiant, the man stared at me. He looked as threatening as a beached seal, especially with the blood trickling onto his chest. I pocketed my phone, walked over to the bed, pulled a card out of my wallet, and before "Lindsay" could stop me slipped it beneath the comforter.

"I can help you."

"Get lost," she said, her voice hard and flat.

I tossed the man's clothes at him and told him to get dressed. When he'd managed the task I followed him downstairs. He walked through the house and out the door without saying a word to Mrs. Fischer, who'd been joined by her suddenly recovered husband, propped up beside her with his cane. When the man was gone I shut the door and turned around and saw Mrs. Fischer pointing a gun at me.

"Is that what you used to kill Jimmy Wooding?"

"I have no idea what you're talking about."

"You better hope you don't. Because there's no potpourri in Marysville. That's where the state women's prison is, in case you failed civics in high school. Very few Christmas sweaters, either."

"Don't move," she said, raising the gun a little. "The police are on their way."

"No, they're not."

"I just called them."

"I don't think so. Town this size, cops could have stopped at the Parthenon for a beer and some pretzels and still been here by now. They're not coming, because if they did you'd have to explain why Lindsay and a guy that looks old enough to be a dirty old man were staining your sheets. And that could lead to all kinds of awkward questions."

"Martha," Garrett Fischer said.

"They'll come if I told them I shot an intruder trying to attack me and my daughter," Martha Fischer said. "Because I don't see any other guy here." Her eyes had gone cold and she no longer looked like a lady who baked Christmas cookies as she hummed along to "The Little Drummer Boy." She looked like the regional production manager who fires that lady for falling behind schedule.

"That guy's not here," I said, choosing my words carefully. "But his blood is, on the upstairs carpet, where I accidentally on purpose bopped him on the nose. It soaked in pretty good. And the thing is, I know the chief detective here. Elliot Mullan. Smart guy. He's going to want to know whose blood that is. But even if he doesn't, which I doubt, a bunch of cops in Columbus are going to start asking a lot of questions real quick if you shoot me. Not that they care about me, mind you. But they care about Jessica Byrnes, and they know I've been looking for her, and they might even know I was coming here today. They'll figure it out."

The room got quiet while Mrs. Fischer let my words sink in. It got so still I could hear the hiss of the gas fireplace and make out almost all the words of "Silver Bells" coming from the other room. She raised the gun. I took a step back.

"Martha," Garrett Fischer said.

"Stay out of this," she said.

"Put the gun down, Martha."

I backed up slowly, reached behind me, and opened the door.

"That's a wrap," I said when I had one foot outside. "Whatever you've got going here, some kind of training school that feeds Saunders & Sons, it's done. Understood?"

Martha Fischer never broke eye contact, keeping the gun aimed at my chest. Her husband looked as if he was going to be sick, or charge after me, or collapse in a puddle of sweat, or some awkward combination of all three. His contorted expression made me feel more uncomfortable than the gun Mrs. Fischer was pointing at me. And this wasn't TV. I was out of snappy things to say. I stepped all the way outside, looked at them both a last time, pulled the door shut, and walked quickly to my van. I backed out of the driveway in a hurry, turned right sharply enough to produce an honest-to-God tire squeal, and left the town-house complex.

Two blocks later I pulled over, donned my Clippers cap and my biggest pair of sunglasses, and got out. A woman pushing a stroller stared at me, startled. I stared back. She had hair the color of red licorice and a teardrop tattoo on her face.

"Got a cell phone?" I said.

"What?"

"A cell phone. There's a fire. Sorry. It's an emergency."

"A fire? Where?" She looked at my van as if expecting to see flames.

"Down the street," I said in my best breathless voice. I gave her the Fischers' address. "I don't have my phone on me. Can you call 911? It looks bad."

"A fire?"

"Hurry. I don't want anyone to get hurt."

She looked at me, looked up the street, looked back at me, and pulled out a phone. I watched while she made the call. I thanked her and got back in the van and pulled away as quickly as possible. I felt a little bad, but I had no choice. Caller ID doesn't work on 911. She could blame it on a funny-looking guy if need be. I didn't think it would come to that.

As I drove back toward the Fischers' town house I called the Mount Alexandria police department. After a minute I had Elliot Mullan on the line. I explained why I was calling.

"I'm not going to be able to just walk in there," he said when I finished. "I'll need a warrant. Why didn't you call me earlier?"

"Don't worry about it," I said, listening to the sound of a siren in the distance. "I think they're having an open house."

41

IT TOOK ME A WHILE TO EXTRICATE MYSELF from Mullan and his questions. He was ex–state police thorough. His head looked more rectangular than ever as I pieced things together for him. He even had a kind of rectangular pen, a four-sided utensil that said "Mount Alexandria Hospital" on it, to go with his rectangular notebook.

I made a number of calls when I was liberated after solemnly promising to postpone any out-of-country luxury cruises for a while. One was to the person who'd rented a white Toyota Corolla from Car Rite Rental. I had to leave a message. Another was to Gretchen Osborne, Jessica's caseworker. She was the one person I had yet to speak to since the revelation about the sixth victim. I needed to talk to her about Garrett Fischer and Saunders & Sons and lots of other things. Her cell phone went straight to voice mail. I left a message and decided, despite her earlier admonition, to try her at her office at Lilyhaven. That's when I got my next surprise of the day.

"Gretchen is no longer employed here," said the woman who answered the phone.

"Are you sure?" I explained who I was and why I was calling. She informed me I'd heard correctly and said Gretchen hadn't worked there for several weeks.

"Can you tell me why she left?" I relayed Gretchen's story of helping Jessica. That earned me a long pause but nothing else.

"I'm sorry to hear that she portrayed herself that way," the woman said. "But I'm afraid that's all I can say."

"But—"

"I'm sorry."

I tried calling Gretchen again but got more voice mail. I kept driving, processing what the woman had told me. Gretchen hadn't worked for Lilyhaven since I'd gotten involved in the case. But if she hadn't, why had she kept up the façade? Did she know more about Jessica's whereabouts than she was letting on? Was she lying about the phone call from Jessica that never came?

When I reached the commercial strip at Sunbury right before I-71, I pulled into a Kroger parking lot. I tried looking up Gretchen's address on my phone but came up empty. I called Bonnie and she picked up right away.

"It's her," she said.

"What?"

"The girl. Mandie Smith. The one in Dayton. We traded some Facebook messages. She knows Jessica Byrnes."

"That's great," I said, and really meant it. "Is she willing to talk? Did you get her number?"

"I brought it up. She didn't sound thrilled, to be honest. She wasn't sure she wants to get involved."

"Would she be willing to talk just to you?"

"Me?"

"Fellow roller derby player and all."

"I could try. I'm not sure what I'd ask."

"Keep it basic. What she knows about the mom and stepdad. Maybe why Jessica left home." I told her about Saunders & Sons and the operation the Fischers were running. "Above all, does she know where she is."

"OK. I'll see what she says."

I thanked her and explained why I'd called. It took her all of three minutes to find Gretchen's address. I wished her luck with Mandie, hung up, plugged the directions into the phone, and got back on the road.

IN LESS THAN AN hour I was sitting in the parking lot of a small complex of up-and-down white stucco units studded with exposed wood beams off Brice Road out east. I knocked on Gretchen's door. I waited a full minute and was about to try again when it opened. A woman who looked to be about my mother's age sized me up for the debt collector, scam artist, or serial rapist she had me pegged for. A strong smell of smoke was coming from the kitchen.

"Everything OK?"

"Just burned some sausage. Did you need something?"

"I'm sorry to bother you," I said. "I'm looking for Gretchen Osborne. I had this down for her address."

"Osborne?"

"That's right."

"No one here by that name." She moved to shut the door.

"May I ask how long you've lived here?"

"Why?"

"It might help me figure out where she is, and if she's OK. It's important I find her."

"You her boyfriend?"

"Just someone concerned about her."

"Like I haven't heard that one before."

"Please."

"Please yourself. What's this about?"

I pulled out a card and my license and showed both to her. Something like a grin replaced the scowl of suspicion. "I used to love *The Rockford Files*," she said. "Now that was a show."

"How I miss the seventies," I said, nodding in agreement. I tried peering inside. The apartment air was hazy from the burned sausage smoke. "You were saying . . . ?"

"I've been here three weeks. Was living with my daughter in Pataskala after my husband died. Then they had a baby and told me I had to move out. Just up and move. What do you think of that?"

"Sounds like one for Miss Manners. You didn't meet Gretchen, before you moved in?"

She shook her head. I asked if the rental office was nearby. She pointed to a building across the parking lot. Then she asked if I wanted to come in for a cup of coffee. She said I favored James Garner. I thanked her and said I heard that all the time and maybe some other day. At that she shut her door sort of hard. I walked over to the office and stepped inside. I was greeted by Bruce Springsteen's live version of "Santa Claus Is Coming to Town" from an overhead speaker. It felt like the nine thousandth time I'd heard it since Thanksgiving. I was sick of it after the first two. A young woman with impressively long fake eyelashes and an even more impressive rock on her left hand looked up from a desk.

"Help you?"

I took out a card and handed it to her. "A woman named Gretchen Osborne was living at 167 until recently. I'm trying to find her. I was wondering if she left a forwarding address. I'd appreciate any help you can give me."

"You're a private investigator?"

"That's right." I wondered if she'd even been born before *The Rockford Files* went off the air.

"Why are you looking for her?"

"She's helping me with a case."

"What kind of case?"

I repeated the missing person spiel for the umpteenth-and-a-half time.

"Don't you have her number? I mean, if she was helping you and all?"

"She's not answering her phone."

"So, like, that's not my problem?"

I tried another tack. "The thing is, I'm worried about her. That she's not answering because something's wrong.

Something related to the woman she was trying to help. That's why I'm wondering if you might know where she is, is all. It's important."

"We're not authorized to give out that kind of information."

"I figured that. I'm not asking for personal details or anything . . . Chrissy?" I said, picking up her business card from the desk. I thought of something. I said, "I can read off her cell number, if you want. See if it matches what you have on file. If it would make you comfortable that I really know her."

She hesitated a moment, and I seized the opportunity to scroll through my recently called numbers. I found Gretchen's and recited it. "So?" I said, when I finished. "How about it?"

She sighed. She played with her computer for a minute. I listened to Bruce finish up and after a blissful moment of silence winced at the opening notes of Paul McCartney's "Wonderful Christmastime." I tuned it out by estimating the candlepower of Chrissy's engagement ring.

"No forwarding address," she said curtly, releasing her mouse and looking first at me and then the door.

"Any idea why she left?"

"I wouldn't be able to say."

"Pretty please?"

"I said no."

"Pretty please and I won't tell the city code enforcement officer there's no working smoke alarms here?"

"What are you talking about?"

I explained about the burned sausage in Gretchen's old apartment. She frowned, looked at her computer, and said, "Gretchen violated her lease. Satisfied?"

"Drugs?"

"No," she said, startled. "Nothing like that."

"It's what I figured. You see a lot of that in a place like this. It looks 'fancy,' but that doesn't stop people from doing stuff they shouldn't. I hope it doesn't get around this is that kind of apartment complex. That plus the smoke alarms."

"It *wasn't* drugs. She had someone else living there. Off the lease. It's not allowed."

"Someone else? Who?"

"I'm not at liberty—"

"Hang on," I said. I pulled out my phone again and flipped through the photos until I found the one I was looking for. I touched the screen to enlarge it and showed her the picture. "Is this the person who was living with Gretchen?"

Reluctantly, she examined the photo. She did her best to disguise her reaction, but it was hard to miss the glint of recognition in her eyes.

"That's her," she said after a moment. "That's really all I can tell you. I'm sorry. Gretchen knew the rules."

It was what I had suspected as soon as she'd told me why Gretchen had to leave. The photo I'd shown her, the one she recognized, was the Reardoor.com picture of Jessica I'd gotten from Bill Byrnes.

42

"HOW'D YOU FIND OUT ABOUT HER?" I SAID to Chrissy. "Did somebody turn her in?"

"Not exactly."

"What's that supposed to mean?"

"Some guy, OK? He came by the office looking for her? He already knew where she lived, but wondered if I had a number for her. I didn't give it to him," she added quickly.

"Did he say what he wanted?"

"Said he had something for Gretchen's sister. I told him it was just Gretchen there, and he said he didn't think so."

"What happened then?"

"I didn't really believe the guy's story, but we're strict about lease violations like that? So I hung around a little longer that day, and when I saw Gretchen pull in me and Luis went over there. He's our maintenance supervisor. We knocked on the door and when Gretchen opened it I told her about the guy and looking for her sister and asked if it was true. She denied it at first. We asked if we could look around. She didn't want to let us but we told her she had to. We found that girl upstairs. She was staying in Gretchen's bedroom. They had an air mattress set up on the floor."

"How did she look?"

"Look?"

"The girl. Her name's Jessica. Was she OK?"

"She didn't look, you know, great. I didn't get too near, in case she was contagious with something?" She wrinkled her nose. I fought the temptation to tweak it like a nasty great-aunt. "I told Gretchen she couldn't have her there. The funny thing was, she didn't argue or anything. She just nodded. And that's it. The next day she was gone."

"The guy who came by. Did you get his name?"

"No."

I described someone I had in mind. She listened thoughtfully. "Yeah. That sounds like him."

"Has he been back since?"

"A couple days later? I could tell he was mad when I explained Gretchen left. He was like you—did she leave a forwarding address and stuff?"

"Do you remember what day that was? The day Gretchen left?"

"Sometime last month."

"Can you check? It's the last thing I'll ask."

She rolled her eyes as if she was all, like, heard that one before. But after a moment she went back to her computer. She tap-tapped her paste ruby-red nails on the keyboard and rolled the mouse around a couple of times.

"November 25. It was a Tuesday, right before Thanksgiving."

Almost two weeks before the story Gretchen spun about Jessica's calls stopping abruptly. I saw now it must have been a ruse. To put me off the trail; make me think Jessica was dead. But why? Why would Gretchen be protecting Jessica? To keep her from becoming the Pleasure Prince's latest victim? To hide her from the other man hunting her? Or some other reason I hadn't yet gleaned?

"Is that it?" Chrissy interrupted. "I really need to get back to work."

"I can tell," I said, looking around the empty office. "You seem swamped."

"I'm busier than I look."

"You're going to be a lot busier if you don't deal with the smoke alarms."

43

I HEADED BACK TOWARD DOWNTOWN. IT was nearly dark and I still had one stop left. One more address I had Bonnie look up for me. I got on the 270 outer belt and took it to 670, on my way to Grandview on the near west side. As the highway veered to the right I glanced at Columbus's small skyline, silhouetted against the setting sun like a construction paper cutout. Many lights were still on in the office towers that overlooked the tangle of interstates to the east and the confluence of the Scioto and Olentangy rivers to the west. I wondered how many men working in those offices had visited Saunders & Sons or its poorer—or richer—relations around town. Had ever engaged a "seventy-niner," as Gretchen called herself. Had maybe even—I paused the thought, then forced myself to continue—paid Theresa or someone just like her. Or, closer to home, had sought out the GFE—the Girlfriend Experience—with someone not their wife. To clear my head I punched in the number for Larry Schwartzbaum as traffic eased. To my surprise, he answered after the first ring.

"Burning the 5:30 p.m. oil, I see," I said.

"Yeah. Thanks to you."

"Me?"

"You and the Pleasure Prince, whose nickname the whole city knows now. Talk about our balls getting squeezed. Even my rabbi wants to know what the heck's going on. Meanwhile I took five new missing person reports in the past two days. It's depressing how many people come to the sudden realization their loved one is gone months after last seeing them. But God help us if their cat's overdue by half an hour."

"Why I'm a dog person. Listen, if it helps any." I told him about Gretchen and Lilyhaven and the apartment complex.

"So Gretchen's been lying the whole time?" Schwartzbaum said.

"Apparently."

"That's just great. Though at least we know Jessica's alive. That's good for you, right?"

"I guess. But if she was hiding from Bronte Patterson, it means she's vulnerable again."

"I see your point there."

"So hopefully Copeland will track him down before he finds Jessica."

"Copeland?"

I explained about the calling card Patterson left me the night at my house and the vice sergeant's promise to find him.

"There a problem?" I said, when Schwartzbaum didn't respond.

"Not exactly. But Copeland's on leave, is the thing."

"On leave? Since when? I talked to him just the other day."

"Since just the other day plus an hour or two."

"How come?"

"Can't say."

"Really? After all the stuff I've told you?"

"I'm sorry."

"Thanks a lot. I've half a mind to put my policeman's ball tickets on eBay."

That got me nothing. There was a long pause on the line. So long that I finally had to ask him if he was still there.

"I'll talk to you later, Andy," he said.

"Larry—" I said. But he'd hung up. And I didn't have time to call him back to ask the million questions crowding into my brain, starting with: why was the vice sergeant on leave not long after he'd promised to hunt down Bronte Patterson?

I didn't have time because I'd arrived at my last destination of the night.

JOHN BLANCHETT LIVED IN a well-kept, nicely landscaped one-story cottage on Mulford Road off Grandview Avenue. Pale lavender clapboard, broad front porch, polished and lacquered brass numbers for the street address. I wasn't sure where top congressional aides were supposed to live, but this seemed right on the money.

"Andy?" he said, a look of surprise on his face as he opened the door.

"Sorry to interrupt. There's been a development in Jessica Byrnes's case. Could I come in?"

"Of course, of course." He stepped aside and let me through. The smell of something warm and delicious drifted in from the kitchen. The TV was turned to the news, and a glass of red wine sat on a coffee table in front of a pale blue couch. The exposed wood floor gleamed like the parquet right before the jump ball of a big basketball game. He had a real fire going in the tiled fireplace. I half expected to see Darlene Bardwell there, her knees tucked under her on the couch, wine glass in hand. But Blanchett was alone.

"Get you anything?" he said. "Wine? A beer?"

"No thanks." I sat down in a leather recliner. I waited for him to sit back on the couch. He muted the TV. "So what's up?" he said.

"What's up is that you tracked Jessica to an apartment complex off Brice Road late last month." I gave him the address. "More to the point, you tracked her caseworker down, who walked away from the place the next day with Jessica before you could do anything about it. You've also been to Mount Alexandria talking to

Jessica's mom and her late stepfather, and then three days ago you were at the Rest EZ Motel, looking for her. Don't waste energy denying it," I added, seeing him about to interrupt. "I've talked to the people at Car Rite Rental. I know it was you. If I was a betting man I'd wager you had a mustache within the past three months that's since gone down the drain. What I want to know is why."

He drew his left knee up and laced his fingers over it. Then he put his knee down and crossed his legs instead and looked at the TV. Suzanne Gregory was doing a stand-up in front of police headquarters.

He said, "I'm sorry, Andy. I should have told you. I've gotten a little carried away with this case. I was really hoping I could find Jessica. For her brother's sake." He paused, not meeting my eyes. "And for the congresswoman's."

"Why? Beyond the obvious, I mean."

"Listen. I know you're skeptical about our involvement. And what I'm about to tell you isn't going to help matters any. You were right about the bill regulating the online sites. It's making an uphill climb look like a walk in the park. Internet sites that aid the trafficking of women have lobbyists too. Surprisingly powerful ones. But we need to get that legislation enacted."

"For the sake of the women."

"There's no need to be sarcastic. But you're right. It would also be a nice feather in Darlene's cap as she launches her Senate run."

Another puzzle piece clicked into place as I recalled the name of her expected opponent. The one with some baggage. A former Democratic state auditor with a golden fundraising touch, but also saddled with a messy divorce because of an affair with a much younger woman. An affair that unearthed youthful indiscretions involving escorts hired for parties at his fraternity thirty-odd years earlier, though he insisted he didn't, in his words, "go all the way." To date, polling had shown him neutral to vulnerable on the allegations. I told Blanchett what I was thinking.

"You've hit it exactly. It's crass, but it's politics. Finding Jessica—*rescuing* Jessica—is important to us because of the campaign. Very important. And because of that, it's possible I went too far."

"Possible?"

"I'm as worried about her as you are," he said, defensiveness creeping into his voice. "I just went about it the wrong way."

"The wrong way? You lied to people." I ticked the names off on my fingers. "Parole officer. Minister. Cop? That last one's a crime, by the way."

"I know, I know. I just couldn't afford to be identified. I wasn't thinking."

"You didn't happen to put a bullet in Jimmy Wooding while you were at it, did you? Get frustrated after a double 7 and 7 failed to do the job?"

"No! Don't be ridiculous. I would never—"

"Because that's illegal too, in case you were wondering. Shooting someone, I mean."

"I said—"

"OK, OK. I believe you, I think. But you realize that by tracking Gretchen down you forced her to go underground? That you probably put both her and Jessica in more danger?"

"I know that now. It wasn't what I intended. You can see that, can't you?"

"I can't see much of anything with this case right now, to be honest. Speaking of which—are you and the congresswoman having an affair?"

"What?"

"Yes or no?"

"No," he said, with what sounded like genuine indignation. "Absolutely not." He was looking right at me, with no attempt to avert his gaze. "Why would you ask me that? Darlene and Barry are perfectly happy."

"Plenty of happy spouses have affairs."

"I guess you'd know that, in your line of work."

"I'm not sure you're in a position to sling mud."

"I'm sorry. I shouldn't have said that. But you're wrong about them. They love each other very much."

I looked at him closely. I'd heard more sincere descriptions of love in hearings for domestic violence protective orders. But his expression gave nothing away.

I said, "I'm glad to hear that. I'm sorry if I falsely accused you."

"It's OK," he said, looking back at the TV. "It's an occupational hazard. Unmarried male head of her Columbus office, not gay, and her in town by herself frequently. You're not the first to suggest it."

I almost felt sorry for him. I said, "So that's it, then? You were hunting Jessica for her own sake but also naked political gain?"

"Sure. If you put it that way."

"More importantly, your hunt's over?"

"Yes."

"Promise? Because we have to start working together. To try to find her before it's too late. For no other reason."

"I said yes."

"Pinky promise?"

"Maybe it's time for you to go," Blanchett said. "My dinner's almost ready."

44

I STAYED IN THAT NIGHT. ANNE SAID SHE was busy, engrossed in final edits of the book she was writing. No boyfriends need apply. Theresa was still staying at Roy and Lucy's. My dad's afternoon nap was turning into bedtime, according to my mom. I cooked up pasta and a Bahama Mama sausage from Schmidt's and sat on the couch with dinner and a Black Label and read *Ohio Colossus* for a couple of hours until I started to nod off. I checked my e-mail a last time and saw that Bonnie had sent me something.

Here's the screen shots of my conversation with Mandie Smith, she wrote. She didn't want to talk on the phone. Not sure if it's helpful.

Thanks, I wrote back.

Hi. Is this a good time? Bonnie had typed, starting off the dialogue.

Sure.

I skimmed a few comments about roller derby. They went over how Mandie knew Jessica. They'd been friends in high school. They hung out a few times, usually at Mandie's house. Bonnie asked her if that was because of Jessica's stepdad.

What do you mean?

My boss, Andy? He said he was abusing her. That that's why she left?

IDK about that, Mandie said. That's horrible if it's true.

Yeah.

It was her mom that was the real problem.

Her mom?

Always yelling at her.

Like what?

Telling her she was fat. She was a slut. She was stupid. It made Jessica cry. It was really bad.

☹ ☹ ☹

Yeah.

How about her stepdad? Did he yell?

Not really. He was just always drunk, when I was there. He sat on the couch while her mom yelled at Jessica.

So that's why she left? Went to live with that family?

I guess. I didn't talk to her much after that. She got really distant. Kind of shrunk up, you know?

Yeah. And you know what happened to her, at that place?

I saw the article you sent me. That's really bad. It makes it even worse.

With what I guessed was more than a little help from Elliot Mullan, the *Mount Alexandria News* had quickly published some of the details about the Fischers' town house.

What do you mean? Bonnie wrote to Mandie.

I mean her mom was so mean to her, but it was her stepdad who told her to go over there?

Don't follow.

I guess they were having money problems. The stepdad knew that guy. Jessica told me the guy said he'd give her parents $500 if they brought her over there to take care of the dogs.

And they believed him? About the dogs?

Maybe. At first.

At first?

I saw her one day after school. She was waiting for that guy to pick her up. Mr. Fischer. I asked her how it was going. She didn't want to talk. I asked her if she wanted to go out sometime, get something to eat. She said she didn't have any money. I asked her about the dog walking and she just laughed it off. Said all that went to her Mr. Fischer and her stepdad.

All what?

The money she made. That Fischer guy gave money to her stepdad every month. I mean, how could he have not known what was going on over there? You don't make that kind of money walking dogs. Not in Mount Alex.

So it was like some kind of reward for her stepdad sending her there?

I guess, Mandie said. Or money for him to keep his mouth shut.

MAYBE IT'S THE MIDWESTERNER IN ME, BUT
mild temperatures after Thanksgiving make me anxious. Fifty
degrees on a December afternoon is like weather insomnia: it's
bedtime for the world, but it can't shut its eyes. Over the past
couple of weeks, the uneasiness I'd felt in my bones at the un-
seasonable weather compounded my growing fears about Jessica
and the men hunting her. And so it was with relief that I listened
the morning of Christmas Eve as blustery winds signaled a cold
front's arrival and the thermometer finally dipped below thirty-
three degrees.

I called Mullan at home first thing. The Mount Alexandria
detective was remarkably even-tempered for a guy interrupted on
the day before Christmas. I imagined him wrapping rectangular
boxes for grandchildren with the paper creases sharp as a salute.
Before I could explain why I was calling, he told me Lindsay's
real name was Sue. That a friend of a friend of the Fischers knew
she was unhappy at home and suggested she could stay there a
while. That the Fischers loaned her a thousand dollars and then
afterward told her the terms of the loan and said they'd show

photos around if she didn't cooperate. When Mullan was done I told him about Mandie Smith. He gave me his e-mail address and I forwarded him the copy of Bonnie's Facebook conversation. If Mandie was right, Garrett Fischer had kept Jimmy Wooding floating in 7 and 7s, and probably a lot more, in exchange for silence about the real goings-on at the town house. My visit to Fischer had raised suspicions about whether Wooding was keeping his end of the bargain. One of them, Garrett or his wife, had taken steps to correct the situation.

So my dad was right. I hadn't killed Wooding. But I was indirectly responsible for his death.

IT WAS SNOWING HARD by the time I left Best Buy early that afternoon with an Xbox I'd found on sale and a couple of games, although that did little to ease the pain of the purchase on my nearly maxed-out credit card. I tried not to think about the debt as I pushed the shopping cart toward my van, the snow stinging my face as the wind whipped up drifts in the parking lot. I'd had to do it. I'd have both boys the next afternoon, and I couldn't afford to break one more promise to them. Late in the day I spent an awkward few minutes at Anne's parents in Grove City dropping off presents for her and Amelia. Anne's mother asked if I couldn't stay for dinner and I said I had another obligation, which was technically true, depending on what you thought of takeout Chinese and a couple Black Labels in front of *It's a Wonderful Life*.

Around ten-thirty that night I reluctantly left home. I'd promised Roy I'd be at Zion for the late service, his first Christmas there as pastor. I respect his calling. I also respect the oyster stew and mulled wine Lucy promised me afterward. Five or six inches of snow covered the sidewalk and the plantings around the church as I got out of the van. I stomped my shoes on the mat just inside the front door, took a program from a man who bore a passing resemblance to Frank Capra, and walked into the sanctuary. It smelled of incense and fir trees and wax. An organ wheezed out the notes of "O Little Town of Bethlehem." I took a seat near the back, next to an old man with thick, yellow hair and three days of stubble. A minute later, Theresa slid in beside me and next to her, Deborah, the girl from the streets who'd tipped us to Saunders & Sons vacuum repair shop. Theresa leaned across me and greeted the man.

The organ stopped and Roy got up from a seat by the altar and stood at the front of the sanctuary and gave an opening prayer. We followed along in the program. The organ started into "O Come All Ye Faithful" as the small choir walked up the aisle. Theresa handed me a red hymnal with a frayed cover pulling loose from its binding. I kept my voice low, not trusting my singing abilities outside of the shower. Theresa couldn't carry a tune much better than me. Deborah wasn't much of a talker, but her voice was surprisingly sweet.

Bible readings followed the singing. Theresa jabbed me twice to keep me from nodding off. We stood up again and sang something else. Roy stepped into the aisle and read a Gospel story about angels and swaddling clothes. When he was done he returned to the pulpit, greeted the congregation, and began his sermon. I tried to concentrate, but my eyes started to glaze over and I was beginning to nod again. "Wake up," Theresa hissed. I sat up straighter, heard Roy speak the words "and they were filled with fear," and felt my phone buzzing. I pulled it out and saw I had an incoming call. It was Gretchen Osborne.

46

I SHOWED THE SCREEN TO THERESA, STOOD up, squeezed past her and Deborah, made it into the center aisle and walked to the back of the church. I answered just before it went to voice mail.

"It's Gretchen," she said. Her voice sounded small and it echoed, as if she were alone in an empty auditorium.

"Where are you? Are you OK?"

"I need help. Jessica's gone."

"Gone?"

"Taken. Kidnapped." Her voice even smaller now, starting to quaver.

"What happened?"

"Bronte Patterson. He was here. I don't know how he found us. I swear I don't. He had a gun. He grabbed her as soon as I opened the door. Told her he'd come back and kill me if she made a sound. Told me he'd shoot her if I called the police."

"Where are you?"

She gave me the address. It was an apartment off Livingston. Not a great part of town. The part where you go when you've been flushed out of your last, best hiding place by a congress-woman's relentless aide.

"Any idea where he was taking her?"

"No."

"You have to tell the police. It doesn't matter what he said." I didn't voice the obvious; it might be too late to help her either way.

"I can't. I was hiding her. You know what's been going on. I got your messages."

"Hiding Jessica may not have been the smartest idea in the world. But it wasn't illegal. And we're beyond secrets now. Hang up and call 911 and I'll be there as soon as I can."

I disconnected the call and walked outside. Almost an inch more had accumulated in the few minutes we'd been in the church. The windshield on my van was already covered. Some-one called my name. I turned and saw Theresa.

"What's going on?"

When I was done explaining, she said, "And you're just going over there? Without me?"

"It's Christmas Eve. I didn't want to—"

"Get weighed down?"

"No—"

"I'm fine, if that's what you're worried about."

"That's what I'm worried about."

"Lightning ain't going to strike twice, QB."

"If you say so."

"But why're we going to Gretchen's?"

"To see if she's OK."

"Didn't you just talk to her?"

"Sure, but—"

"What about Jessica? Ain't it her we're looking for?"

"We don't know where she is."

"She's with Bronte. She just told you that."

"We don't know where Bronte is. That's the whole problem." I thought of Marc Copeland, the vice sergeant, and his mysteri-ous leave. "He moves around. No permanent address."

"Hang on," Theresa said.

She disappeared back into the church. I waited only a couple of moments before following her inside. It wasn't a blizzard yet, but it was close. In the outer vestibule, Theresa was talking to Deborah. Through a window on one of the swinging doors leading into the church I could see Roy in the pulpit, gesturing as he spoke.

"You sure?" Theresa said. Deborah nodded, defiant.

"Phone?" Theresa said to me. I nodded. "Plug this in."

"What is it?"

"It's where Patterson's been staying."

I looked at Deborah. "She gave us the address? I thought she was scared of him."

"She is scared of him. Terrified. But she's more scared about Jessica."

I thought about Patterson, boasting about how he was untouchable. About his reputation for hurting people. About the real hurt he put on me.

"Thank you," I said to Deborah. To Theresa, I said, "She should stay here. We don't know what we're going to find."

"Lucy's gonna take care of her," Theresa said. She reached out, hugged Deborah, and gently pushed her back inside the sanctuary, where Roy's wife was waiting.

"Let's go," Theresa said, turning around. "We ain't got all night."

THE ADDRESS WAS OFF Kelton north of East Main. Not far from corners that Jessica had worked. As had Lisa Washington. As we got close an SUV raced by, almost hitting us, before turning off into an alley in the next block. It left the only tire tracks on the narrow, snow-covered street.

"Idiot," I said. I drove past a red-brick house corresponding to the address Deborah gave us. I had to park three houses down. I got out, shouldered my Louisville Slugger, and jogged along the sidewalk, kicking up small rooster tails of white powder, Theresa right behind me. The street glowed orange from the lights reflecting off the falling snow. I saw a single light on inside, in the living room. I went up to the porch and tried the door. Locked. "What if this is another trap?" I whispered to Theresa.

"Then we're probably fucked."

"And a Merry Christmas to you, too."

We went around to the side. A car was parked back there, a nondescript four-door sedan, nothing fancy, but I noticed right away it had a limited amount of snow on the windows and top. It hadn't been sitting there for long. Which was why I recognized it. I'd seen it a couple weeks back on East Main, suspecting the driver was tailing us. A driver that turned out to be Marc Copeland. I noticed something else. Another car had been parked behind it recently, the tire tracks still faintly visible even as the snow fell. I thought of the SUV speeding past us in the street. I thought about running back to the van and giving chase. Then I looked at the side door and turned and nudged Theresa. The jamb was splintered. The door opened easily.

We found Copeland in the living room, crumpled on the floor like a piece of furniture dropped off the end of a truck. We rushed to him. Blood was everywhere. He'd been shot in the side. A handgun lay beside him. His lids fluttered but his eyes stayed open.

"Who did this?" I said.

He shook his head.

"Was it Bronte Patterson?"

He shut his eyes and opened them again.

"Where's Jessica?"

Lips moving now but no words. I repeated the question and leaned in, trying to hear. He shook his head again.

I took out my phone. I showed him the keypad. I dialed 911. When an operator answered I explained where we were. I said an officer was down and gave her Copeland's name. I said the scene was secure, that there was no reason for the squad to wait for responding officers to go first. I hung up before she could ask me my name.

"Help's on its way," I said. I looked around the room. The window to the right of the fireplace was shattered.

"You got a shot off, at Patterson, didn't you?" I said.

His eyes shut and opened again.

"Is that why he took off?"

Copeland's eyes shut and I wondered if that was it, if even the effort of contemplating my questions expended the last bit of energy before death took him. Then he opened his eyes and looked at me.

"Bronte," he said.

"What?"

"Bronte took her."

"What happened?"

He spoke in hoarse fragments, pausing between each statement. "I found out where she was. Told him to go get her. Told him I'd meet him here. He came in without her. Shot me. Stupid. But at least I—"

"You told Bronte to get her?"

"Stupid," he repeated.

"How did you know where she was?"

"I'm sorry. Didn't mean to."

"Didn't mean to what?"

"Too deep. Sorry." His voice was fading, as if he were walking downhill, away from us, as he talked.

"Hang on, Marc." I heard a siren in the distance. "What was too deep?"

Bronte's mocking words in my house came back to me. His fearlessness when it came to being found. Copeland's repeated yet fruitless promises that he'd locate the pimp.

"Were you protecting Bronte?" I said.

He might have nodded, but it was hard to tell. A red bubble formed at the edge of his mouth.

"They're almost here. It's going to be OK."

Still nothing.

"How did you know where she was? Where Gretchen was?"

"Guy. Called me."

I heard a sound. I looked up and saw flashing lights in the street. A moment later someone was pounding at the front door.

"Who?"

"Guy," he said.

Copeland's eyes closed and then opened again. But the light in them was starting to dim, like taillights smudged by exhaust. I ran to the door and opened it. Two blue-uniformed paramedics rushed in. We stepped outside. I was back on my phone trying to reach Larry Schwartzbaum when Theresa tugged at my sleeve.

"The car that nearly hit us. That must have been Bronte, taking Jessica out of here. After Copeland returned fire. It had to have been. We can follow him."

"Follow him? Where? He's long gone."

"Follow his tracks. There's no cars right now. It's snowing too hard and everyone's inside the churches. But that ain't going to last forever, because those churches are going to let out soon and then we won't be able to find shit."

I looked inside the house, where the paramedics were kneeling over Copeland. I listened to the sound of oncoming sirens. Once cops got here we'd have no chance of leaving. There was a good possibility we'd be in handcuffs and in jail just in time for Christmas. No amount of explanations would suffice with a wounded police officer on the floor, on leave or not. Dirty or not. And then it would be much too late for Jessica, wherever Bronte had taken her.

I was trying to decide what to do when a sound interrupted me. I looked up the street. A man was running down the sidewalk in our direction. I did a double take. It was someone we'd seen before. Someone who hadn't seemed capable of breaking into a slow trot, let alone sprinting like that through the snow. The shopping-cart bum. The conspiracy theorist. He was gesturing at us and shouting something. I took Theresa's hand and pulled her off the porch and onto the snow-covered walk.

"Stop!" I heard him yell. "Police."

I traded glances with Theresa. Another couple of moments and he'd be on us. "Let's get out of here," I said, and started running.

"Stop!" he yelled, and then I heard him swear. I turned and saw he'd slipped and fallen on the icy walk. As soon as I saw him raise his head I figured he was OK and we started running again. We dashed past the ambulance blocking the street and through the snow to my van. Once inside I drove farther north until the next side street. Away from the oncoming sirens. I turned right and almost immediately braked, cursing as the van started to slide, and just made the turn into the alley to follow the still-fresh tracks. I drove down to the next intersecting alley and turned left, seeing the tracks that Patterson's SUV made. We barreled east in pursuit. We went three blocks before the tracks turned onto a side street and went down to Main. From there it didn't take a professional tracker to figure out where he'd gone. We'd emerged right by the abandoned grain silos. The silos next to the street where Leonard Lortz said he'd taken Jessica the night he paid her for a blowjob. We followed the tracks to the side of the fenced-in property and pulled up beside a dark SUV that had jumped the curb and was parked half on the street and half on the snow-covered grass. The SUV that had nearly sideswiped us earlier. I put on my brights to illuminate the vehicle. There was no one inside. We got out. I looked around, wary. Even though the access street was still well-lit, between the heavy snow, the time of night, and the distance from Main Street, it felt far away from anything, including anyone who might stop to see if we needed help. Bat in one hand, flashlight in another, I approached the car, Theresa right behind me. At the same moment we both pointed to the footprints in the snow leading toward the fence surrounding the back of the silos. The tracks were fresh and easy to follow. I kneeled to examine them. I reached out and touched something dark smudged into the compacted snow left by the smaller of the two sets of shoeprints. I lifted my finger to examine it. The tracks were indeed fresh, as fresh as the icy-red crystals melting on my skin.

47

WE FOLLOWED THE SHOEPRINTS ACROSS A
short expanse of snow to the chain-link fence surrounding the
property. The trail continued on the other side. But how? It was
Theresa who spied the loose flap of mesh at the bottom corner
of a pole, reached down, and pulled it back to reveal a gap big
enough to slide a coffin through. A thought flicked in and out of
my mind, like heat lightning on a late summer afternoon. Patterson couldn't have made that opening just now. He wouldn't
have had time. Had he planned this all along? Or—. But Theresa
interrupted me. She was pointing with urgency across the field of
snow to the silos.

We hunched over, squeezed through the fence, and started
tracking again. The prints, already filling with snow in the heavy
storm, led to a small, white, corrugated metal shack at the corner
of the silos a few dozen yards away. We approached carefully. I
brought out the flashlight and shone it in front of us. It illumi-
nated a closed door two steps down, streaked with rust. I stepped
down, reached out, turned the knob, and pulled. Nothing. I
tried again. I flashed back to the house on the east side and the

basement door that hadn't given. I tried a third time, and a fourth, and then started yelling in frustration—we were so close!—pulling on the knob as hard as I could, before staggering back and half falling as it wrenched open and I lost my balance. I heard Theresa swear. I'd nearly knocked her over.

Through the doorway, we heard a woman scream.

I stood up and used the flashlight to reveal a set of descending stairs leading to an open doorway. I walked down a couple of steps before pausing.

"Jessica!" I yelled.

I took a few more steps down. I hesitated again. Despite how far we'd come, how close we were to rescuing Jessica, I didn't want to go through that door. Not yet. Patterson had a gun and nothing to lose. Any doubts I had about that fact had evaporated at the sight of Copeland's bleeding body on the floor of the house we'd just been inside. Patterson had shot a cop. All bets were off now. One decent shot at us and everything we'd worked for was over.

"Let's go," Theresa hissed.

"Wait."

Focus, Andy, focus.

Why repeat history, but why bank on second chances either? I'd already used up enough for a lifetime. Why gamble on somebody else's life?

Focus . . .

"We don't have time."

"Hold on," I said, listening.

"He's going to get—"

Jessica screamed again.

"*Now,*" I said, charging down the stairs and through the door.

48

WE WERE IN A TUNNEL LIKE SOMETHING OUT
of a submarine movie. Ahead of us a set of metal steps rose to a
metal walkway. I listened for a moment, hearing a faint clanking
sound ahead. The sound of people running. I dashed up the steps,
guiding my way with the flashlight in my left hand. The walkway
disappeared into the darkness, running past metal pipes the size of
old furnace ducts and massive concrete pillars and circular cranks
that opened or shut some type of valves. I realized we were in the
heart of the complex, on a path directly through and under the
silos. Below us, light reflected in water pooled four or five feet
down. Up ahead, I caught a glimpse of a man's retreating back.

"Let her go, Bronte," I called, as I pounded down the walkway. I heard a shout in response and stopped. I yelled again. This
time I heard his reply.

"I'll shoot. Go back."

"Hurting her will only make this worse. We'll help you figure
things out. But not like this."

A flash of light, a boom, a metallic clanging just above my
head. He hadn't been kidding. I was trapped, with nowhere to

turn. But it was hard to see in the tunnel and he was under pressure himself. He was no longer the hunter. Turning to be sure Theresa was all right, I switched off my flashlight, jammed it into my pocket, grabbed the metal railing, and started feeling my way forward. Theresa crept behind me.

"I got your back, QB," she said.

"Thank God somebody does."

As we advanced I realized it wasn't completely dark down here. A gray light permeated the air. I saw the silhouette of Patterson and a glimpse of Jessica in front of him as they walked. I found I could see another entryway in the distance. There were two ways in and out. Like a good rat hole. I called out again, telling Patterson to stop.

"We can figure this out."

"Not gonna happen."

"You forgetting what you told me? 'Ain't nothing can't be renegotiated.'" I stopped, trying to think of something else to say. Theresa whispered in my ear.

"Copeland," I said, taking her cue, my voice echoing in the enclosed space. "You can give them Marc Copeland. He's alive. He's going to make it."

"Bullshit."

"I'm telling the truth. We called the paramedics. I was there when they were treating him. I know he was protecting you. Think how much you can tell the police."

"Like they gonna listen."

"Let her go and find out."

"Think I'm stupid?"

"Think you're smart enough to know when to cut your losses." I prayed I was right.

Things got quiet again except for the lapping of water against the concrete, as if we were walking over a creek in a cave.

"Just give me Jessica, then," I said. "Let her go and you keep going. I can see there's an exit. You go one way, I'll go the other."

They were almost at the end of the walkway. I could see the other door clearly now. For a second I thought I saw a shadow pass in front of it: the swirl of snow outside playing with the light. Or was it someone come to help us? Had the police, with the assistance of Gretchen, and maybe Copeland, figured out where we were? Deciding to risk it, I turned on the flashlight. Patterson was just a couple of dozen yards head of me, glaring. He blinked with the ferocity of a predator trapped with nowhere to go. I saw the gun in his hand. He moved his other hand and I braced, and with a sudden, savage move he pulled Jessica into view and pushed her onto the walkway. She screamed and for a minute I thought she was going to lose her balance and fall into the cold water below. Instead she got to her knees with a low whimper, looked at me, and started to crawl in our direction like the survivor of a car wreck scrabbling to get to safety. She was smaller than I'd imagined, and thinner, and more exhausted looking, if that were possible. She was wearing a gray sweatshirt and sweatpants and sneakers without socks. No coat. Blood streaked her face and one of her eyes was blackened. But it was her, unquestionably. And what struck me just then was how much more she looked like the picture from high school than the booty shot from Reardoor.com.

As she crawled, Patterson backed away, toward the far entrance. For a full count of ten I thought we were in the clear. Jessica was almost to us. Then I saw Patterson raise his hand and point the gun toward her.

"Bitch," he said, extending his arm.

"No!" I cried. I lunged forward, landing on top of her, feeling her grunt as the air went out of her body, so tiny compared to mine. My bat went clattering away, falling into the water with an ominous splash. The walkway was slippery and I felt our bodies slide and I grabbed a railing just before we too went off the edge. I looked up and caught Patterson's eyes in the dim light and saw the gun and waited for the explosion and the stink of cordite. Instead I heard Theresa scream and Jessica moan and Patterson make an odd coughing sound, as if a swallow of water had gone down the wrong pipe. He fell backward out of sight, pulled by some invisible force. I stood, lifted up Jessica, and dragged her back down the walkway.

As Theresa wrapped her arms around Jessica I looked ahead, trying to see Patterson. I couldn't find him or hear anything in the gray light. I called his name. I started to take a step forward when a guttural cry stopped me in my tracks. I froze. The cry became a choking sound that went on for several more seconds before ending abruptly, like a phone thrown out a car window mid-argument.

"Bronte?" I said and inched ahead. I stopped at another sound. But not of someone in pain. Of someone singing.

"In and out, twist and shout, you know that's how it is."

The notes of the clear tenor voice hung in the air of the tunnel like one of the soloists in Roy's cold, stone church.

"Feel the pain, feel the hurt, feel that naughty pinch."

I backed up, a primal fear flooding my guts like ice water, overriding any obligation to help Patterson. I flashed back to the night in the abandoned house looking for Theresa. The shock of pain as Lortz had attacked me from behind. The odd cough I'd emitted, as if a swallow of water—

"Love the touch, love the push, of the good-time Pleasure Prince."

The singing stopped and time stood still and I relaxed just long enough to retrieve my flashlight and probe at the shadows. In the next second I yelled in shock as Patterson's body dropped onto the walkway, hitting the metal with a wet smack like a side of beef cut in one motion from a hook. A cord hung loosely around his neck. A moment later, Leonard Lortz stepped into view, both hands around Patterson's gun.

49

"RUN," I SAID.

Theresa said something I couldn't make out. I kept my eyes glued on Lortz's face, willing myself not to break eye contact. Of all the gin joints in all the towns in all the world. Of all the places Patterson could have taken Jessica to finish her off. To hurt her the way he hurt girls who disobeyed him. How had Theresa put it? Who'd gotten out of pocket with him. We'd stumbled into Lortz's own rat hole. His real hole; the house where he'd captured Theresa either a backup or a decoy. This place was perfect: so close to the women he hunted. I kept looking at Lortz. He smiled. He looked like a schoolboy caught in the boy's room with his hand down his pants who couldn't care less. Like a guy who wasn't going back to managing a convenience store. Like a guy who'd figured out how to get even with the women he felt ruined his life—

"In and out, twist and shout . . ."

"Run!" I yelled. I turned and saw Theresa and Jessica, transfixed by the sight of Lortz slowly walking toward us. Jessica's face was a mix of confusion and fear, but Theresa's expression was twisted by revulsion as she glared at the man who'd already tried once to kill her.

"Run, goddamn it!"

"*Feel the pain, feel the hurt,*" Lortz sang, his voice down to a whisper, taking another step closer as he raised the gun. His face was as placid as if he were straightening boxes of cereal on the shelf at Dollar & Done.

"*Love the touch, love the push—*" he sang, and stopped. Something had interrupted him. A sound. I'd heard it too. He looked up and then behind, as if half expecting to see Bronte rising from the dead. Which he did. Patterson—definitely not soft as a bunny —was struggling to his knees in the dim, gray light like a boxer with nothing left to lose trying to defy the count. Lortz turned and aimed the gun at Patterson and fired and Patterson's body jerked once and twitched twice. But still he kept moving. His hands reached out and grabbed Lortz's left leg and pulled just hard enough to tug him off balance. Lortz recovered, dragged his leg free, and fired again, his back now completely turned toward me. It was the only chance I'd get.

I flung myself on him and the two of us went down hard on the grated walkway, landing just past Patterson's convulsing body. For a terrifying moment I thought we were going to slide into the cold water below. As I tried to find the nearest railing, Lortz twisted himself around and won just enough room to maneuver the gun between our bodies. I should have known how strong and quick he was. Burn me once . . . Panicked, I felt the weapon shifting in Lortz's hand as he tried to push the barrel against my ribs. I dug my left hand between us and strained to push the gun down against his own stomach. He pushed back and ice gripped my spine and I thought of all those ridiculous pull-ups I prided myself on each morning and I pushed back harder. In the heat of the struggle I caught a glimpse of his face. He was still smiling. A smile that at least six women had likely glimpsed in their last moments on earth. A smile you saw in nightmares you didn't wake up from. I didn't know what else to do. I smiled back. Confusion flitted in and out of his eyes, and his grip eased for the length of a heartbeat. I pushed my right hand as hard as I could and he pushed back and we struggled for a century or two and then something exploded and my body jerked and for a moment I couldn't hear anything. Then I realized the pressure from Lortz's hand had lessened and he had relaxed beneath me, like a man drifting off to sleep on the couch. I moved away from him, feeling something warm and sticky on my jacket. I reached out and took the gun and slid it behind me. I got to my knees. I looked and in the gloom saw my flashlight nestled in the crook of Patterson's lifeless right arm. I picked it up, trained it onto Lortz, and watched blood spurting from his chest. I studied his face. He was still smiling, but it was different now. The smile of a man used to telling jokes that people were forced to laugh at who realizes the room has grown silent for the first time.

I grabbed a cold railing and hauled myself up. I turned and nearly collided with Theresa, standing beside me, looking down at Lortz. She was holding the gun. Behind her, Jessica crouched in the middle of the walkway, her head tucked into her knees.

"Leave him," I said. "It's over."

She said something I couldn't make out. "What?"

"Knees."

"I'm sorry?"

"Uncle Knees." She stared at Lortz. I blinked in confusion. Had the strain of the case finally caught up with her? The encounter with Lortz snapped something inside? I said, "Listen to me. We need to leave. Jessica—"

"That's what I had to call him."

"Who?"

"'On your knees,' he used to say."

"He?"

"My uncle. A blowjob every morning, after my mom left for work." Her voice level and calm, steady as a cashier reciting gas points and money saved from coupons. "'On your knees,' he'd say. 'On your knees, you dirty fucking slut.'"

I exhaled, watching my breath form a small cloud in the chill of the tunnel. "It wasn't a neighbor."

She shook her head.

"Your uncle."

"I was fourteen years old. My mom yelled at me when I finally told her. Said it was all my fault."

I said nothing.

"I tried to apologize. She wouldn't listen."

I waited for a couple of seconds. I said, "We need to go. We need to get Jessica out of here. She's not dressed for this. And she's hurt."

Theresa kept looking at Lortz. He was still smiling but his eyes had closed.

"We should help him," she said.

"Yeah."

"Or maybe you already did."

She wiped her eyes, handed me the gun, and walked back to Jessica. She pulled her to her feet. I took off my coat and wrapped it around the trembling young woman. Together, we limped slowly back down the metal walkway without looking behind us. In another minute we were outside in the middle of a Christmas Day blizzard.

50

WE MADE IT BACK ACROSS THE PERIMETER
yard, trudging through filigreed curtains of falling snow. We
squeezed through the fence and got into my van. I started it
and blasted the heat and called 911. I texted Gretchen, telling
her what had happened. No one said anything as we waited
for help.

The cruisers got there first, occupied by the unlucky third
shifters who'd pulled Christmas Day overnight duty. The squads
came next, followed in surprisingly quick time by the detectives,
starting with Larry Schwartzbaum. Right around 2 a.m. a couple
of TV trucks rolled up to make it a real party. I saw Suzanne pile
out of one of them and beeline for us at an impressive clip, four
months pregnant or not. Now that was Christmas spirit.

I gave Schwartzbaum the highlights of our ordeal inside the
silos. As I spoke, Jessica sat silently beside us, gripping a coffee cup
with hands that were thin and a troubling gray and pitted with
scabs. A few minutes later Gretchen arrived, and after some nego-
tiation between me and Schwartzbaum, she was allowed briefly
inside to see Jessica. She burst into tears when she saw the woman

she'd tried so hard to harbor from danger. It was difficult not to notice the dull look in Jessica's eyes in response, the flat affect she showed the person who'd tried but failed to be her savior. After a couple minutes Schwartzbaum nodded at a patrol officer and the woman politely but firmly took Gretchen away.

We were getting our final going-over from the paramedics when one other person arrived. He was backlit by the kaleidoscope of emergency lights outside the squad that seemed to be multiplying every minute. Our conspiracy theorist. *The government knows. Goes all the way up to the White House.* He didn't offer his name, and I didn't ask. He asked some hard questions about why we didn't stop when he yelled at us outside Patterson's house. I asked him some hard questions in return. Schwartzbaum intervened. Turned out he was an undercover officer with the state, brought in to investigate rumors that someone in the police department was protecting a pimp and trafficker on the east side. Someone who turned out to be Marc Copeland. Who turned out to have a serious oxycodone addiction thanks to aggravating a back injury a while ago. I asked how he was doing. Gonna pull through, came the gruff response. Unlike Leonard Lortz. And then he was gone.

It took another hour, but we were finally allowed to leave the scene just before 3 a.m. Roy had arrived and was going to take Jessica and Theresa back to his house, at least for the night.

"Ask you something?" I said to Theresa as we stood outside Roy's car.

"No."

"What's your mom's name?"

"My mom?"

"Yeah."

"Why should I tell you?"

"No reason. If you don't want to."

"Don't want to."

"That's fine. I was just curious, is all."

"Patty," she said after a moment.

"Patty?"

"You deaf on top of stupid, QB?"

Patty. Theresa's name on the streets.

The name of the person who refused to believe what Theresa's younger self said her uncle—her mother's brother—was doing to her each morning.

The name that helped her tolerate the taste of dick.

51

CHRISTMAS DAY MIRACLE! SCREAMED THE headline on the press release faxed and e-mailed and tweeted and probably hand-delivered by Congresswoman Darlene Bardwell late on the morning of December 25. The news conference was the next day. She held it at her Columbus office, in the Town and Country Shopping Center on East Broad, which liked to call itself the first shopping center in the country. It was a nice touch, Bardwell having her local headquarters there. The room was filled with reporters when Theresa and I walked in ten minutes before it was scheduled to start. Bardwell was up front, talking to Jessica. Her brother and her son stood next to her. John Blanchett, the congresswoman's aide, was nowhere to be seen.

"Andy?" Bardwell called out, gesturing for me to come forward.

I walked up reluctantly. As I situated myself on the edge of the officials gathered for the event, I made eye contact with Kevin Harding. True to my word, I'd texted him after I'd gotten home Christmas Day, even before I collapsed into bed, giving him a couple things Suzanne and the other TV reporters hadn't gotten at the scene. To my surprise, he was already up, but then he had twins and lots of presents under the tree. He nodded at me. I nodded back. Our engagement was back on.

Bardwell was trading glances with one of the videographers to see if they were ready when the door to the office opened. Gretchen Osborne walked in. She didn't look relieved or grateful or rested. She looked as if she'd just thrown up in the parking lot. She searched the room for faces until she settled on mine. She gestured at me. I gave an apologetic shrug to the congresswoman. "Just one more second, folks," Bardwell said brightly, though I could hear the pique creeping in.

"I'm sorry," Gretchen said as we stood in the corner. Theresa came up beside me. "I screwed everything up."

"You did what you thought was right. Unlike almost anyone else involved in this case."

She shook her head. "I was wrong about Jessica. I thought I was hiding her from Bronte. I knew she was scared of him. But she was just as scared of something else."

"What?"

She pulled a tattered backpack off her shoulder. She opened it and retrieved a black composition book. "This," she said.

I took the notebook from her, opened it, and started flipping through the pages.

"Andy?" Bardwell called out.

"This is from Saunders & Sons," I said, ignoring her. I realized I'd seen its replacement the day I dropped off my Hoover. "Did Lisa Washington give her this?"

Gretchen nodded. "Lisa stole it when she left that place. She was owed money and was hoping to use it as leverage. She gave it to Jessica for safekeeping one night. The night she disappeared. The night Lortz . . ."

We waited. Gretchen said, "Jessica thought Lisa was killed for the notebook. And she thought she'd be next. That's why I tried to hide her."

"Who's in here?" I said.

"A lot of names, going back a few years. I recognize some of them. But that's because I always liked reading the business and sports pages. Saunders took down all their real names. It was protection against them ever telling anyone about his operation. He'd out them."

"*Andy?*" Bardwell said. I opened the book and started reading. The entries were chronological, by date and name of girl and type of transaction and amount. It would take a while to read. I paged through and got to the end. I stopped, seeing a different set of listings. A kind of crude index. Here, the names were alphabetical, with several blank lines between names in case more were added. *Adams, Anderson, Archer.* I turned the page. *Banks. Barber. Barclay.* I stopped at the next entry.

I said, "How did Bronte find you the other night?"

"Blanchett."

"The aide?"

"I knew he was trying to locate Jessica. He told me, the night of the vigil, asked if I knew anything. But like he was trying to help her. I think he knew I was hiding something. Christmas Eve, I just got desperate. I didn't know how much longer I could manage. I figured maybe this"—she gestured at the notebook—"was enough to protect us if I gave it to him."

"But Blanchett didn't come."

She shook her head. Something was wrong here. The call to a congresswoman's aide had ended with the arrival of a violent pimp at Gretchen's apartment.

"Andy!" the congresswoman said. "Some of these good folks are on deadline."

I turned and looked at her and nodded. I walked past the reporters to the podium. I opened the composition book so Bardwell could see it. I realized now why Blanchett had been hunting Jessica. Why he'd disguised himself as a parole officer. A minister. A cop. Had even broken into a grieving woman's house on the day of her murdered granddaughter's funeral. Not to make hay out of a political bill. To save the congresswoman's career, which was about to go off the rails through no fault of her own. I whispered to Bardwell, explained what the book was. I flipped to the end and moved my finger to the entry after Barclay. *Bardwell, Barry.* I looked at her. She stared at me, puzzled. At least I thought she was puzzled. I realized after a moment she was frozen in place, uncertain what to do.

"Could I—" she said, and stopped. She swallowed. "Would I be able to keep this?"

"No," I said, and closed the book.

"What are you going to do with it?"

"Wait for you and Barry to do the right thing," I said, putting it under my arm. I nodded at Theresa, who walked over to Jessica and whispered something to her. A moment later Jessica and her brother and little Robbie and Gretchen and Theresa and I walked out into the cold, sunny day, a line of reporters following us. I turned but couldn't see Bardwell for all the people between us.

52

A MAN I DIDN'T RECOGNIZE ANSWERED THE door at Gloria Washington's house the next day, shortly after noon. Still, I thought he looked familiar. I introduced myself and my guests.

"Ben Washington," he said, shaking my hand. "I'm Gloria's oldest son. Lisa's uncle."

"It's nice to meet you." I entered first, and turned and beckoned toward Jessica. She stepped inside, followed by her brother, Bill, holding Robbie in his arms. Theresa brought up the rear.

It was warm inside the house and smelled of baking. We took off our snow-covered boots and shoes and sneakers and gave our coats to Ben. We settled ourselves in the living room. Gloria set out a plate of Christmas cookies, cups, and a carafe of coffee. Gloria let her son serve us while she went over and stood before Jessica.

"I'm so sorry about what happened," she said, taking up her hands. "I'm so glad you're OK."

Jessica lowered her eyes and nodded.

"When they found that last girl. I was so worried. And then, when I saw her picture. . ."

Jessica nodded again.

The news had broken right after the congresswoman's scuttled news conference. The coroner's office identified Leonard Lortz's last victim. "Darla," the woman we'd met our first night canvassing the streets. The one from the suburbs who'd looked so much like Jessica. Who'd claimed she wasn't worried. Her real name was Emily Shoemaker. She was twenty-two.

"But you're OK, and that's what matters," Gloria said. "It was good of you to come by. I wasn't expecting it. After everything you've been through."

"We weren't quite sure what this was all about," Ben added, sitting beside his mother with a cookie on a plate.

I cleared my throat. "We had something we wanted to tell you. Or actually, Jessica did. Something I didn't know when I was here before."

"Is it about the names?" Gloria said. "All those men? I never knew Lisa had that book. I'm sorry if that put you in danger."

"It ain't," Jessica said, and stopped.

"Not the book, exactly," I said. I couldn't see the point in going into all that right now. It would come out eventually. Gloria was right: the names had almost gotten Jessica killed. Shit started rolling downhill after Barry Bardwell offered to buy the book from Mr. Saunders. The book containing the record of his visits to the vacuum cleaner store at a low point in his not altogether happy marriage. Employing a Hoover even older than mine that he'd picked up at a secondhand shop.

"If not the book, then what?" Gloria Washington said, interrupting my train of thought.

"It's about Robbie," I said.

"Robbie?"

"The, ah, boy," I said, gesturing at Bill Byrnes and the child sitting on his lap, munching a cookie.

"It ain't his name," Jessica interrupted. "Robbie."

Gloria looked at her and waited.

"It's Robert."

"That's a fine name," Gloria said. "It was my husband's name. Lisa's grandfather."

Jessica shook her head in frustration. She said, "Robert's his name, because Lisa named him for your husband. He ain't my baby. He's Lisa's boy. He's your—" Jessica stopped, trying to think.

"Great-grandson," Bill Byrnes said. "Robbie—Robert—is your great-grandson."

"How is that possible?" Gloria said.

"Lisa didn't know she was pregnant," Jessica said. "She was in a bad way. We both were. We were staying off Main Street, working for Bronte, when it happened. Bronte like to kill her. Like to kill him," she said, pointing at the boy. "Said Lisa was wasting his time and costing him money. Lisa always did better than me, out there. She had him on the bathroom floor. I said I'd take him. I brought him to Bill. I didn't know what else to do."

"The father?" Gloria Washington said.

"Not sure Lisa ever knew," Jessica said.

I said, "I know it's a lot to process right now."

"Yes, it is," Gloria said. She looked at the boy. The child's resemblance to Ben Washington, his great-uncle, was striking. As it was to his great-grandmother. I kicked myself for not having noticed it before. I'd looked at the childhood photos of Lisa, and her mother, and Ben, and all the other relatives whose pictures lined the mantel, the day Theresa and I visited Gloria the first time. Robbie—Robert—looked like every one of them around the same age. It was like so many aspects of this case. A clue, a vital one, had been hidden in plain sight yet impossible to see. And with it, a life had hung in the balance. I'd been hunting blind, not realizing how much was right in front of me.

53

"ALL THAT FOR A PROSTITUTE," MY FATHER
said with a grunt.

"Her name's Jessica."

"What's going to happen to her?"

"I'm not sure. She's not going to have it easy."

"I'm supposed to feel sorry for her?"

"Let's not get into this again," my mother interrupted. "I
think we can figure out how each of us feels about it. Maybe we
could be thankful Andy was there. To help her."

"I'm just saying," my father said.

"Don't," my mother said.

We were sitting in my parents' living room later that day, after
dinner. My father had been in a bad mood since I'd arrived. He
was in a lot of pain. Shelley had left that morning to go home to
Cleveland, and it had upset him, though he wouldn't say as much.

"The pimp," my father said.

"What about him?"

"How'd he know where the prostitute was?"

"Jessica. From the cop. Copeland."

"How'd *he* know?"

"The congresswoman's aide. Blanchett. He had a deal with him."

"A deal?"

I explained what we'd learned in the aftermath. After Barry Bardwell told Blanchett about the notebook stolen from the brothel with his name in it, Blanchett nosed around with some vice guys who knew some guys. Found out Marc Copeland had a problem. Told him if he could find Jessica and the book, he'd do what he could to call off the internal investigation Copeland faced. After Gretchen called Blanchett on Christmas Eve, the aide called Copeland. Copeland, seeing a chance to kill a couple of birds with one stone, told Bronte where she was and instructed him to bring him the girl. Bronte, figuring Copeland was up to something, double-crossed the officer, shooting him in the house while narrowly avoiding getting shot himself. Knowing from Copeland that the silos were one of the places the Pleasure Prince might have operated out of, Patterson decided to go there for a perfect copycat murder.

"Lowlifes, all of them," my father said.

I inched the dining room chair I was sitting in across the carpet to get closer to my dad's recliner. "Is there anything I can get you?"

"I'm fine."

"Jessica's not perfect. She made a lot of mistakes. But she didn't have it good at home. It's understandable, what happened to her."

"People make choices. You did."

"This is not about me, believe it or not."

"You're just making excuses for her."

"I'm not making excuses. I'm explaining the way I see it."

"You've always made excuses. For others. For yourself."

"Maybe. Probably. Not so much anymore."

"Not how I see it."

"Bud," my mother said. "For God's sake shut up."

I got out of the chair. I walked out of the living room and into the kitchen, lifted my coat off its hook, opened the side door, and went outside. The light was fading. Intermittent flurries had swirled around all day, and the air outside my parents' house was filled with flakes floating to the ground like ash from a distant fire. More snow was forecast for overnight. I reached into my jacket pocket and felt for my car keys. I found them and gripped them, squeezing them like a talisman. I looked across the road at the snow-swept field, almost all the corn stubble hidden under a white blanket. My father was right in one regard. I used to make a lot of excuses.

"Asshole," I said, and turned and went back inside.

54

"IT'S A FUNNY PLACE TO BREAK UP."

"I'm sorry," Anne said. "I didn't mean it to happen like this."

Story of my life, I said to myself, but aloud, told her, "It's OK. I get it."

We were strolling through the Nativity scene set up each year on East Broad by State Auto Insurance, across Washington Street from the art museum. It was a Columbus tradition. The life-sized plaster sculptures were almost ninety years old but still in pretty good shape. Piped-in carols serenaded us as we walked. I had fond memories of my mom bringing Shelley and me here as kids, after a day spent Christmas shopping at the old Lazarus on South High. It was a custody night. I had the boys with me. We'd ended up here after I pried them out of my house after an afternoon of video games, looking for something to do, anything, that was outside and free. On a whim I texted Anne, and to my surprise she said she and Amelia might stop by. The kids were up ahead, getting hot chocolate.

Ironic thing was, I'd been feeling pretty good when I pulled up. I'd just gotten a call from Bonnie, who told me the meeting with Jessica Byrnes and the dog Troy had been working with had gone well. Jessica's new caseworker thought a pet was a good idea, especially one that protective. A companion that didn't want to hurt her for once in her life.

"The thing is," Anne said, and stopped. I waited.

"You know what they say," she said, trying again. "It's not about me. It's about you."

"That's honest."

"I'm kidding. I'm not going to give you a bullshit line about needing space or anything like that. I just want a little bit more stability right now. I'm up for tenure next fall, and trying to finish the book and everything . . . And I'm thinking about trying to buy a house." A pause. "My parents said they'd help."

She waited, but I didn't say anything. I thought about my conversation with Roy at O'Reilly's. A heavy truth was settling in. But it was preceded by the pettiest of realizations. I couldn't see myself moving in with her. Not that she'd invited me, but the suggestion hung in the air like mist at twilight, a concept just out of reach and quickly fading. As we stood there in silence my phone buzzed, and instinctively I pulled it out. I read the text message that had just arrived. After a long moment, I replied, then pocketed the phone.

"Everything OK?" Anne said.

"Yeah. Just needed to make a call on something."

"So what are you thinking?"

"I'm thinking I'm sorry. But I understand what you're saying. I don't have a nine-to-five job, a.m. or p.m. And sometimes I don't even have a job, period."

"There's an opening, by the way. I meant to mention it to you. At Columbus State. Head of security. I thought—"

It was a nice gesture. Perhaps even a final lifeline. It was just like Anne to suggest it.

"Don't think I'm cut out for that."

"I kind of figured."

We strolled for a few more minutes, arm in arm, before catching up with the boys and Amelia. We got ourselves some hot chocolate. As Anne chatted with Mike and Joe as though nothing had happened, I pulled my phone out and looked again at the text message I'd gotten while standing with Anne by the Three Kings.

Me again. I'm coming to Columbus tomorrow. Ready for that Christmas ale?

Mary Beth. The Parthenon bartender. *Nice lady,* according to Elliot Mullan.

I looked at my reply. The message I'd sent after Anne had all but broken up with me. But before she'd held out one last bit of hope.

How had Roy put it? *You're fixing problems, not scoring touchdowns, but what's the diff?*

Sounds good, I'd written. Text me when you're in town.

Read on for a sample chapter from *The Third Brother*

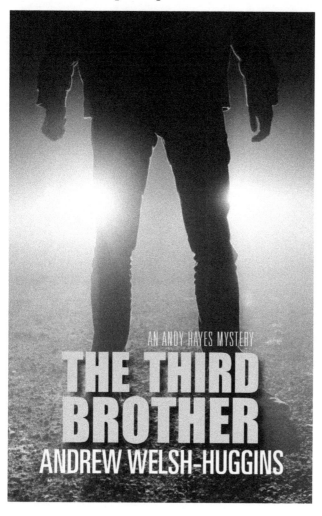

AN ANDY HAYES MYSTERY

THE THIRD BROTHER

ANDREW WELSH-HUGGINS

1

"GO HOME!"
"Go home!"
"Go home!"

I blinked in the late afternoon sun, processing what I was looking at across the parking lot. Two men shouting at a woman, one of them with something in his hand. The woman shouting back, struggling to retrieve what the man was grasping. Behind her several children, a couple of them wailing. Whatever was happening, it wasn't even the second cousin twice removed of a fair fight. I let go my shopping cart and started to run.

"Go home!"
"Go home!"
"Go home!"

She was black—I was guessing Somali—wearing a flowing yellow dress and orange head scarf. The older of the two guys was chanting while a younger and skinnier man tugged at the scarf like an old-fashioned vagrant trying to steal laundry off the line. Both of them white. She was no pushover; she was yelling at them as she tried with one hand to keep the garment from being pulled off while shielding her kids with the other. As I ran I looked out at Broad, hoping for a cop, but saw only a steady stream of cars speeding in each direction past a jumble of west-side fast-food restaurants, car lots, and payday loan joints.

"Go home!"

"Go home!"

"Go home!"

"Stop it," the woman said over the crying of her children. "Stop it!"

"Hey!" I said as I reached them a few moments later. I took a second to catch my breath. "What the hell do you think you're doing?"

"Go home . . ." The older guy said, the chant dying on his lips as he stared at me. He was a hard-living fifty or so, dumpy and balding with patchy grizzle coating his face and chin. He wore loose-fitting tan cargo shorts and a blue checkered button-down short-sleeve shirt with the bottom two buttons undone, exposing a flash of belly as white as butcher-shop lard. The kid with the scarf in his hand was scrawny, midtwenties maybe, in jeans shorts and a white ribbed wifebeater, with a shaved head and a thin face I might have paid more attention to had my eyes not been drawn to a prominent tattoo on his neck that seemed to involve rifles, barbed wire, and the sun. I couldn't tell if it represented a branch of the military or a prison break fantasy.

"The fuck are you?" Grizzle said. His eyes were glassy and he swayed as he spoke. "Some kind of raghead lover?"

Up close, I noticed for the first time the gun in a holster on his right side. Ohio's an open carry state, making it perfectly legal. I took a step back. Legal, but cause for concern with a guy in that condition? That was another matter altogether.

"I'm someone telling you to leave this lady alone."

"We'll leave her alone when she goes home. Where she belongs."

"She is home, you nitwit. That's probably why she's buying groceries."

"How do we know she don't have a bomb under that?" said the scrawny guy with the tattoo, tugging on the scarf as he pointed at her dress.

"Stop it!" she said.

"How do we know you don't have shit for brains?" I said. "Do everybody a favor and beat it."

"Free country," Tattoo said. "Except for *terrorists*."

"The only terrorists I see are you two clowns. Why don't you crawl back under the rock where you came from and we can all go about our business?"

"Make us," Tattoo said, grinning.

"Are you deaf on top of stupid?" I said, reaching out and tearing the end of the scarf from his hand. He looked at me in surprise, as if I were a magician at a kids' birthday party who'd just pulled a penny from his ear. I turned toward the woman, who rewrapped her scarf without meeting my eyes. I was turning back to face the cowboys when out of the blue Tattoo leaped onto my back. I reached around to try to pull him off, wobbling like a top at the end of its spin, and then gasped as he wrapped his right arm around my throat and cut off my air. *What the hell?* I thought. This was supposed to be a simple grocery run. I gasped as black specks floated before my eyes like flies hovering over dogshit. I staggered, spun around once more, summed up my available options, settled on one, and fell backwards, hard, into the car behind me. The kid made an "oof" sound like a guy who didn't realize the medicine ball he was catching was quite that heavy, and dropped off me like a leech doused in sea salt.

I stepped away from him, inhaling deeply. "I said, beat it."

"Let's hold it right there," Grizzle said, the gun out of the holster and in his right hand. *Lesh hol' it right there.*

"Easy now," I said, backing up.

He didn't reply. He nodded at Tattoo, who slowly righted himself, walked over to the woman, grabbed her scarf again, and this time pulled it clean off. He shrieked in triumph like a movie

Indian counting coup as the woman cried out and put both hands on her head.

I stepped in front of her, keeping my eye on the gun.

"Why don't we all calm down a little? No one wants to get hurt."

"Sure about that?" Tattoo said, charging up to me, scarf balled in his hands as he stuck his face in front of mine. I saw bloodshot eyes and smelled breath that would have wilted poison oak. "You shouldn'a gotten involved."

"And you should try picking on people your own size for a change."

"That's what I'm about to do."

"Have it your way—"

"Let's get out of here," Grizzle interrupted.

"What?" Tattoo said.

"I said, let's go." He held up a phone in his free hand.

"Gimme one minute with this douche. Just one fuckin' minute."

"Forget it," Grizzle said. He waved the phone at Tattoo. "He's saying JJ's, now."

Reluctantly, Tattoo took a step back, though his eyes never left mine.

"Don't try anything stupid, ya dumb shit," he said. "Raghead lover. Traitor."

"There's a cop," I said.

"What?"

"Behind you." He looked around. As he did I grabbed the scarf out of his hands for the second time that day.

He twirled back, eyes blazing, right arm cocked. But Grizzle whistled and held up his phone again. "JJ's," he said. Lowering his gun, he turned and limped toward a rusted brown pickup truck three rows over. Too far to see the plate.

"We ain't done here, douche," Tattoo said, following his partner.

"I'm free most Thursdays," I called after him. He flipped me the bird. A minute later they were gone in a squeal of tires and cloud of diesel and a long, defiant blast of their horn.

I took a breath and turned to the woman.

"You all right?"

She nodded unconvincingly, phone already pressed to her ear as she made a call.

I'd had worse shopping trips, I consoled myself, reaching for my own phone. I was conscious, anyway.

Then it hit me: I'd forgotten to use my coupons at checkout.

Shit.

Acknowledgments

I'm grateful to Jen Del Carmen, Bill Parker, and Dawn Stock, who read an early draft of *The Hunt* and offered suggestions that improved the manuscript while catching some embarrassing mistakes. Any hiccups after all their help are entirely my fault. David Holtzapple, an engineer familiar with the structural integrity of the silos on East Main, generously provided photographs of the complex and assistance in understanding what people might face inside on a dark winter's night. Dr. Scott Mackey helpfully explained ejection fraction numbers and other elements of heart attacks and their treatments.

Several people educated me on the realities of human trafficking in Columbus and Ohio, including Andrea Boxill through her former work at CATCH Court, a Franklin County Municipal Court rehabilitation program for victims; Elizabeth Ranade Janis, antitrafficking coordinator at the Ohio Department of Public Safety; and Michelle Hannan, professional and community services director at the Salvation Army of Central Ohio, and Kelli Trinoskey, the Salvation Army's community relations director. Above all, I'm appreciative of former trafficking victims I spoke to either for this book or in my work as a reporter. I admire their willingness to tell their stories in an effort to spread awareness about the hard realities of prostitution. In that vein, I recommend *Paid For: My Journey through Prostitution*, by Rachel Moran, as the best of several books I read about trafficking and its impact on women.

As always, I'm thankful to everyone at Ohio University Press for their suggestions, recommendations and encouragement, including director Gillian Berchowitz; acquisitions editor Rick Huard; managing editor Nancy Basmajian; promotions and events manager Samara Rafert; sales manager Jeff Kallet; and production manager Beth Pratt.

A reminder there's a reason they call it fiction. The actual roller derby teams in Columbus and Ann Arbor go by different names, but are no less exciting to watch. Most of the restaurants in *The Hunt* are real, although in Resch's case I chose to glaze over the truth: it's not actually open on Sundays; in this case delicious doughnuts trumped the truth. You'll search in vain for Jury of Your Pours, though it's not far from where the late, great Jury Room sat.

Pam, my partner in crime for life, once again made several winning observations in the short run as my first reader, for which I'm grateful as always. Finally, thanks to our children, Sarah, Emma, and Thomas, to whom this book is dedicated, for continuing to inspire us with their own adventures, endeavors, and dreams.

WITHDRAWN

CPSIA information can be obtained
at www.ICGtesting.com
Printed in the USA
FFHW02n0214070918
48117648-51846FF